The Legacy

The Legacy

A Raleigh Killen Mystery

Jemma Lansing

Copyright © 2009 by Jemma Lansing.

Library of Congress Control Number: 2008911664
ISBN: Hardcover   978-1-4363-9535-9
               Softcover   978-1-4363-9534-2

All rights reserved. No part of this book may be reproduced or transmitted in any form or by any means, electronic or mechanical, including photocopying, recording, or by any information storage and retrieval system, without permission in writing from the copyright owner.

This is a work of fiction. Names, characters, places and incidents either are the product of the author's imagination or are used fictitiously, and any resemblance to any actual persons, living or dead, events, or locales is entirely coincidental.

This book was printed in the United States of America.

To order additional copies of this book, contact:
Xlibris Corporation
1-888-795-4274
www.Xlibris.com
Orders@Xlibris.com

Prologue

Raleigh Killen was relieved when she pulled into the driveway of her new home in Pine Grove, Washington. Her flight out of Phoenix had been delayed three hours, then fog at the Seattle airport caused her plane to be diverted to Portland. After four hours there, the plane took off again and this time managed to finally land in Seattle.

After waiting at baggage claim it became clear that only one of her two bags made it down carousel. Raleigh didn't even try to wait out the line of other angry passengers with missing luggage; she headed for the car rental area.

One thing finally went right—Raleigh was able to secure her rather bulky rental Cadillac without delay and she drove off into the Seattle afternoon, heading south. Her MapQuest directions were on the seat beside her and OnStar was the push of a button away in case she got irretrievably lost. Getting lost was a good possibility at any time with Raleigh's poor sense of direction, but after the prolonged trip and being unfamiliar with the area, getting lost was almost a certainty. In fact, the only reason she had rented this boat of a gas-guzzler was because it came with OnStar.

By the time Raleigh reached Pine Grove two hours later she was exhausted, she felt grimy, her eyes were bloodshot, and she had consumed far too much caffeine. But she was finally home. Her new home on Conifer Drive, Pine Grove, Washington.

Being so late to arrive at the house, Raleigh wasn't surprised that Dahlia Bible, her real estate agent, wasn't there to meet her and turn over the keys. She rummaged through her carry-on and located her cell phone and called the real estate office. Maybe Dahlia was waiting there for Raleigh's call.

After a confusing phone conversation with Violet Bible, the owner of the real estate office and Dahlia's mother, Raleigh was en route to the strip mall that housed Bible Real Estate.

As Raleigh walked through the door of the tiny office she could see the desk in Dahlia's cubicle was overflowing with unopened mail and the message light on her answering machine blinked steadily.

Violet Bible, whose name aptly matched her violet-dyed hair, was sniffling into a handkerchief printed with violets and dressed in something purple and multi-ruffled. She looked up when the bells on the door jingled and her expression was one of sheer panic.

Raleigh had now been traveling for a total of ten hours and wasn't surprised that her own appearance was likely the cause of Mrs. Bible's panic. She did not, however, take her fatigue and frustration out on the older woman, as much as she wanted to take it out on someone.

"Mrs. Bible, I'm Raleigh Killen. We spoke on the phone a few minutes ago . . . ."

"Yes, dear . . . yes, I remember you. I remembered you right away. Dahlia doesn't get many clients."

"Mrs. Bible, Dahlia apparently didn't get my message, or she couldn't meet me at the house with the keys, so I came to pick them up. The house on Conifer Drive, twelve-thirteen?"

"Yes, dear, well, I suppose they're in Dahlia's office . . . somewhere. I don't . . . really . . . know." Mrs. Bible stopped stammering and burst into tears.

"Mrs. Bible, I've had a very long day and I want to go home and soak in the tub." Raleigh was not an unfeeling woman, but ten hours in transit were enough to try her never-too-saintly patience.

Violet Bible continued blubbering and she laid her head down on her desk. Raleigh rolled her eyes and spotted the bathroom at the back of the office. She grabbed a coffee mug, filled it with water from the tap and walked back to Mrs. Bible's desk. Raleigh heroically resisted the urge to dump the water on Violet Bible's head and merely shoved the mug unceremoniously into the older woman's hands.

"Take a drink and calm down, Mrs. Bible . . . please," she added belatedly. "Is it Dahlia? Has something happened to her?"

Mrs. Bible raised her head from the desk and took a big gulp of the water. She swallowed too quickly and started to cough. Raleigh whacked her vigorously on the back.

"She's gone!" Violet Bible finally seemed capable of rational speech. "She ran off to Las Vegas!"

"Las Vegas? Oh, she eloped?"

"I only wish. Oh Lord, I only wish. She has shamed the entire family." At that Mrs. Bible looked up at the framed, faded photograph of her dead husband and founder of Bible Real Estate, Duie Bible. Duie's untimely death ten years ago had left poor Violet and Dahlia to carry on the family business, such as it was.

"She ran off to Las Vegas with the UPS driver."

"Oh . . . but they didn't elope?" Raleigh didn't see how this was so shameful, embarrassing maybe, to her mother. Though the idea of Dahlia with her stringy brown hair, scrawny shoulders and grating voice having anyone want to run anywhere with her was mind-boggling. If Raleigh hadn't felt so sorry for Dahlia she wouldn't have let her handle her home purchase in the first place. Once escrow closed, all Dahlia had to do was check up on the remodeling contractor Raleigh hired and confirm that the agreed-upon work had been completed. Even Dahlia could handle that and Raleigh had paid her in advance for her services.

Violet Bible looked around, as if someone might be eavesdropping, then she lowered her voice. "The UPS driver is a . . . woman." At this point she burst into tears again.

Raleigh felt like joining her, though not for the same reason. Instead, she located a bottle of aspirin in her purse, got herself some water and downed two.

"Oh. I'm sorry, Mrs. Bible, really, I am. It's not that bad . . . I'm sure she's . . . charming. But right now I really need to get the keys, to my house. I'm sure everything will work out."

"Of course, dear, of course. You need your keys. In Dahlia's office somewhere." Violet Bible made no move to get up from behind her desk, only waved one hand limply toward her daughter's cubicle.

"How about I go look? You just stay here, take a few deep breaths. I'm sure the keys are in my file."

Violet Bible nodded weakly and Raleigh escaped into Dahlia's cubicle and tackled the overflowing desk. Catalogs, bills, everything was mixed together and, with a rising sense of panic, Raleigh unearthed various overnight envelopes that she herself had sent to Dahlia, all unopened. Further down in the messy stack of paperwork she found a file with her name on it, but everything was jammed inside without any rhyme or reason. There was a sealed, lumpy envelope from the escrow company and she opened it to find a set of house keys tagged with her Conifer Drive address. *Why hasn't this been opened? What keys did Dahlia give to the contractor? She must have gotten others from the listing agent, mustn't she?*

"Mrs. Bible, when did Dahlia . . . leave?" There wasn't any response. "Mrs. Bible . . . ?" Raleigh raised her voice.

Violet Bible edged into the doorway slowly, holding onto the doorjamb like she was on the deck of a sinking ship. "Five weeks or so ago. Right after she got her commission check from Worthy Title."

"Five weeks ago? But she was supposed to be supervising the contractor."

"What contractor, dear?"

"Marty Hammer, the contractor who remodeled my house. She was supposed to supervise the work. I hired him before I flew back to Phoenix, but I left her in charge. All she had to do was make sure the contractor followed my instructions."

Mrs. Bible looked completely baffled. "But, dear, she left as soon as she got the check. Everything is just as she left it. She gets real put out if I open her mail or listen to her messages. Everything is just as she left it so when she comes back . . . I'm sure she'll call you."

Well, that explained the mess of unopened mail. And now Raleigh was doubly anxious to get inside her house and see what Mr. Hammer had done without any oversight. They had a contract, but . . .

Raleigh grabbed the keys and left the cubicle, almost knocking Violet Bible down. "I'll call you later, Mrs. Bible. I have to get back to the house."

"Yes, dear, you go be happy in your new home while I . . . ."

Raleigh didn't wait for Mrs. Bible to burst into tears again. She bolted across the strip mall parking lot to the Cadillac.

* * *

Raleigh wrestled with the stubborn lock, something Mr. Hammer had neglected to repair or replace. Of course, if he had replaced the lock her key wouldn't work. The lock finally released and Raleigh opened the front door of her new home.

She took one step inside and *she* burst into tears.

Chapter One

Raleigh settled back against the plush, beige leather airplane seat and made herself comfortable. The alarmingly young-looking copilot carried the padded nylon backpack case containing her laptop down the aisle and gave her a questioning look.

"Can you put it over there?" Raleigh indicated the seat across the aisle from her. "I'll need to check my e-mail later—if that's okay."

"No problem, ma'am. You can plug in right here." He pointed to the jack in the wall near her footrest and the adjoining power outlet. He buckled her backpack safely in the seat.

"And if your batteries run low, feel free to run your laptop off the outlet. The tray table comes out of the wall and adjusts." He demonstrated how the tray table was released from the wall and the various positions. *Ooh, dual cupholders.* Then the copilot recited the routine safety procedures lecture, which Raleigh listened to in case it was different for a private jet—it wasn't.

"This is quite a change for me," she told the copilot, "traveling by chartered jet. One time I was stuck at the screening checkpoint for three hours because of the underwire in another woman's bra."

The copilot chuckled obligingly, gave her a nod and walked back to the cockpit and took a seat. He donned his headphones and started flipping switches and entering data into what looked like a small computer fitted into the dashboard, if planes can be said to have dashboards.

The jet seated six and Raleigh could easily see a map of their route appear on the computer display up in the cockpit. Their location blinked with a red star right on Pine Grove, Washington, and a white dotted line snaked south along the Pacific coast, then east across the country to their ultimate destination, Greenhaven, Ohio. This was marked with an unblinking red star.

The pilot, who appeared to be fourteen and therefore older than the copilot, climbed on board and walked back to Raleigh, stooping slightly to accommodate the low headroom.

"Are you all set, ma'am? Can I get you something to drink, a snack before we take off?"

"I don't think so. I'll wait until we've been airborne for a while." Flying was difficult enough for Raleigh, even under these luxurious conditions, and the last thing she needed was a breakfast of Diet Pepsi and cheese curls in her stomach while they took off.

Raleigh had eaten a cup of yogurt about an hour ago, a little before five o'clock, but she didn't usually have breakfast until seven anyway. Once the sun was up and they reached cruising altitude she would take a chance on eating something.

"Well, the beverages are here—the ice and glasses over here—and the snack pantry right next to the cockpit. Help yourself when you're ready." The pilot indicated a bank of wood cabinets along the opposite side of the plane.

The pilot touched the bill of his cap and walked backed to the hatch, raised the steps and closed the door. He took his seat and conferred with the copilot for a moment, then they both flipped a few switches and talked to the tower as the two jet engines roared to life. The pilot turned back briefly and shouted over the noise, "You ready, ma'am?"

Raleigh nodded and the plane taxied slowly away from the hangar and toward the runway. It was still quite dark and all she could see outside the window were the runway lights, then the tower lights in the distance on their left.

Raleigh opened her package of child-sized EarPlanes—child-sized to accommodate her undersized ear canals—wedged one firmly in each ear and tightened her seat belt. She watched outside as the plane crossed the lighted tarmac and made a turn, then taxied slowly to the end of one of the two runways. There they paused for several minutes while garbled chatter passed back and forth between the copilot and the tower. Then the pilot pushed a lever forward slowly and the plane started to move, gaining speed quickly, down the runway.

At this point in any flight Raleigh closed her eyes and hoped for the best. The plane jolted along the runway for a time, then the nose lifted, then the entire plane. They banked sharply and climbed. Raleigh practiced her deep breathing, making sure she didn't hyperventilate, and tried to make her body relax.

The climb out of the small, regional airport was quite jolting—apparently there was more wind up here than on the ground—but the plane soon leveled off and continued climbing at a more gradual, smoother pace.

Raleigh opened her eyes, took a few deep breaths and relaxed the tension on her seat belt slightly. The digital readout screen for the passengers showed the time and place of departure, the airspeed (she didn't want to think about that), the altitude (another piece of information she didn't really want), and the flying time to their destination. Almost four hours, but with the plane to herself and the wide, reclining seat this would likely be the best flight she had ever taken.

To start this trip, Raleigh had been picked up at the hotel in a limousine and whisked directly to the private hangars at the Pine Grove airport where *her* jet awaited. No standing in line at a ticket counter, no checking her luggage and wondering if she'd ever see it again, no suspicious looks from the screeners (as if a fifty-three-year-old woman in jeans and a "Love me, love my cat" sweatshirt looks like a terrorist), no being herded like cattle into a too-small waiting area, and then straining to understand the unintelligible announcements and wondering if her flight had just been called.

This was the way to fly, a whole plane to herself, a whole luggage compartment to herself, unlimited snacks and, as would soon become clear, a pilot and copilot who liked to point out interesting highlights of the geography below. Raleigh deemed it time to remove her EarPlanes, then she rummaged in her traveling bag and located her noise-canceling headphones, put them on, and activated the switch. The drone of the jet engines almost disappeared and Raleigh could hear the pilot and copilot talking in the cockpit.

This was the one disadvantage to the headphones; she could overhear conversations very easily. Conversations that were no one else's business. She hadn't heard anyone plan a murder, not as yet, but she knew far more about the affairs of strangers than she cared to. Luckily, the pilot and copilot were talking about where they would be staying in Greenhaven before heading back to Washington State the next day.

Though Raleigh couldn't see through the cloud cover below the plane, the jet was following the coast of Washington, then Oregon, and eventually would turn east about midway along the California coast. She stifled a yawn, then reclined her seat and slid it forward so she could kick off her shoes and rest her socked feet on the facing seat. Raleigh had been up since four, far too early even for an early bird like her, and she was still sleepy. She checked the onboard clock—6:01—and closed her eyes.

* * *

The sun coming through the window woke Raleigh and she blinked blearily, then remembered where she was and looked outside. The land below was brown and barren. *We must be over California.* The pilot noticed her stirring and pointed out the right side of the plane.

"We crossed over the mountains. Now we're heading east. If the prevailing wind holds we may land early."

The clock said 7:20.

Raleigh nodded to the pilot and took off her glasses and rubbed the last of the sleep from her eyes. She checked the back of her head with her hands—as usual, the dreaded bedhead. Her short, fine hair, gradually touched with gray over the last five years, mashed down so easily. Raleigh wasn't vain, but she didn't think it was fair that she was cursed with both bad hair and wrinkles.

Raleigh unfastened her seat belt and knelt in front of the seat across the aisle and unzipped the exterior pocket of her backpack. She withdrew a legal-size manila envelope and resumed her seat. Undoing the envelope clasp, she pulled a thick sheaf of papers free and opened the plastic-bound document on top. It was the last will and testament of George Durbin Mobley, a man of whom she had never heard. A *relative* of whom she had never heard.

An only child, and orphaned over thirty years ago, Raleigh hadn't known she had any living relatives, even as distant a one as George Mobley. And, in fact, he had never known of her either. His will simply left his entire estate to any living relative. As indicated in the cover letter from the lawyer, Andrew Newton, Esq., the connection, though very slim and through marriage only, was valid and Raleigh inherited everything. What constituted "everything" seemed fairly meager, the tiny house being the only real asset. There might be little left once the estate was settled, including the expense of the chartered jet which was she was enjoying, but Mr. Newton stressed that time was of the essence and his paralegal made all the travel arrangements without consulting her. Raleigh was sure Mr. Newton's bill would be a hefty one, too.

But she had nothing better to do for several weeks since her new home was being remodeled, so she agreed to fly at once to Greenhaven. She was not inclined to try to live in the house while the work was being done, not with the kitchen and both of the bathrooms being completely gutted. And *this* time the work was actually under way and Raleigh was supervising the remodeling herself, albeit from a distance.

The list of her erstwhile cousin's assets was short—a savings account that had been converted to a checking account in the name of the estate; the house, which had been paid off some time in the last decade; the contents of the house and a Honda Civic from the 1980s.

Not much of a legacy, but settling her cousin's estate was a welcome distraction from the fiasco that greeted her when she arrived at her new home in Washington.

George Mobley had been living on Social Security and a small pension of three thousand dollars a month. With the cost of living in small-town Ohio, she imagined he had a comfortable enough life before his sudden death five months ago. Mr. Newton had seen to the funeral arrangements, so Cousin George was buried in January, but it took quite a lot of detective work to locate her, his only living relative. *Another expense billed to the estate.* Raleigh would be lucky to have enough for a return flight to Washington, even traveling standby.

It was somewhat fortunate for Raleigh that she had served as an executrix before, both for her parents' estate when she was twenty and for an elderly aunt's seven years ago. She knew what was necessary to settle George Mobley's estate. An appraisal of the house, arranging the sale, interviewing estate sale agents, perhaps calling in an antiques dealer if any of the furniture or knickknacks looked valuable, paying the bills and distributing the remainder, if there was any, to the heirs—her.

How odd it was that someone would pick as their heir *any* relative. George Mobley made no provision for a secondary heir, no friends, charities, nothing. If Mr. Newton hadn't located her the estate would have gone to the state of Ohio. Yes, Cousin George must have been a weird sort of duck, maybe a hermit. No friends, no connection to the outside world other than grocery store clerks, his doctor—she wondered if he had a cat or dog. There was no provision in the will for the care of a pet, so, probably not.

In her conversations with Mr. Newton she asked about George Mobley, but the lawyer merely drew up the boilerplate trust and will as directed last year, a bare two months before her cousin died. Mr. Newton knew nothing personal about the late, and seemingly unlamented, George Mobley.

Raleigh looked up at the clock and saw that a whole hour had elapsed since she started reviewing the paperwork. The pilot was pointing out something thousands of feet below. Raleigh couldn't tell what he was saying, she hadn't replaced her headphones, but she nodded and took a quick look through the window to be polite, trying not to really note the ground so far below.

She got up and stretched the kinks out as best she could without hitting the ceiling, then replaced the file in her backpack and walked carefully forward the few steps to the rosewood cabinets that held the earlier-indicated refreshments. Raleigh pulled a Diet Pepsi from the minibar, her way of getting caffeine, and checked out the snack pantry. Honey-roasted peanuts, granola bars, M&M's, Gummi Bears, three flavors of potato chips in minicans, red licorice sticks, Doritos, sunflower seeds, cheese crackers and more. Raleigh decided on a blueberry granola bar for her belated breakfast and took it back to her seat with the Diet Pepsi, a cut-glass tumbler and a minican of low-fat potato chips she intended to save for later. She settled back into the plush leather splendor with a sigh.

Now the copilot pointed out the left side of the plane at what might have been Texas or Oklahoma and she took another quick look just to be polite.

Raleigh adjusted the tray table, opened her granola bar, then got the latest Tamar Meyers paperback from her tote and settled back to read. With yellow highlighter close at hand to record errors.

By the time Raleigh finished the book, and Mama's crinolines and pearls were back in place, another hour had passed and she hadn't had to use the highlighter even once. Raleigh put away her book and stowed her trash in the pullout bin, then plugged in her laptop and checked her e-mail. Nothing urgent was waiting, but she sent a brief message to Pam Bergman back in Phoenix, who was confused because she couldn't reach Raleigh in Pine Grove. Raleigh explained the change of plans and added the phone number for the hotel in Greenhaven where she would be staying, at least for this first night.

Raleigh hadn't been the least bit sorry to leave the suburb of Phoenix where she had lived for the last ten years, but she would miss the friends she made there, among them Pam, a professor of environmental science who had supported Raleigh's decision to go back to school at the advanced age of fifty-three.

* * *

A slight jolt and a gentle dip of the nose of the plane woke Raleigh suddenly from her self-induced stupor of computer solitaire. She scrambled to replace her EarPlanes for the descent and raise her seatback to a full and upright position. In spite of her being the only passenger, she was a person you could count on to follow the rules and regulations, at least when it suited her.

Raleigh looked out the window briefly and saw as the plane dipped down through the clouds that it was quite overcast and drizzly. But it was green, so very green below. While she had no use for the Midwest, where she had been raised, she did appreciate how green and verdant it was in the spring. For a mere day or two before the weather got suffocatingly sticky and hot. Before every mosquito within ten miles used her for a snack bar. That was one of the many things she appreciated about what would soon be her new home in Washington, the rainfall and rich greenness—without the heat. Raleigh had done her time in the desert climate of Arizona and she was quite happy to make the move to the Pacific Northwest, though her well-laid plans had gone quite awry and the move-in was being delayed for a month by the remodeling.

The plane banked sharply and Raleigh assumed her usual landing position—eyes closed, breathing, trying to relax. Lower and lower they went until the plane finally jolted onto the tarmac.

She opened her eyes then and saw that they had landed at what must be the smallest airport in the country. No landing tower in sight, just a few hangars and several dozen tied-down single-engine propeller planes. They taxied to a stop at one of the hangars, where a limousine was waiting. The copilot shut the engines down and the pilot got up and opened the hatch and lowered the steps. Raleigh removed her EarPlanes, swallowing hard several times to get her ears cleared completely.

"You wait here for a minute, ma'am. We'll get your things and have them pull the car right up to the door."

Raleigh remained seated, but unfastened her seat belt, stowed her laptop and checked her tote and backpack.

"How was the flight for you, ma'am?" The copilot came back and got her things.

"I'll never want to travel commercial again. Is it okay if I take a bottled water?" she asked as she got up and followed the copilot toward the hatch.

"Ma'am, you can empty the whole pantry if you want."

Raleigh limited herself to the bottle of water, then a second one as she remembered her bedhead, and waited for the copilot to clear the stairs. The pilot reached out a hand and helped her down to the tarmac where the limousine had been pulled up to the luggage compartment of the plane and several of her oversized bags were being unloaded. Ordinarily Raleigh traveled light, but she didn't know how long settling George Mobley's estate would take and she preferred to be prepared for any type of weather in Ohio. One minute it could be eighty degrees with 99-percent humidity, the next there could be frost on the tulips.

The copilot stowed her tote and backpack in the limousine and he and the pilot waited with her in the mist while the limousine driver adjusted the luggage in the trunk.

"When you're ready to go back give me a call," the pilot said as he handed Raleigh a business card. "We won't be more than five hours away."

"Ma'am, we can leave whenever you're ready," the limo driver said as he walked over and opened the rear door for her. She shook hands with the pilot and copilot and got into the limousine. Raleigh wondered if she should have tipped them. But even a meager ten percent of the cost of the flight must be at least a thousand dollars! The driver got behind the wheel and Raleigh was on her way, still wondering about the gratuity.

Chapter Two

The limousine glided smoothly down the two-lane road toward the city of Greenhaven as Raleigh reset her watch. It was one o'clock here, ten o'clock back in Pine Grove. She cracked open one of the bottles of water and gingerly dampened the back of her head and tried to fluff her hair a bit. Even on a good day her hair didn't fluff well, but it start to feel a bit less flat. As her hairdresser used to say, "There's nothing worse than walking around with poodle butt on the back of your head."

Fields of onions in rich, brown muck passed by on either side of the road, newly planted by an army of laborers, their boots and hands crusted in mud as they pulled clusters of the sets from the back of a flatbed truck and jammed them into the soil one at a time. Further on other workers were taking a break for lunch, sheltered from the drizzle underneath a tarp canopy, while a tractor plowed the next muddy field into rows ready for planting.

A sign alongside the road welcomed her and everyone else to Greenhaven, Ohio, Population 54,349, Salad Bowl City. At this point the farm fields stopped abruptly and were replaced by an unfortunately unimaginative, cheap, housing development. Instead of row after row of onions, row after row of cheaply-constructed homes sprouted three feet apart. They had the obligatory patch of anemic grass in front, but there wasn't a single tree in sight. Raleigh hoped all of Greenhaven didn't look like this.

And the housing developments did give way to more appealing neighborhoods as they reached the city proper where the homes were older and trees lined the streets. Here there was some personality and individuality—a Craftsman bungalow next to what looked like a former farmhouse with a wide porch that would provide even more welcome shade in the summer. A Victorian carriage house looked like it was being used as a residence, then a Midwestern foursquare, not a bit of vinyl siding or cookie-cutter concrete patio in sight. Raleigh could see huge stands of lilacs that would fill the air with their scent the minute the sun came out and the old-fashioned white hydrangea were budding. Tulips and daffodils stood guard at the base of the shrubs and the grass was rich and dewy.

As they approached the business district of Greenhaven it was clear that some of these lovely old homes had been converted to offices, but most retained their charm due to thoughtful conversions. It was in front of one of these, a two-story Craftsman house, that the limousine came to a stop. A discreet brass plaque on one of the porch pillars held a single line—Andrew Newton, Esq.

"We're here, ma'am."

The driver got out and opened the door for her and handed her onto the sidewalk. The drizzle had let up and Raleigh didn't bother to put up the hood on her jacket. She reached back into the limousine and retrieved her tote and slung it over her shoulder.

"Are you going to wait here for me? I don't know what Mr. Newton arranged."

"Well, my instructions are to take your bags to the hotel, check you in, then return here and take you to the hotel when you're ready."

"You'd better wait here for a moment while I talk to Mr. Newton. I may be staying at the house instead."

"Certainly, ma'am, whatever you wish. I'm at your disposal."

The driver closed the door and almost stood at attention while Raleigh walked up the steps and to the front door.

Raleigh rang the bell and waited a moment, but no one answered so she tried the knob. The door was unlocked and she let herself into what must have been the original vestibule of the house. The inner door was also unlocked and when she walked through she was in the former parlor. Everything from the carpet to the drapes and the furniture were all appropriate to the Craftsman style; the computer on what looked to her like a genuine Stickley desk was not. Nor was the man behind the desk.

Raleigh waited for her presence to be acknowledged, but as the man continued working at his computer she realized he was wearing a tiny headset and was apparently transcribing something. She walked closer and edged into his line of sight, not wanting to startle him. She failed in that intention.

"Yaaahhh!" The man jerked back from the desk, pulling the tiny headset from his ears. He punched quickly at the transcription machine and stopped the tape. "What do you think you're doing, sneaking up on me like that? You nearly gave me a heart attack!"

"I'm sorry . . . I rang the bell . . . The doors were unlocked . . ."

He crossed his arms over his faded, inside-out Nebraska Cornhuskers sweatshirt and glared at her. She noticed he had three earrings in one ear. Rather a lot of hipness, in her opinion, for someone who looked like he was forty-five.

"I can't hear the bell with headset on." He looked at her as though she should have known that and started to replace the headset.

"Wait, please, I'm here to see Mr. Newton. I have an appointment. I'm Raleigh Killen."

"As Judy Garland said in *A Star Is Born*, 'I just don't care.'" The lanky man gave a good imitation of Judy Garland.

"It wasn't *A Star Is Born*, it was *I Could Go On Singing*, directed by Laurence Harvey. But you gave a very good imitation."

"So it was. And so I did. Who did you say you are?"

At least she seemed to have his attention now. "Raleigh Killen. I'm here about the George Mobley estate. And you're . . . Mr. Newton?"

"Mobley . . . Mobley . . ." The man got up from behind the desk, all six feet three inches of him, and took off his glasses while he rummaged through a Stickley-style file cabinet. Raleigh was pretty sure Gustav never made legal-size file cabinets, but they were very convincing all the same.

"Ah, here it is." The man turned back to her with several file folders. Without his glasses, she could see that he had dark brown eyes almost the same shade as his hair. She took in the sweatshirt, the faded jeans, the Birkenstocks on his bare feet.

"Are *you* Mr. Newton?"

That question was now met with a snort, but not an entirely unfriendly one and he suddenly extended a hand toward her.

"Bluff, Jon Bluff, no *H*."

"I'm pleased to meet you, Mr. Bluff." Raleigh wasn't at all sure that she was pleased, but she was determined to observe the niceties.

"Likewise, Miss Raleigh Killen. You're the heiress, now I remember. Since you're an heiress, you can call me Jon."

"Uh, thanks. I'm . . . honored."

"You should be. I don't generally allow such familiarities."

He scanned the contents of the first folder, then checked the other three.

"Everything should be here, but it always pays to be sure. If Newt-face got his hands on these who knows if it's intact."

Raleigh didn't comment on the nickname Jon used for the absent lawyer, she was too busy rummaging in her tote, from which she finally withdrew the minican of potato chips and the bottled water she had liberated earlier from the plane.

Jon looked up as the vacuum seal on the potato chip can burped. "What are you doing? You can't eat in here. This is a business office."

"Sorry, but I didn't have lunch and I'm starving." She tucked a whole potato chip into her mouth and crunched.

"You can't eat that!" He reached across the desk with his gangly arm and snatched the can from her hands before she could get another potato chip.

"Mr. Bluff," she addressed him with the authoritative tone that she often used with dogs, misbehaving children and, eventually, most of the men she ever dated, "I have not eaten lunch and from the looks of those files lunch is not in my immediate future. I would be very obliged if you would return that." She held out her hand for the potato chips.

"Here." He shoved the files toward her instead and strode through a swinging door with her potato chips.

"Hey! Come back here!" She ran after him and found herself in a dining room, also furnished with Stickley. Raleigh could see Jon through another doorway in the vintage 1950s kitchen feeding her potato chips into the garbage disposal. She barely noticed the change in decades of the décor.

"I don't think Mr. Newton would approve of your behavior, Mr. Bluff, and I will inform him of your extreme rudeness the minute I see him."

Jon ignored her threat and opened the Sub-Zero refrigerator and got a carton of eggs, a bunch of scallions from the crisper, a carton of sour cream and what looked like hash browns covered with plastic wrap.

"You'll have a long wait to 'inform him of my rudeness.' He's in Texas, consulting on a copyright infringement case."

Raleigh dropped into one of the fifties-vintage chrome chairs and set her bottled water on the red boomerang-pattern Formica tabletop.

"He's not here? But he has to be here. He has to go over the estate with me." She was more than a little dismayed at the lawyer's absence. "I . . . I was counting on him to help take care of things."

Jon cracked three eggs into a bowl, setting aside two of the yolks, and whipped the remainder into a froth. He put a copper omelet pan on the stove to preheat, popped the hash browns onto a paper towel and into the microwave, then diced the scallions. The beaten eggs went into the pan, sizzling and cooking as Jon swirled them around. Two slices of sourdough bread were inserted in the Dualit toaster, a big spoonful of sour cream landed on top of the nearly-set eggs, then the scallions and the hash browns from the microwave. One flip of the wooden spatula and Jon slid the omelet onto a Vernon plate, brown-eyed Susan pattern, and placed it in front of Raleigh. A white napkin, cutlery, pepper mill and saltcellar followed. The toaster popped.

"Wal-lah!"

Chapter Three

Raleigh polished off the last bite of toast and heaved a very unladylike sigh of satisfaction. She had lost all inclination to vent any wrath on Jon Bluff, though she might find a bit to spare for Andrew Newt-face, Esq.

"Thank you, Jon, thank you very much. I'm sorry I snapped at you, but . . . what am I going to do without Mr. Newton? When will he be back?"

Jon collected the dishes and rinsed them in the sink, then stacked them in the dishpan. "Never fear, dear lady, you are in my capable hands. Dessert? I have a slice of Meyer lemon tart in the fridge."

"I know most people seem to like chocolate best, but give me lemon any time."

"A kindred spirit. You'll split it with me."

He got a square Tupperware container from the Sub-Zero and plugged in an electric teakettle and scooped tea from a canister into two clear glass mugs.

"Is there anything I can do to help?"

"It's a little late for that," Jon said as he placed the Tupperware container on the table, added two forks, poured water into the mugs and brought them over to the table.

Jon dropped into the chair next to her, burped the Tupperware lid off and dug in. He gestured for Raleigh to help herself. She did.

"Ummm, this is fantastic . . ."

"Made it myself."

"Really?"

"Escoffier, class of 1999."

"You're a chef? Then why are you working for a lawyer? Why aren't you running a restaurant?"

"I did for a while, *Heaven* in San Francisco. Wasn't worth the stress. Every night was an *opera tragique*."

"But still . . . from Escoffier to small town, Midwest law office? That's quite a change."

"Not really. I grew up here, you see. Graduated from Juilliard, decided being a professional pianist wasn't my thing after all. Harvard MBA after that—didn't like the suit life, though. Cop for two years in Cleveland—'nuff said about that."

Raleigh stopped believing Jon's story as they swapped the lemon tart back and forth and she had trouble stifling the laughter that was welling in her throat.

"Became an architect specializing in restoring historic homes—you're sitting in an example of my work—and the decorating of same. Which brought me back here. While I was working on this place for Newt-face I filled in answering the phones and he kept wanting to share my lunch, so I started cooking him dinner, too. He wasn't going to bother restoring the upstairs, uses a lot of it for file storage, but I squeezed in an apartment for myself and moved in while he was out of town. It took him nearly two weeks to notice.

"I toil like a dog for mere room and board and health insurance—and the pension plan—and a percentage of all business I bring in. The senior citizen trust/will package was my idea. It's a snap to prepare, mostly fill-in-the-blanks, and we collect when the senior citizen becomes the dearly departed.

"In the case of George Mobley I prepared the trust and the will; he died two weeks after he signed the documents. We already took our fee from the estate, as you will see when we go over the updated financial statements, and I set about finding you. Actually, we didn't make as much as I hoped from this one, it took quite a while to identify you and then determine there weren't any more heirs. None of that was cheap—and chartering a jet? Don't get me started. But it's part of the package, estate settlement for a flat fee. More than half the time we come out ahead."

Raleigh looked up at the vintage clock on the wall over the sink—5:30. Jon noticed, too.

"Oh-my-gosh, I'll be late for class!" He quickly wiped his hands on a dish towel and ran out of the kitchen.

Raleigh followed him through the dining room and into the outer office, where Jon shoved the file folders into her hands and pushed her toward the door. "Go through these tonight, we can talk tomorrow."

She grabbed her tote bag on the way out and they were suddenly on the porch with him locking the front door.

"Have you checked her in?!" Jon shouted to the driver, who was holding the limo door for Raleigh.

"It's done, dude. I went right after you messaged me. Don't get your shorts in a twist."

Raleigh got into the limousine and tried to make room in her tote for the file folders. "I'll go over these tonight and we'll . . . ?"

"I'll meet you at the Mobley house tomorrow at nine." Jon didn't wait to wave good-bye, he jumped into the green PT Cruiser parked in the driveway and backed out.

"You can take a look around and head back to Washington!" Jon shouted from the open car window and he was gone.

Chapter Four

The following day dawned far too soon for Raleigh. She was snuggled into a surprisingly comfortable hotel bed sound asleep when the phone rang with her wake-up call.

Raleigh stretched and yawned and struggled free of the down comforter and sat on the edge of the bed. In spite of eating healthy most of the time, taking her vitamins, yoga practice every day and regular, vigorous walks—she was getting old. Mentally she had felt old as long as she could remember, but now her body had decided to start catching up—with a vengeance.

Oh well, some forward bends to unkink her back and she was able to walk to the bathroom without too many pops and snaps. She started the water running in the Jacuzzi tub, went into the sitting room and pulled a bottle of water from the complimentary mini-bar and stretched upward and yawned again.

Two extra-strength aspirin now, the vitamins would be taken with her breakfast. The sitting room was covered with papers and files and she started to replace everything in the proper folders while she waited for her laptop to boot up. It was chained to the flimsy piece of furniture with a tamperproof, she hoped, cable. Once online, Raleigh checked her e-mail and found a message from her friend Rachel and another from Marty. Rachel could wait, but the contractor couldn't find her spec sheet for the faucet in the kitchen—would she send it to him again? She located the original message and resent it to the contractor, with what she hoped was tactful reminder of the schedule. Raleigh intended to leave Greenhaven, Ohio, in four weeks or less and move into the house in Pine Grove. Her addendum to the contract penalizing the contractor one thousand dollars a day for each of the first five days he was late might be sufficient motivation for timely performance of his duties, but the bump to five thousand a day after that should really keep him on track. Though it wasn't Marty's fault that the remodeling wasn't done immediately after escrow closed, he seemed to understand Raleigh's frustration and annoyance and agreed to her terms.

Raleigh logged off and went back to the bathroom and adjusted the water temperature, adding a scoop of lavender bath salts from the container on the edge of the tub. Her toiletries were scattered on the vanity, all that she had unpacked besides her nightshirt the previous evening. She knew she wasn't supposed to have jet lag going from west to east, but she did anyway. A long soak in the tub to get the last of the knots out and she'd be ready for breakfast in her room.

While the Fairview Hotel wasn't the Four Seasons, not that Raleigh had ever been inside a Four Seasons, she had a two-room suite with a very comfortable bed, plenty of fluffy pillows, free beverages in the mini-bar and a gloriously oversized bathtub. Raleigh eased herself into the hot, slightly purple water and sank back with a sigh and wondered how much the estate was paying for this. But for the moment she would enjoy it.

* * *

Raleigh was out of the tub and dressed, her short hair still damp, when she left the hotel room and took the somewhat-creaky elevator down to the first floor. Seven o'clock was apparently early here; the only person she saw was the desk clerk. They exchanged good-morning nods and Raleigh walked out onto the street.

The Fairview Hotel was located in the center of downtown Greenhaven, as shown on the hotel brochure, and Raleigh set off to explore the surrounding streets. She walked briskly for thirty minutes, circling the block where the hotel was located, then expanding outward a block at a time. The downtown was four extended blocks long with two short blocks running parallel to the main street. She passed five antique stores in the first two blocks, a gourmet food shop, the ubiquitous Starbucks on the second corner being the only business open at this early hour. The lone barista was poring over a textbook and nodding sleepily. Raleigh pressed on and was rewarded with an art gallery featuring local artists—she would return later when the gallery was open—the original Carnegie library, with an unfortunate concrete block wing shoved onto the back, one dress shop and men's clothing store, a tea shop and several two-story vintage buildings that had been salvaged from the wrecking ball and converted to office space. Down one street was a sign indicating the beginning of the historic homes district and she recognized it as yesterday's route from the lawyer's office.

Raleigh checked her watch and saw that her allotted thirty minutes had passed and she headed back the way she came toward the hotel. She preferred to retrace her steps to avoid getting lost when she was in an unfamiliar town. Raleigh was well-aware, as were her friends, that her sense of direction was so faulty she could get lost backing out of her own driveway.

The day was starting to warm up already and it was slightly humid, so Raleigh was tired and sweating when she got back to her hotel room. She was still used to the dry air of the southwest and had forgotten how difficult it is to breathe when the humidity was high. She grabbed a Diet Pepsi from the mini-bar and popped the top. *Who needs coffee?*

The sharp knock on the door startled her and she walked over to the door and looked through the peephole—a waiter with her breakfast. She opened the door and cleared a space on the coffee table for the tray. She signed for the breakfast and was careful to use all the locks after the waiter left.

Raleigh sat down to her breakfast of oatmeal with brown sugar, scrambled eggs, a pot of tea and a dish of strawberries. The scrambled eggs were runny, yuck. She set them aside and poured soymilk on her oatmeal. While she ate, she tried to review the updated balance sheets, but she wasn't able to concentrate on numbers this early in the day, not without a calculator.

Raleigh gave up on the paperwork and switched on the television to look for some local news. All she could find were the network morning shows with attractive anchors whose white teeth blinded you when they smiled, which seemed like most of the time, whether a smile was appropriate or not.

Maybe the Cartoon Network . . . ? *Yu-Gi-Oh!*. She hated Japanese animation, it was so flat. TV Land . . . ? Bingo, *Mister Ed*, one of her favorites. Raleigh had probably seen each of the episodes at least ten times, but it was better than being bored by the big three networks or terrified by the blood, violence, rumor-mongering, and unrelenting sensationalism found on CNN and its analogs.

Old TV shows had a lot of appeal to Raleigh, though when she first saw many them it was as an adult. Her mother and father had been older than her peers' parents and by the time she started public school she had already been indoctrinated into the joys of reading and playing outdoors and spending what would now be called "quality time" with her parents and aged aunts. Television viewing was reserved for an hour on Saturday and Sunday nights. Her upbringing was surely to blame for her early-onset maturity and her inability to understand other children even when she was one. She never felt superior to her peers, but she didn't see the charm of comic books, a Betsy Wetsy doll, Silly Putty, or any of the myriad of things that seemed to entrance other children her age. Though never a budding athlete, Raleigh could jump rope with the best of the girls and climb the monkey bars and swing for hours while she daydreamed. There were chemistry experiments at home, growing colorful crystals on chunks of coal, exploding baking soda volcanoes—she thought it was baking soda, maybe it was baking powder. Anyway, her parents encouraged her to make messes whether in search of scientific breakthroughs as she did when she imagined she was Marie Curie, or her artistic endeavors as she tried to imitate Salvador Dali and ended up Jackson Pollock. Though eager to try and wanting to succeed, she realized she would never be a scientist or an artist. She majored in English almost by default.

When reruns of the black-and-white TV shows started to hit the air Raleigh was in her thirties and *Father Knows Best*, *Ozzie and Harriet*, *Mister Ed* and the others were new to her. She had been a fan of most of the fifties shows ever since—even *Have Gun Will Travel*, which appeared within the last two years on a new channel offered by her cable service. And she didn't generally like Westerns.

Perry Mason, especially the earliest episodes, was a show she really enjoyed. The mysteries he solved, with the able assistance of shapely Della and stolid Paul, seemed almost funny now, but mysteries were her favorite form of entertainment, whether on television or in print. On *Perry Mason* the guilty party was always caught and punished, too. Not at all like real life. And Perry was a hunk with that wavy, dark hair and those sultry eyes.

Raleigh scraped the last of the oatmeal from her bowl and poured another cup of tea and tried one of the strawberries. Much to her surprise, it was actually good, not tasteless as early strawberries usually are. She popped another one in her mouth as the phone rang. She muted Wilbur and Carol and picked up the receiver.

"Ms. Killen, this is the front desk. Your car is here."

"Oh, thank you. I didn't realize it was so late. Tell the driver I'll be right down." Raleigh switched off the Thanksgiving story according to *Mister Ed* and stuffed the papers into her tote. She grabbed her jacket and hurried from the room, wishing she had taken the time to make the bed. Though she never made her bed at home, she didn't want the housekeeping staff to think she was a slob.

Chapter Five

Raleigh didn't wait for the creaky elevator, she took the fire stairs two at a time, hating herself for losing track of the hour. She bolted from the stairwell, startling the janitor who was mopping the tile floor, and stepped carefully around the wet area.

"Good morning, ma'am." The earlier desk clerk had been replaced by a young woman who was far too perky for any time of day. Perhaps she was another Katie Couric in the making. Raleigh walked across the lobby and through the entrance.

The limousine was waiting at the curb, motor running. She apologized to the driver for keeping him waiting and jumped into the backseat. He got behind the wheel and they pulled down the drive and onto the street.

The driver took a route that wound toward the outskirts of town, then the bypass took them quickly north of town into a residential area of hills, tall evergreens, and curving, narrow roads. Near the top of one of the hills they pulled out of the shade of the overhanging maple trees and into Sunrise Hills, a WWII-era development of bungalows on neat lots, most with well-tended yards, some with a motor home parked alongside the garage.

At the end of Spruce Circle, the limousine stopped. Jon's PT Cruiser was parked in the driveway of what had to be George Mobley's former house and was now hers, at least until she managed to sell it. The house was quite compact, probably only two bedrooms and one bath, but the outside was freshly painted, gray with white trim, a red front door with a white screen door and a pair of red wooden shoes nailed up on either side of the bay window. A chain-link fence encircled the yard, a practical choice considering the weather in Ohio, and a detached one-car garage was visible at the end of the cramped driveway. The yard was well established without being overgrown, lilacs flanking the front steps, narcissus at the base of the shrubs, somewhat patchy, weedy grass recently mowed.

The driver handed Raleigh out and retrieved her hastily-loaded tote bag. Jon must have heard the limousine door slam because he came through the front door and waited on the porch for Raleigh to climb the steps. Once she got onto the porch Raleigh saw that there was a white porch swing at one end with a red, metal glider chair nearby.

"Miss Raleigh, you found the palatial manor that is now all yours. You're late."

"Good morning to you, too. I'm sorry I'm late, but I went for a walk through your downtown."

"It isn't my downtown, but the office conversion on 3rd and London? I will take credit for that.

"Well, Miss Raleigh, are you ready to take possession of the old homestead?" He dangled a ring of keys from his hand.

"You of all people should know that this is not my old homestead. Until your boss called, I never knew George Mobley existed."

"Newt-face is not my boss, we're . . . collaborators."

"Collaborators, huh? Like in the French Resistance?"

Jon rolled his eyes and ignored Raleigh's joke. "Back to the issue of your legacy. Your aunt's marriage to Dick Mobley was perfectly legal, but why she never divorced him after he deserted her . . . you would know more about that than I."

"I suppose I should know, but I don't. Aunt Sue was already in her seventies when I was born, she was my mother's oldest sister, and she and Aunt Lily had lived together in their parents' house since they were born. I always thought they were old maids, but since you discovered Dick Mobley's marriage to Aunt Sue, that clearly wasn't true." Raleigh sat on the porch swing and looked out at the neighborhood.

"Maybe George Mobley's father took everything Aunt Sue had and she couldn't afford a divorce, or was too embarrassed he left her, or maybe she wanted to pretend it never happened. Having been through a divorce myself, even an amicable one, you do want to put that part of your life behind you."

"That was eight years ago. It took you a while to move on . . . or move."

"How did you know that?"

"It came up in the research."

Raleigh's aunt was forgotten for the moment.

"Oh, really? That's very thorough research."

"I like to know who I'm dealing with."

"Yes, well . . . well, when Aunt Sue died, Aunt Lily went on as usual, she was a seamstress. She passed away seven years ago. And left a real treasure trove of old photographs, correspondence, postcards, all kinds of paper records, some of it from the 1800s! I still haven't had time to sort it out and compare it with the photo albums from my parents, but it's one of my projects after I get settled. If those boxes hadn't already been in storage I would have looked for a marriage license or something when Mr. Newton first called.

"As though I need another project. First I need my own house finished, then I need to register for classes . . . I must like living in chaos."

"Well, you won't find much chaos here. I haven't gone through the house except to look for financial records, which you already have in the statements I gave you yesterday. I couldn't locate the deed, but my nephew over at the county office got me a new one, the bills come to the office, the car registration is in the glove compartment, I put the title to that in your name already. Nope, you won't find a treasure trove here, Miss Raleigh."

"The car is Honda, right?"

"A Honda? Not just a Honda, a cherry Honda Civic, 1984, with only eight thousand-something miles on it."

"That's not possible. It must have zeroed out at least once."

"Nope, I had the mechanic check when I took it in for a tune-up. It's the original mileage. Maybe George was smart enough to realize he was too old to drive anymore. It runs like a dream and if you decide to sell it I can take care of that, too."

"Well, I will sell it, but why don't I use it while I'm here? I'll be here a month and that limousine is nice, but I'd just as soon drive myself around. The town's small enough, even I can't get too lost."

Jon looked taken aback. "A month? I can sell the house and everything for you. You don't want to hang around here for a month."

"The remodeling on my new place started only last week and I would prefer to stay out of the way until it's over."

"It's your decision, Miss Killen." Jon spoke stiffly and disapproval was written all over his face.

Raleigh wondered briefly why Jon's attitude changed so suddenly, but she mentally shrugged it off.

Jon held the screen door open. "Now, shall we take a look inside?" He smiled charmingly, but his eyes were cool.

Raleigh got off the porch swing and saw a curtain fall back into place at the house on the other side of the driveway. Jon noticed, too.

"They've been watching since I got here."

"They?"

"Neighbors on both sides."

"I hope they come over and say hi. I'd like to know something about Cousin George. And if they're elderly, so much the better. They'll have the scoop on everyone who ever lived in the neighborhood."

She shouldered her tote and Jon ushered her into the house.

Chapter Six

Though Jon arrived earlier and opened the doors and windows the house still smelled musty and probably would for a while. There was a thick layer of dust everywhere, but all appeared neat and somewhat Spartan.

There was dark, cheap paneling in the entry, which was carried into wainscoting in the living room, the walls topped with dingy wallpaper that may have been original to the house. In this case, original was not a plus. The carpet was an indeterminate color of drab shag, probably the same vintage as the Sears paneling and dust-coated "satin" drapes, color also uncertain.

The furniture was sparse and shabby, a sofa positioned facing the front windows, upholstery faded and grimy where hands had rested for decades; a matching chair and ottoman, equally grimy; a coffee table with peeling veneer and cigarette burns; two floor lamps with cracked, yellowed shades—and when Raleigh turned away from the sofa—a large console TV, covered with dust, a cable box on top.

"Does it work? It can't work. We had a TV like that once, the back was full of tubes."

"As unlikely as it seems, it does work. Black-and-white, though."

"When something went wrong we took the tubes down to the drugstore and plugged them into the tester, then bought whatever new tube we needed."

"The cable's still on, as are all the utilities. Since you're going to sell the house, prospective buyers will want to check everything, so I left that as is."

Raleigh nodded and walked into the dining room, which was occupied by a bare early American table with one chair and a matching hutch. There wasn't anything displayed on the hutch, nor were there any pictures on the living room or dining room walls. George Mobley, though an old man when he died, obviously didn't believe in saving things, or buying things in the first place.

"I guess George Mobley was a minimalist."

Jon snorted.

The kitchen was a bit less dusty, but much grimier than the living room and held a small wooden dinette set painted a dingy mint green, dated Harvest Gold appliances, an old, corroded chrome toaster and percolator, a small countertop microwave and a pitted enamel sink. As they walked across the floor the cracked brown linoleum crunched under their feet.

Raleigh checked the kitchen faucet, which worked, and flipped a light switch. A not-so-dazzling 40-watt bulb struggled to illuminate the dingy pantry. There was a wealth of food, canned and boxed, on the shelves, staples in reused glass jars, spices in smaller jars, and rusted metal tins that held who knows what. She took a glass jar of something white and granular off a shelf and could see minute spiderwebs inside.

"How long do you has this food been here? It looks like it came over on the *Mayflower*."

"From my own observations, George Mobley was a 'thrifty' man. If he bought something he kept it, well . . . until he died. But an agent will be able to see past the dirt."

"I'm going to clean all of this out before I let a real estate agent in here. Maybe that funny smell will go away. What do you think it is?"

"Well, mold, for one thing. Cigarette smoke, sweat. Something kind of chemical, too. Some of those plastic containers in there are deteriorating."

"All this food has to go and definitely a good cleaning, top to bottom."

"Before we venture into the cellar, let's finish this floor. The smell down there is even worse."

They walked past the back door and Raleigh could see a rusting washer and dryer sitting on the porch. "Those go, too. Can you arrange to have a dumpster brought in?"

"Sure thing, Miss Raleigh, your wish is my command." Jon's tone was deliberately light.

There was a bathroom in the hall, sandwiched between the two bedrooms. Raleigh looked inside briefly and was surprised to see that, though dirty, the bathroom had an old clawfoot tub and pedestal sink—both apparently in good shape. The toilet was the old variety with the water for flushing in a tank suspended from the wall overhead. She stepped in and pulled the chain. It worked.

"I've been stopping by every other week to run water in the sinks, flush the toilet, make sure none of the pipes were leaking over the winter. Someone spent a lot of money when they installed the plumbing, all copper pipes."

"You're very conscientious."

"It's all part of our service, Miss Raleigh."

The bedrooms were both tiny, only one furnished as a bedroom, with a twin bed, two mismatched nightstands, a dresser with warped drawers and peeling veneer, then a tiny closet. The closet was barely the depth of the clothes hangers and the clothes on those hangers were moth-eaten and decades old.

Cousin George had obviously not been a fashion plate and most of the clothes appeared to be work clothes.

"What did he do for a living?"

"I don't know exactly, but he worked for Atlas Manufacturing starting in 1940, a factory worker I guess. Atlas was a subcontractor for the auto industry, but they moved their operations overseas maybe fifteen years ago. Whatever he did there involved exposure to something toxic, that's how you get the type of cancer that killed him."

"Do you know if any of his friends are still alive?"

"No one was mentioned in the will, but you could ask the neighbors—if they'll talk to you. As I've been coming and going I've noticed one or more of them watching me, though they pretended not to be home when I knocked on the door across the way." Jon nodded toward the house across the driveway that could be seen through the smoke-streaked bedroom window.

They looked into the second bedroom, stacked with mismatched boxes.

"I took a good look around when he first died, had to find the current bills and bank statements, and I checked into the boxes for valuables, but it all seems to be mildewed magazines and crumbling papers. I did see some old photographs, but I don't remember where. If you do find anything of value, let me know. We'll need to update the numbers for tax purposes—in case you find a stash of diamonds, or IBM stock certificates or something. Unless I can take a cut."

"Besides the house, there doesn't seem to be much of value. The few thousand left in the checking account . . . it isn't much for eighty-five years."

"Maybe that's the way it should be. Spend your money while you're alive, die when you're broke. Are you ready to see the cellar?" Jon wiggled his eyebrows dramatically.

"Sure, why not. It can't be worse than this."

"Wanna bet? Around the back. You have to get to it from outside."

They went through the back door and into the barren backyard. Raleigh could have sworn she saw someone duck out of sight behind the rotting back fence.

"There are eyes all around us." Jon's light tone seemed forced.

"I noticed."

Jon led her over to a warped door set into the foundation and unlocked it.

They stepped down into an old root cellar with dirt floor and walls. Ramshackle shelves were buckled and rotted. Jon switched on the bare lightbulb that hung from the ceiling, this one probably 25-watts. Raleigh could barely see a very old gas furnace and the remnants of a coal bin and chute. She nodded toward the furnace.

"Does that work?"

"Surprisingly well, I suppose because the house is so small. It's quite noisy, but I had it checked and it ran fine all through the winter."

Raleigh turned and walked out of the cellar with some alacrity.

Jon relocked the cellar door and they walked back into the house.

At the front door, Raleigh paused. "I didn't realize there would be so much work to do to get the house in shape to sell. This is a couple of weeks of cleaning at least."

"I can get a crew in if you like, but you'll still want to sort through things. Or not. I can trash everything and have the house cleaned and take care of the sale for you. You can still fly back to Washington today."

"That's tempting, but . . . no. Cleaning will keep me occupied here."

They stood there silently for a moment and Jon finally dug in his pocket and handed her two sets of keys. "The car keys and the house keys. The blue one opens the bedroom doors. Double deadbolts on both. Why, I don't know so don't ask. And let me show you how the alarm system works." He closed the front door and now she could see the keypad mounted on the wall.

"An alarm system? For what? There's nothing in here worth stealing."

"Maybe he was paranoid, or crazy. Or both. Here . . ." Jon showed her how to arm and disarm the system and gave her one of his business cards. "As you see, the alarm code is the last four digits of my office number. The code word, if you set the alarm off accidentally—and the monitoring company will call to check, is 'Georgy Porgy.' I gave them your cell number."

"You've made it easy to remember."

"Just so you know, the estate prepaid your accomodations for two days. Beyond that, the expense is on you."

Chapter Seven

Raleigh stayed behind at what was now her house after Jon left, in his PT Cruiser, and the driver, in his limousine. The garage had contained the aforementioned Honda Civic, in near-perfect condition as Jon stated. Jon located a Greenhaven street map and, at Raleigh's insistence, dismissed the limo driver, who was also his cousin, and left her to her own devices. She intended to drive to the closest grocery store and stock up on cleaning supplies, then head back to the hotel and let them know she would be checking out of her room.

Though Raleigh didn't tell Jon, she decided to move into the house. There was so much cleaning to do that she'd have to be here most of the time anyway and she had to sort through the boxes containing George Mobley's life, which would take at least a week. Besides, Jon's eagerness for her departure had aroused her suspicions and she thought it would be best for the house to be occupied. Her caution was probably unnecessary, but his reaction to her taking an active interest in the estate might indicate that she should take a closer look at the financial statements.

Yes, staying at the house made the most sense and she could cook for herself once she cleaned out the kitchen. The hotel food would pall very quickly for her, even if she wasn't a vegetarian.

Raleigh backed the Honda down the driveway and onto the street, then went back to close the garage door—no fancy automatic opener for George Mobley—when someone jumped out of the shadows inside.

The someone, an elderly man, couldn't move fast enough to make his escape and Raleigh stood between him and the door. He looked as startled as she was sure she must have, but after an awkward moment he brushed his blue-veined, gnarled hands on his elastic waist jeans and extended one toward her.

"Um . . . welcome to the neighborhood. I'm . . . um, Hash Peters. From next door." Hash jerked his head toward the house on the left.

"Hello, Mr. Peters, I'm Raleigh Killen. George Mobley's cousin—second cousin-in-law, to be exact. At least that's what the lawyer told me."

They shook hands briefly.

"Oh, yes. The heir. Figured there must be one."

She nodded cordially and waited for Hash Peters to explain himself. He rocked back and forth on his heels for a moment.

"Never heard old George talk about any relatives."

"I daresay he never knew about me any more than I knew about him—until Mr. Newton contacted me a couple of weeks ago."

"Didn't waste no time, did you?"

"Well, it happens that . . . ," Raleigh started to explain, but decided the story was none of this geriatric trespasser's business.

"Were you looking for something in here, Mr. Peters?"

"It's Hash. Everyone calls me Hash. Short for Hamish." Hash looked somewhat desperately around the garage and grabbed a rusted set of branch loppers. "Old George borrowed these last fall. Needed 'em back."

The story was perfectly plausible, but Hash's expression was so guilty that Raleigh couldn't believe him. The loppers were corroded beyond being useful to anyone, but if he wanted to pretend they were his she didn't really care.

"Well, it's a good thing you found them, Mr. Peters . . . Hash. And it's nice to meet one of my cousin's friends. Since I didn't know him I'd like to talk to you about him when I have more time." She nodded meaningfully toward the garage door and stepped out of his way. He made a break for it as fast as he could at his age, certainly eighty plus. By the time Raleigh got the garage door back down and the lock secured he was long gone.

Hash Peters had been up to something in the garage. The question was—what?

Raleigh liked most elderly people, they reminded her in some way of her parents and their friends. That was probably why she was going to study gerontology instead of childhood development or something; she already knew a lot about the elderly from her own personal experience. Too many people dismissed them, forgetting their lives could be far more fascinating than some dot-com millionaire's—if anyone took the time to listen.

Raleigh walked back down the driveway and got into the Honda. She spread out the map and oriented herself so she could follow the route Jon had drawn to Kroger, the closest grocery store. When Raleigh came back to drop off the cleaning supplies perhaps she would knock on the neighbors' doors herself. She was very curious about what Hash Peters had really been looking for in the garage. She could see the silhouette of a figure behind the lace curtains at the house on the right side as she pulled around Spruce Circle and drove away.

Chapter Eight

Raleigh walked across the McDonald's parking lot with her cup of diet caffeine. The day was quite warm now and she shed her jacket and left the car door open for a moment while she rearranged her map and looked for a cup holder—to no avail. Apparently cupholders weren't as ubiquitous in 1984 as they are now. She took another drink and wedged her cup on the seat between her tote bag and her jacket. She double-checked the map and pulled out of the parking lot in search of the grocery store.

* * *

The Kroger was as well stocked as Jon said and Raleigh loaded her cart with cleaning supplies, all in the largest sizes she could find. She didn't remember seeing even the most basic tools for cleaning at the house—mop, broom, pail, sponges—so she loaded up those, too. And the jumbo packages of paper towels and cleanser, scrubbers, a couple of gallons of bleach—it all teetered alarmingly in the overstuffed cart as she wrestled it toward the checkout.

The checker took pity on her and got a bagger to help unload everything onto the belt, then reload it into two carts after it was scanned.

The total rose steadily on the cash register readout, but they took credit cards so she decided to charge everything. Raleigh brought some cash with her, and a few traveler's checks, but until she located a compatible ATM, she didn't want to run short. By the time the checker was done, her total was just over two hundred dollars.

The bagger pushed one cart, Raleigh the other, across the parking lot to the Honda, where another problem arose; how to fit everything inside the tiny hatchback. By folding down the rear seats and pushing the passenger seat forward, they managed to load it all, though one window had to be rolled down to accommodate the mop and broom and the hatchback took all of the bagger's weight to close it. The bagger nested the two carts and started back toward the store. "Good luck getting it back out, lady!"

Raleigh waved, checked her map, and pulled out of the parking lot.

* * *

It was too bad she didn't have the bagger's assistance once she got back to the house. While the paper towels had fairly exploded from the Honda when she opened the hatchback, everything else had gotten jammed in so tightly it now didn't want to come out. She carried the paper towels and one bag onto the porch and came back to the car to see what else she could free.

While Raleigh unloaded and carried things up onto the porch she could see curtains twitching on both sides of the house and at one house across the street. You'd think the neighbors' curiosity would get the better of them—and she could use some help. She sat on the porch steps for a moment to rest and looked first at one house, then the others. She sighed and wished she hadn't made Jon dismiss the driver. Or that Jon would come back to see how she was doing. Reminded of her lawyer, or whatever Jon actually was, Raleigh made another mental note to recheck the estate paperwork when she got back to the hotel. She stood and stretched, then headed back to the car.

The side door of Hash's house opened and he paused in the doorway. It looked like someone nudged him from behind and he walked out into his driveway followed by a woman in her seventies with the most beautiful white hair Raleigh had ever seen. Her hair was pure, bright white and fluffy, surrounding her head in a halo. The woman nudged Hash Peters again, but this time he didn't budge. She sniffed loudly, straightened her calico cobbler apron trimmed in rickrack, and walked down their driveway and over to Raleigh.

The woman's expression was neutral as she extended her sturdy hand. "I'm Flossie Peters. You already met my husband Hash." Flossie jerked a thumb toward Hash, hovering in the background.

"Yes, I did, Mrs. Peters. I'm Raleigh Killen, a distant cousin of your former neighbor, George Mobley."

"Call me Flossie, Mrs. Peters is my mother-in-law." Flossie looked at Raleigh appraisingly.

"You don't favor George."

"It's not surprising, we were related only by marriage. His father married one of my aunts. George was his son by a previous wife."

"Oh, so you're not really kin." Flossie looked inexplicably relieved.

"Not in the natural sense, just on a technicality. Richard, that was George's father, apparently deserted my aunt."

"That sounds like a Mobley. Probably took her for every penny, too." Hash added his two cents from a safe distance.

"I wouldn't really know. All of my relatives have been gone for some time, so there isn't anyone with whom I can check."

"Hash! Come on out here! Give the girl a hand with this stuff!"

Hash looked like helping Raleigh was the furthest thing from his mind, but he obeyed his wife and walked out to the Honda.

"It's okay, Hash. You heard her, she isn't really kin."

"Well . . . I suppose that's something." Hash admitted it grudgingly and walked closer. "What is all this mess?" He gestured at the bags in the car.

"Cleaning supplies. The house is, well, pretty dirty. I'm guessing that housework wasn't a high priority for George Mobley."

"Not that we'd know. Never been inside." Hash wrestled with the bags and started handing them out to Raleigh.

"Oh, you've not lived here long? I was hoping to talk to his neighbors, find out what he was like, you know?"

"Dear, me and Hash have lived here for going on fifty years. George was here almost that long—right after the war started."

"Not that old George got a piece of that. I went, so'd Bailey, Emmett, all of us. We went, got shot at while old George milked that one arm bein' shorter than the other for all it was worth." Hash set the last of the bags on the ground and walked around the car to try and release the mop and broom.

"Don't you pay any mind to Hash, dear. Everyone did their part. It wasn't George's fault about his arm."

"But if you've lived here all this time, I don't understand. Was he . . . well, peculiar?"

"Peculiar? The man was pure mean. He was pure mean. Not crazy, though, if that's what you're asking." Hash barely missed breaking the hatchback window with the mop handle when it popped free abruptly.

"Now, Hash, you stop talking like that. Raleigh here may not be blood kin, but it's not nice talking so about the dead."

Hash pulled the broom from the car and shoved it and the mop into Raleigh's hands. "George Mobley never let anyone in that house and we're all more than a mite curious about just what's inside," Hash hinted broadly.

"Since you've been so kind to help me unload the car it would be rude of me not to satisfy your curiosity. I'll carry the last of this up and we'll go inside."

Both of the Peters blinked in surprise and waited on the sidewalk for a moment, then followed Raleigh onto the porch. Flossie beckoned across the street and to the house next door.

When Raleigh unlocked the door and turned around there were two more people standing at the base of the steps. A frail-looking woman in her seventies or eighties, her sparse gray hair drawn back in a very tight bun, and a man in his seventies, potbelly hanging over his sweatpants.

"Raleigh, honey, this is Doretha Bean. She lives next door."

Raleigh nodded to the woman, whose expression was clearly one of fear.

"And this is Bailey Wahl. From across the street."

The man's jowls shook as he nodded. Raleigh nodded back.

"Were you all friends of George Mobley?"

Mrs. Bean stepped back abruptly and would have fallen over if Bailey hadn't caught her.

"Dot, it's okay. She's not his real kin. She never even knew George." Flossie's tone was reassuring.

Mrs. Bean pulled herself together with a visible effort. She seemed about to say something, but Flossie shook her head warningly and Mrs. Bean closed her mouth.

"Here, let's get inside." Raleigh quickly opened the door and they were assailed by the sound of the security alarm. Raleigh darted around the door and disarmed the system, then went back to the porch and held open the screen door.

The neighbors started to follow her inside the house.

"Hash! Bailey! Bring some of that stuff with you."

Hash and Bailey each grabbed an armload of bags, bending somewhat creakily.

The neighbors stopped short in the vestibule, then walked suspiciously into the living room.

"Criminetly!" Flossie exclaimed, "Look at the davenport. I bet dirt's the only thing holding it together."

"Well, I never woulda thought . . . ," Bailey trailed off, dumbfounded. "I expected . . . I don't know what I expected, but not this."

"I know it's pretty dirty and I don't know that a good cleaning will improve it much, but that's what I'm planning to do. Let's put everything in the kitchen." Raleigh led the two old men into the kitchen where they dropped their bags on the dirty, greasy counter, then returned to the living room.

"Hash, what'd he do with all the money? He could have fixed up the place ten times over with what he had." Bailey looked around with confusion.

"Ask her." Hash jerked his head toward Raleigh. "She ought to know what happened to the money."

"Were you under the impression George Mobley was rich? There was only the one bank account. And most of that is already earmarked to pay the rest of the estate expenses."

"You're being cheated, kiddo." The raspy voice belonged to a newcomer, a man whose age Raleigh couldn't guess. He leaned heavily on a cane with one hand and rolled a portable oxygen canister with the other, the plastic tubes taped beneath his nostrils.

"George Mobley was richer than anyone in all of Sunrise Hills. Your lawyer's cheatin' you. No way in hell there isn't a shitload of money. You'll forgive my language."

Bailey Wahl stepped over and made the introductions. "Miss Killen, this here's Emmett."

Since both of Emmett's hands were busy supporting himself in an upright position Raleigh didn't offer to shake, but she did smile at him pleasantly. "I'm pleased to meet you, Mister Emmett."

"Ain't Mister, it's just Emmett." To Hash he said, "Dot gimme a call *she* was back, got up here quick as I could. Those stairs liked to kill me gettin' up 'em. I gotta sit."

Raleigh rushed to brush the dust off the chair, then thought better of stirring it up. It didn't seem to matter to Emmett, he dropped heavily onto the chair, dirt and all.

"This place is a pesthole. What was George up to, livin' like this? He could have took better care of the place. Why'd we bother paintin' the outside last summer when the inside looked like this?"

"Emmett, Miss Killen here never knew George," Hash volunteered.

"You're lucky for that, kiddo. This house is just like George. A good front on the outside, rotten on the inside."

"I don't know if you want to see the whole house, but you're welcome to look around while I bring in the rest of the bags."

Raleigh started ferrying the bags into the kitchen. Mrs. Bean seemed frozen in the vestibule and Emmett stayed glued to the chair, but the others walked carefully around, opening cupboards and cabinets, almost tiptoeing. They reassembled in the living room, shaking their heads. Flossie put an arm around Mrs. Bean's thin shoulders.

"You've all been so kind to stop by for a visit, but as you can see, the house isn't really . . . looking its best. And I have a lot of cleaning to do, so . . . ," Raleigh hinted with a smile.

Flossie had the good sense to recognize the "here's your hat what's your hurry" in Raleigh's voice.

"C'mon, Hash, let's leave the young lady to her cleaning. Bailey, help Hash get Emmett down the stairs."

"I don't need no help, Floss. I got up here by myself."

Emmett shook off Hash and Bailey and made his way to the front door unassisted.

"Honestly, Emmett. Boys," Flossie addressed Hash and Bailey. "Stand at the bottom and see he doesn't fall and break something."

Bailey laughed. "If he falls, we'll be the ones who get something broke." But Bailey and Hash went down the stairs first and kept an eye on Emmett's careful descent.

"Now, Raleigh, we'll leave you be for now. You certainly got your hands full if you're gonna clean this place up proper. But we'll be back, help you out as we can. And if you need anything, just come around to our side door and give a knock."

"Thank you, Flossie. There'll be plenty of time for us all to get to know each other. I'll be moving in as soon as the place is clean."

It's a good thing that Emmett had reached the sidewalk because Raleigh's announcement stunned everyone and Emmett nearly fell.

"You're not moving into this dump?! Are you crazy, kiddo?"

Chapter Nine

Crazy? Raleigh was starting to think Emmett was right. Three hours of work and the only clean place in the house was the bathroom. No small accomplishment for her or anyone else. The clawfoot tub gleamed, but the fixtures were beyond salvation. They worked, thank goodness, but were badly corroded as she discovered when she scrubbed them with steel wool as a last resort. And the pungent aroma of bleach was permeating the house and at last overtaking the mustiness and odor of stale cigarette smoke. There was an uninspired, but serviceable, black-and-white tile floor beneath the years of dirt, but nothing improved the dingy bathroom wallpaper. The dirt had bonded with the paper and removing it would be the only solution—a project that could be undertaken by the new owners, whoever they might be.

She had shredded two sponge-backed scrubbers, the mop head already needed replacing, she was out of bleach and scouring powder and when she tried to remove the bathroom curtain from the rod it fell apart in her hands. The old roller shade was yellowed with age, but it provided the necessary privacy and the new owners could also tackle their own window coverings. This house was going to be an "as is" sale, no doubt about it.

Raleigh suddenly heard her cell phone ringing and looked around for her tote bag, finally finding it in the dining room. "Hello." She was a bit breathless from inhaling so much dust and she started coughing.

"Miss Raleigh, is that you? I bet you didn't remember to buy any of those paper masks, did you?"

"No, Jon, I didn't think of it, nor did I think of rubber gloves." She looked at her reddened hands ruefully. "And the neighbors think you, or more correctly, Mr. Newton, is a crook . . . are crooks? Whatever."

"What?!"

"The neighbors are under the impression that George Mobley was quite well-off."

"Miss Killen," he said with an icy tone. "You have all the financial reports. His pension and Social Security, that's all he had to live on. Frankly, I wasn't too surprised when I first saw the inside of the house. He maintained the outside for appearances, but I don't see how he could have kept up with the cost of living."

"Yes, the statements are quite clear, Jon." Raleigh wasn't sure she could believe him or the statements he had supplied.

"It is curious, though. They all seem to really dislike him and were ready to dislike me. But once they knew I wasn't a blood relative they weren't exactly friendly, but neither were they downright hostile.

"They were all very anxious to get into the house, 'all' being the neighbors on both sides, one from across the street and another who must live around here somewhere. I let them come in and they were all flabbergasted. You said you'd never met any of them, right?"

As Raleigh talked to Jon she started to corral all the remaining cleaning supplies in the kitchen, which, judging by how long scrubbing the bathroom had taken, would be a two-day project.

"The dumpster will be in the driveway by seven in the morning and I've seen to it that you have help tomorrow. Don't get all excited, the help won't be me. I may be a Renaissance man, but I don't get dirty on purpose."

Jon was being charming and perhaps too helpful, Raleigh thought. "What help do you have in mind?" She tried to keep the suspicion out of her voice.

"My niece and nephew. They're both working their way through college and can always use a few bucks under the table. I told them to be there by one—morning classes, you know. Randy can do the heavy lifting and Naomi can clean if you tell her how you want it done."

"Okay, I'll try them out."

Raleigh was about to sit on the floor, then realized she probably wouldn't be able to get up again.

"Hold on while I find a place to sit. I'm too tired to keep talking standing up."

Raleigh walked into the living room. There wasn't a clean place to sit, but she was so dirty she decided it wouldn't matter. She eased herself into the only chair in case it collapsed beneath her, but it had held up under Emmett's weight earlier so she relaxed for a moment.

"Why don't I take you out for lunch tomorrow, Miss Raleigh? We can go over the paperwork then."

Lunch? Tomorrow? Raleigh suddenly remembered she missed lunch today.

"There's a great little Mexican place in the mall by Kroger."

"Okay. As long as I'm back by one."

"I'll pick you up at eleven."

Raleigh heard a knock at the door.

"Gotta go, Jon, someone's here."

Raleigh dropped her cell phone in her tote bag and walked over to the open front door. Mrs. Bean was standing on the steps with a napkin-covered plate in her hands.

"Hello, Mrs. Bean."

"Here, I thought you might be hungry. These were George's favorites." She picked up the napkin and showed Raleigh several large peanut butter cookies underneath.

Raleigh opened the door, but Mrs. Bean didn't come inside. She held the plate out to Raleigh and walked back down the steps.

"Thank you, Mrs. Bean," Raleigh called out as the elderly woman tottered back to her own house.

Flossie must have been waiting in the driveway because the minute Mrs. Bean's door closed she was up Raleigh's steps. And she took the plate from Raleigh's hand before the younger woman could react.

"Dot tries, but she can't bake worth a lick. If you ate these you'd have the bellyache for a week—or end up in the hospital."

Flossie stuffed the cookies into her pockets and kept the empty plate. "I'll give it back to her tomorrow. You just remember not to eat anything if it comes from Dot." Flossie wagged an emphatic finger at Raleigh.

"I understand. Sally's grandmother was like that. She loved to bake for all the kids in the neighborhood, but her doughnuts could have been used for hockey pucks. Some of the boys tried it once, worked fine. Girls weren't allowed to play hockey when I was in school."

"Me, I'm a good cook. You can tell by looking at me I don't make people sick."

"I'm sure you're a great cook, Flossie. And all this talk about food reminds me I haven't had lunch. I wonder if there's anything in the pantry that's still edible."

Raleigh walked into the kitchen and Flossie followed quickly behind her.

"You're not eating anything outta that pantry while I'm around. You're coming with me."

Flossie grabbed Raleigh by the arm and almost dragged her through the house and to the front door.

Unwilling to get into a wrestling match with a septuagenarian who could probably beat her two out of three, Raleigh went along without further protest, pulling the door closed behind her.

* * *

Comfortably ensconced in Flossie's kitchen a few minutes later, Raleigh watched while the older woman bustled around.

"You really don't need to feed me, Flossie. I can send out for a pizza or something."

"Nonsense! You're not having some cold, greasy pizza when I'll have you a nice hot meal in five minutes."

As it turned out, Flossie's idea of a nice hot meal was a can of Campbell's tomato soup, the condensed variety, and a grilled Velveeta sandwich.

"At least let me help. I can slice the cheese." Though Raleigh used the term "cheese" loosely when it came to Velveeta.

"You've been working all day. You just sit there and keep me company."

Hash walked into the kitchen, clearly surprised by Raleigh's presence. Flossie pulled the peanut butter cookies from her apron pockets and thrust them into his hands.

"Here. Make yourself useful and put these out in the trash."

Hash's expression was one of pure puzzlement.

"Dot made 'em for Raleigh here. They're *George's favorites.*"

"Right." And Hash exited the kitchen through the side door.

Raleigh could hear the trash can lid bang down. Hash returned and hovered in the doorway.

Flossie slapped an old aluminum griddle on the stove top and lit the flame underneath it.

"Doretha used that artificial sugar when she baked for George. Awful stuff, but he was diabetic. I'll go over later, see that she throws it out."

"Looks like Floss's makin' you a grilled cheese. I can't have the Velveeta anymore, all the salt. Boy, I'd sure like a grilled cheese, too." Hash looked wistful.

"Not with your blood pressure." Flossie flipped the sandwich and ladled tomato soup into a bowl. "Here, start on this." She set the bowl on the table in front of Raleigh with a paper napkin and a teaspoon.

"Thanks, Flossie. This is just like my mother used to make when I was little. It brings back memories." Raleigh tried the soup. The recipe probably hadn't changed in forty years—unfortunately.

"Do you fix it for your kids, carry on the tradition?"

"Oh, I never had children, Flossie. Never did get along all that well with them, even when I was one. My parents were quite old when I was born—I was a 'change of life' baby and all my memories are of my parents' equally old friends, a couple of aunts, an uncle on my father's side."

"You missed one of the joys of life." Flossie flipped the sandwich onto a paper plate. "Diagonal, I bet."

"How did you guess?"

Flossie sliced the sandwich and put it in front of Raleigh.

"If you think children are a joy, you must have had a houseful." Raleigh took a bite of the greasy creation.

"I had one . . . before. *We* had the three. One boy and two girls."

There was a moment of dead silence, finally broken by Hash. "I'll go see if the mail's here."

"Did I say something wrong?"

"No, no, dear. Our son Davey died young, real young."

There was another long silence and Raleigh took a spoonful of the unnaturally red soup.

"Sure wasn't fair to Hash. Me, it was my cross to bear, but not Hash."

Flossie sat on one of the kitchen chairs and wiped her hands nervously on a dish towel. "Before Hash and I were married, before I even met him, I was seeing this older boy. Thought I was in love, of course. What does a fifteen-year-old know about love? The minute I was in the family way . . . off he went. Hopped on a train and I never saw him again."

"My folks sent me to a home for other girls in the same situation, had the boy. He was adopted out. It was okay with me, mostly okay, what business did a teenager have with a little baby?"

Raleigh didn't know what to say. Hash had returned and was standing outside the side door listening.

"I was so disappointed when we lost our son, but . . . you got to take what life hands you sometimes. I'd done wrong before and this was, I don't know, the cost of me being so stupid when I was a kid. Shouldn't have cost Hash his son, though. Thank the Lord, the girls are fine. One's out in California, the other's down in Columbus."

"But that George found out. About the boy," Hash added through the screen door.

"George Mobley? What did he have to do with it?"

"It must have been the clippings, that's my guess. I wasn't supposed to know who adopted the boy, but I snuck into the office at the home one night and memorized their names. Don't know why."

"It was the Toledo paper that brought it all up again. We get it down at the drugstore most Sundays. There in the obituaries, the couple who adopted the boy, dead in a Trailways bus accident." Hash came back into the kitchen and put a hand on Flossie's shoulder.

"It mentioned the boy, too. He was married by then, had three kids of his own."

"I started watching the paper, read it down at the library, bought it when there was something about the boy in it and cut it out. Don't know why I did it . . . I just did it." Flossie shook her head in bewilderment.

"She kept the clippings in the hall desk. No one used to lock their doors around here. We all do now."

"George took the clippings, threatened to tell on me." Flossie clenched her hands on the tabletop.

"Please forgive me for saying this, Flossie, but an out-of-wedlock baby . . . ? Even if it was shameful back then . . . these days it isn't."

"Back then? This was just ten years ago."

"Ten years ago? Now I really am confused."

"George didn't want money, he wanted Floss to fix his meals. Not that the food didn't cost money, but it seemed little enough to keep him quiet. *I* would have preferred to punch him in the nose."

"Now, Hash. Don't let Raleigh be thinking you're a violent man." She patted his hand. "Dear, it wasn't the shame, I didn't care about that, not after all this time. It was for the boy's sake, and his family's."

"You see," Flossie paused dramatically, "the boy thinks he's Jewish. He's a rabbi for crying out loud! His folks never told him different, I suppose, or he wouldn't be a rabbi. How could I let him find out he's really Lutheran?"

"And to keep George quiet you fixed his meals for ten years?"

"Don't you be thinking Floss didn't tell me before we got married. She's as honest as the day is long. She just didn't want the boy to find out and I figured it was her decision. I sure would have liked to punch George in the nose, though."

Flossie heaved herself up from the table and hugged her husband tightly. "Isn't he a pistol? He couldn't punch a fly, let alone a person. Me havin' the boy never mattered one whit to him. I'm the luckiest woman in the world."

Hash blushed up to the roots of his hair. "Now, Floss, you're embarrassing me. And in front of company."

"First, I'm not company. Second, it's nice to see a couple who are still happy together after being married for . . . how many years?"

"Going on fifty-two, isn't it, Hash?"

He nodded in agreement. "And I hope we have another fifty-two together."

"A few meals here and there, what did it matter? I had Hash and the boy was safe. That's what was important. Figured it was all part of paying for my sin." Flossie sniffled and pulled a handkerchief from her apron pocket. It was covered with cookie crumbs. "That Doretha. Do you believe in lying . . . sometimes, Raleigh?"

"To be kind? Certainly. Let me take the plate back tomorrow and tell her how good the cookies were." Raleigh picked up the plate from the counter where it was sitting.

Flossie nodded and sniffled loudly.

"Now you go on and leave me start Hash's supper, otherwise he'll talk me into a grilled cheese sandwich and it isn't good for him."

Raleigh dropped her paper plate and napkin into the wastebasket and set the soup bowl and spoon in the sink, then left by the side door. Flossie was giving Hash another hug.

Chapter Ten

Raleigh had a lot to think about as she walked back to her house and collected her things. Her cousin hadn't been a kindly old man, he hadn't been even a benign one. He had been a thief when he stole those clippings from the Flossie and Hash Peters—and an extortionist when he used the information to force Flossie into fixing his meals for all those years. Raleigh would have poisoned him, had he tried to blackmail her. No, she didn't know what she would have done in their shoes. Contacted "the boy," maybe. Though she didn't approve of them knuckling under to George Mobley, she could understand why they did.

Which brought her thoughts to Emmett. He had been open in his dislike for her cousin—maybe he was one of George's victims, too.

For now, she was exhausted. She pulled the shades and checked the doors, relocked both bedroom doors though she didn't know why she bothered, set the alarm and then locked up the house. Back at the hotel, that huge tub beckoned her and she hoped the lavender bath salts had been replenished, she could use their supposedly calming influence.

The sun was low in the sky as Raleigh drove back toward the hotel, taking a wrong turn only once, and it was with relief that she pulled into the lot and parked. Room service and a soak, that's what she needed.

Raleigh walked across the lobby and vetoed her first impulse to take the stairs. Creaky though the elevator was, she was just too tired to walk up the stairs and tomorrow she would have to contend with more cleaning and filling up the dumpster. With Jon's niece and nephew helping, Raleigh intended to supervise and let them do the heavy lifting.

When Raleigh entered her room she noticed the light on her phone was blinking, so she paused in her beeline for the bathroom to check her messages. Pam had called wanting an update, the contractor told her he had sent her pictures of kitchen sinks via e-mail, and Jon berated her for not answering her cell phone. He must have called while she was with Flossie and Hash. It was just a reminder about lunch tomorrow—she'd have to remember to take a change of clothes with her in the morning, there was no telling how dirty she'd get by lunchtime.

Raleigh started to fill the tub, giving unspoken thanks that a new container of lavender bath salts was on the vanity. She peeled off her filthy clothes and caught a sudden look at herself in the mirror. She had a streak of dirt across her forehead and a smear on one cheek and several wisps of cobweb in her short hair. If there were any spiders they'd better abandon ship now or drown very shortly.

The tub had only a couple inches of water, but she got in anyway and let it fill up around her, all the way to her chin. She dunked herself under the hot, scented water for as long as she could hold her breath to dispatch any spiders or dust bunnies that may have hitched a ride, then came up for air and turned on the jets. They made a lot of noise and didn't provide much discernible massaging action, so she turned them off and simply soaked for a while.

Raleigh woke with a start to the ringing of the phone in the other room and found the water had cooled considerably. Through the door she could see that it was dark outside and she grabbed a towel and padded over to the phone, trying not to drip too much on the carpet.

"Hello?"

Great. Heavy breathing. She hung up and ran back to the bathroom and dried herself off and drained the tub. There was a substantial ring of dirt visible all around the white porcelain. Maybe she'd take a shower tomorrow in lieu of scrubbing two bathtubs in one day.

Raleigh closed the drapes and located a pair of flannel pajamas in her bag, then called room service and ordered a salad and lasagna. There weren't many vegetarian options on the menu and she was glad she had decided to move into the house—after it was clean. A trip to the local health food store for groceries and she could eat more as she usually did.

While Raleigh waited for her dinner to arrive she logged on and checked her e-mail. The pictures from Marty, her contractor, were there and she selected the chef's sink with one side larger and deeper than the other, with a matching white Grohe pull-out faucet. The contractor seemed to be on the ball. When the supply house was out of the sink she had initially specified he took pictures of two similar ones and the faucets that would fit best. He confirmed that her "confetti" solid-surface countertop was in stock and had already sent in the measurements for fabrication. As soon as the cabinets were primed the countertops would go in, the plumbing and electrical work having been completed that morning. Glossy white paint on the cabinets would follow, bright yellow on the walls of the breakfast nook, and the kitchen would be almost done. The vinyl flooring she had picked out for the kitchen was now discontinued and the contractor was sending several alternative samples by Priority Mail to the hotel.

Raleigh sent an e-mail to Marty and gave him the address of the legal office instead. She fully intended to check out of the hotel as soon as possible and didn't want her flooring samples lost in hotel mailroom limbo. She was glad to learn that the work was half a day ahead of schedule and thanked him for staying on top of the workmen.

There was a knock on the door and Raleigh was relieved to see a waiter there with her dinner. The soup and grilled "cheese" sandwich had saved her life, but hadn't filled her up and now she was starving again. As soon as the waiter left she switched on the TV and pulled the cover off her lasagna and dug in.

Chapter Eleven

Raleigh was up before the bedside alarm went off, in and out of the shower, and had taken her morning walk and had a mediocre breakfast from the buffet in the atrium restaurant, all by eight.

Back in her room, she dumped her tote bag on the floor and reorganized the estate paperwork, taking only what she would need that day. But nowhere could she find the shopping list she had made the previous day and she couldn't remember what, besides lots more bleach, she needed. As she stacked the remaining papers on the desk she realized she had inadvertently stuffed Mrs. Bean's cookie plate into her bag. She got up and washed it quickly in the bathroom sink.

* * *

When Raleigh pulled up in front of the house later she saw that the dumpster had already been delivered and left in the driveway near the front porch. She dropped her bag on the porch and walked next door to Mrs. Bean's, hoping it wasn't too early to pay an uninvited call. Although the way the neighbors dropped in on her unannounced and en masse—it was time she turned the tables on at least one of them.

Raleigh walked onto the red-painted cement porch and knocked on the door. She thought she heard someone moving around inside, but no one came to the door. She knocked again.

"Mrs. Bean? It's Raleigh from next door? I brought your plate back."

She knocked again and waited, then gave up and walked back toward her house, slipping the plate back into her tote bag.

Inside the house the bleach smell had dissipated and the mustiness and other odors were back, Raleigh noticed after she had disarmed the security system. Now if she could find her list and get to Kroger she would tackle the kitchen on her return. She located the list on the kitchen counter, added a few more items and was about to leave when she heard footsteps, lots of them, coming up the stairs and onto the porch.

"Hello? Raleigh, are you in there?" It was Flossie's voice.

"Be right there, hold on." Raleigh shoved the list into her bag and walked back through the house to the front door.

Not only were Flossie and Hash Peters on the porch, so were Bailey from across the street and two men she didn't know. Mrs. Bean was rushing down the sidewalk to join them wearing a sweat suit with a puff-painted garland of flowers around the neck of her top. Both Flossie and Mrs. Bean were carrying purses and Flossie had a jacket on over her dress and apron.

"Good morning." Raleigh didn't know what these seniors had in mind today, but she was determined not to get sidetracked by any of them today. Good manners dictated that she open the screen door and invite them in, though for only a minute. "Please, come in. I'm just leaving for the store, though . . ."

They all filed in and the newcomers had a good look around.

"Raleigh, dear, I want you to meet Al Vitello, he knew your cousin George from the church, St. Stephen's, and Gus Trout. They both used to play poker with George and the rest of the boys. Raleigh suddenly noticed that all the men were carrying cleaning supplies, mops, pails, etc.

Al Vitello was a short man with dark hair, a small mustache and dark eyes, who looked rather younger than the others. His face was sunburned and creased, but he had an air of suppressed energy.

"Pleased to meet you, ma'am. Your cousin started coming to St. Stephen's shortly after he retired; he converted not long after. He ran our Thursday night bingo game for several years and helped me with the books." Al punctuated his words by looking her up and down in a somewhat-leering manner.

Raleigh imagined Gus Trout had once been a big, burly man, but age had done its work and he was now somewhat heavy and drooping. All the same, he reached out and grasped her hand firmly, his blue eyes still alert and piercing beneath their hooded lids.

"Pleased as well, ma'am. I used to coach football over to the high school. Knew George from the regular Monday night poker game."

"Well, I appreciate meeting you two . . . and seeing the rest of you, but I'm heading out to Krogers . . ."

"No, you're not," Flossie said firmly. "Leastways, not without us. Me and Dot. We all talked it over last night and decided it was our duty and our privilege to help you out here."

"Help me out? Flossie . . . I . . ."

"The boys here are gonna stay and clean things up for you and Dot and I'll take you to the Krogers. And no argument, young lady."

What was wrong with the people in Ohio? Or at least the ones in this neighborhood. Or with her, letting them steamroll right over her?

Feeling like she was being herded by a bunch of geriatric border collies, her protests ignored, Raleigh was swept through the front door and into an old two-tone green Chevy Impala. Flossie and Mrs. Bean shoved her into the front seat and got in on either side of her, Flossie behind the wheel. Raleigh was glad of that, at least, she wouldn't have been too sanguine with the frail Mrs. Bean driving.

"Now don't you worry, Raleigh. My Hash knows how to clean—I trained him. Bailey, too, he raised both his boys himself after Lou left in '59."

"Flossie," Mrs. Bean piped up quietly, "will it take long enough? The Krogers?"

"Ladies, I really appreciate you helping me out, but I can go to Krogers myself. And I have some college students coming this afternoon to help me out, the heavy lifting, throwing out the trash . . . And Jon is picking me up at eleven. He's taking me to lunch."

"Is Jon your young man, dear?"

"No, Mrs. Bean. Jon Bluff works for George Mobley's lawyer, Mr. Newton."

"Well . . . does he like cookies, dear?"

Oh please, no more toxic baked goods. Raleigh's prayer remained unspoken.

"No, ma'am. He can't have cookies, he's . . . allergic."

"To cookies? Nonsense, dear." Flossie elbowed Raleigh none-too discreetly or gently.

"He'll like them, Raleigh. I helped Dot throw out all that sugar substitute she was using."

"Hated to waste all that saccharine, but Flossie says I don't have to use it now that George is gone."

Raleigh was pretty sure saccharine had been banned back when she was a child. If Mrs. Bean still had some it had to be more than toxic by now.

"All right. But I have to be back at the house by eleven." Raleigh gave up with a sigh.

"Will that be enough time, Flossie?" Mrs. Bean wrung her handkerchief in her thin hands.

"The boys'll do what they can. Don't you fret, Dot."

Raleigh shuddered to think what kind of cleaning mayhem four old men could inflict, but she supposed they couldn't make the house any worse than it already was.

"They'll get rid of all that nasty stuff in the pantry, clean out the cupboards, scrub the floor, wash the dishes. You'll be surprised, Raleigh. You'll be surprised."

Though Flossie drove maddeningly slowly, they arrived at the grocery store without incident. Raleigh grabbed a cart and consulted her list, mentally subtracting a few things that now might not be necessary. Everything she needed was in the cleaning aisle, but Flossie and Mrs. Bean insisted on going up and down every aisle—"just in case." A trip that would have taken at most half an hour by herself had taken an hour by the time the bagger loaded everything into the trunk of the Impala.

Raleigh caught Flossie checking her watch. "What time do you have?"

"It's just ten, dear. We have another whole hour before you have to be back. Let's see, where else can we go?"

"This is everything I need, Flossie. Let's go on back and see how Hash and the others are doing."

"No, no, we can't go back yet. They won't be done." Mrs. Bean sounded quite panicky, which Raleigh couldn't understand.

Flossie gave Raleigh a look and nodded her head toward Mrs. Bean. "There must be somewhere else you need to go, Raleigh . . . ?"

"Oh, sure. Let me think." What made Raleigh believe she could make a career of working with the elderly? A day and a half around this bunch of senior citizens and they had her wrapped around their collective little finger.

"Do you know where the health food store is? Natural Farms? I think it's on Harrison somewhere. I'd like to take a look there."

"I think that's the hippie place across from the Home Depot. Sure thing. Dot, it's clear across town."

Mrs. Bean seemed relieved and they piled back into the Chevy and were off, albeit slowly.

* * *

Natural Farms was more than Raleigh had hoped for and well worth the trip. Now she was the one who wanted to go up and down every aisle, delighted that they carried her favorite peanut butter, nonfat yogurt and soymilk. She'd be able to stock the house with real food, make a decent salad, scramble eggs the way she liked them and not search high and low for a restaurant with something vegetarian.

When she checked the phone book yesterday for restaurants she was dismayed to find they ran to national chains which, at best, could offer steamed vegetables over rice or pasta and salads made of iceberg lettuce and a wedge of unripe tomato smothered with some horrible bottled dressing.

Though they checked every aisle in the store, and the bulk bins, it was obvious to Raleigh that they needed to kill more time. Perhaps this trip out was a treat for Mrs. Bean and Flossie didn't want to take her back too soon. They reached the last aisle and were in luck, a deli/bakery section with several small tables clustered near the window.

"Ladies, I don't know about you two, but I could use a cup of tea. How about I treat us all? Please, I insist."

Flossie was obviously grateful for the suggestion and Mrs. Bean looked like she needed a rest after all the walking they had done.

"Here, you ladies take a seat and I'll get the tea."

Raleigh walked over to the counter and ordered a pot of tea. When she was rummaging in her tote for her wallet she came across Mrs. Bean's plate and added six assorted cookies to the order. The clerk helped carry everything over to the table and Mrs. Bean's eyes lit up when she saw the cookies.

"Oh, thank you, dear." Mrs. Bean's hand hovered the plate, undecided about which cookie to pick.

"Is it okay? She isn't diabetic, is she?" Raleigh whispered to Flossie while she poured the tea.

Flossie spoke equally quietly. "No, she's fine. I'd like to get some meat on those bones. She went downhill right after Buddy died and that was almost forty years ago. Just started caring about things again when George took sick. Funny how that happened . . ."

"What are you two whispering about? Mrs. Bean squinted at Raleigh. "For a minute there you looked just like Lou, dear." Mrs.

Bean took two cookies, one oatmeal with raisins and the other chocolate chip.

"Lou?"

"Lou Wahl, Bailey's wife," Flossie explained and took a molasses cookie. "The three of us girls used to pal around, especially during the war when all the men were gone."

"That Lou, she was a pistol. You could tell just by looking at her that she'd never settle down. She was a Ralston—they never amounted to anything. None of 'em."

"Remember when she got on the picnic table down at the Kiwanis and did a hoochie dance?" Flossie smiled at the memory. "She was a fast one, she was. But so much fun."

"I could understand why Bailey married her, but did you ever see her settling down?"

"No, Dot, can't say that I did. Poor Bailey, he deserved better'n that."

"Were they married long?"

"Three years, wasn't it?" Mrs. Bean brushed the crumbs daintily from her fingers and took a peanut butter cookie from the plate.

"No, it was more like five years before she took off. They went across the state line when he was home on leave, remember?"

"Yes, he went back to the war then, didn't come home for another year or so."

"Lou had the first boy right off the bat, the other one after Bailey got back for good."

"She lit out before Joe was weaned."

Raleigh drank her tea and listened to the two women reminisce. "Was George living here then?"

"George? When was it he showed up, Flossie, right before the war?"

"Right after it started. The company moved him in from somewhere in Indiana . . . Illinois. All the local boys were drafted or volunteered, needed someone to take charge of things. George must have been the only one left to send to the plant here."

"That must have been an interesting time, women going to work in place of their men."

"Dot, Lou and I all worked over to Atlas, on the line. That's where we met George. And didn't he love to lord it over everyone that he was in charge of the floor—and 'inspect' our work a little too close, if you know what I mean."

"He wouldn't have dared if our boys had been here."

"He and Lou had a thing going for a while. Except for Bailey, she never had any sense about men. And she threw him over, left him with a toddler and a baby."

"She wound up in prison, you know, forgery or something."

Great, I remind Mrs. Bean of a hoochie dancer and a convicted felon.

"That was all after the war. The boys came back and most of us lost our jobs at the plant. And Lou up and left poor Bailey . . . all us wives pitched in and helped raise his two, both stayed in Greenhaven, started families."

"Mrs. Bean, do you and your husband have children in the area, too?"

Mrs. Bean gulped and looked like she was going to faint.

"Settle down, Dot. Here, take a drink of tea. Slowly."

"I wasn't going to say anything," Mrs. Bean began, "you being so nice to me and all, Raleigh."

Flossie got up and pulled Mrs. Bean to her feet. "You hush, Dot. Raleigh doesn't need to hear about that."

"She does so. She ought to know about Faith. She ought to know George killed my Buddy. Murdered him."

Faith? Who is Faith? Or Buddy? And her cousin a murderer?

Mrs. Bean was clearly unbalanced, Raleigh thought as Flossie nearly carried her friend from the store. Raleigh retrieved Mrs. Bean's plate and followed the two elderly women back to the car.

* * *

The ride back to the house was quiet, with Mrs. Bean leaning her head against the window, eyes closed and Flossie concentrating on her driving.

Flossie pulled in front of Mrs. Bean's house first and helped her from the car.

"Mrs. Bean! Your plate!" Raleigh scrambled out after them and pressed the plate into Mrs. Bean's hand.

"And thank you again for the peanut butter cookies. It was very thoughtful of you."

Mrs. Bean smiled wanly at Raleigh's thanks.

"You go on over to the house, Raleigh. I'll get Dot settled in first." Flossie hustled Mrs. Bean up the sidewalk.

Raleigh watched Flossie unlock Mrs. Bean's door and help her inside, then walked over to her house. She could hear swearing from inside, even before setting foot on the porch. And was nearly knocked over on the front steps by Al Vitello hurtling through the front door and down, his arms laden with food from the pantry.

She dodged out of the way and Al pounded down the steps and over to the dumpster, where he hurled the cans and jars on top of the previous loads.

"You're back!" Al's expression was one of alarm. He threw himself back up the stairs and she followed him into the house. "Boys! She's back!"

In Raleigh's absence Emmett had arrived and was ensconced on the now sheet-covered sofa, oxygen tank at his side. The sofa had been turned to face into the room.

"I see they enlisted you in this project, too, Emmett."

"Hell, no. Heard all the noise across the fence, come on over to see what was happening. Figured I'd better stay and supervise this bunch before they hurt themselves."

Through the doorway, Raleigh could see the men scrambling around in the kitchen and figured she'd better get a closer look. Emmett read her mind.

"You go on. I'll stay put here."

Raleigh walked into the kitchen and was pleasantly surprised to see that it seemed to be intact. She was unpleasantly surprised that they didn't seem to have accomplished much in almost three hours. Someone had given the floor a rough mopping and pushed the dirt around. And there was a stack of dripping, but clean, dishes on the not-clean counter. Bailey and Hash were drying them and putting them back in the cupboards which hadn't even been wiped out.

Gus was on his hands and knees in the pantry, unloading the lowest shelves and pitching things into a bushel basket. Al Vitello ran hot water into a bucket and dunked a mop, ready to mop out the pantry.

As far as Raleigh could see, the kitchen was the only room on which they had worked. Elsewhere in the house furniture had been moved, drawers opened, but . . . nothing more.

"Floss told us to dump all the food. Stunk something awful in there." Hash jerked his head toward the pantry. "Washed some of the containers, but the plastic ones were kind of sticky and funny, dumped those, too."

"You have all done such a wonderful job, I don't know how to thank you." Raleigh couldn't help wondering what they had really been doing while she was gone. Gossiping, most likely. *Men.*

"Didn't get past the kitchen, though. Except for the bathroom all the other doors are locked, even the cellar. If you got the key we can get started in there next." Al Vitello was eager to continue working, but Gus groaned as he struggled to his feet with the last of the pantry contents and headed outside.

"I wouldn't hear of it, gentlemen. I have an appointment and he should be here any minute."

Gus returned with a grocery bag, followed by Flossie with another. Hash finished wiping a dented aluminum pot and took the bag from her.

"Here, Floss, let me take that."

"Is Mrs. Bean all right?" Raleigh asked when she spotted Flossie.

"Dot? What happened to Dot?"

"Nothing, Hash. You know how excitable she is. Raleigh took us to tea at that hippie grocery store and Dot ate too many cookies. Too much excitement I expect."

Flossie made no mention of Mrs. Bean's accusation against George Mobley. She wiped a hand across the countertop, did not nod approvingly.

"Four or five more bags in the trunk." Hash and Al headed through the house while Flossie took a look around the kitchen. She checked the cupboards and drawers, the pantry.

"There's nothing to be done for that floor except replace it. Should come up easy, though. Well, what do you think, Raleigh? Do the boys know how to clean?" Flossie's disapproving expression belied her words.

"The boys" didn't, but Raleigh was quickly getting used to lying to these odd, kind-hearted people. "They did a great job, Flossie. I don't know how to repay you all except to shoo you out of here with my thanks. Jon should be here any minute."

"That the tall, scrawny guy who's been hanging around here? He your boyfriend or somethin'?" Emmett was standing in the doorway.

"No, he works with my lawyer, Andrew Newton. We're going to have lunch and go over things concerning the estate."

"You be sure and ask him where the money is. George had plenty, that I know. Where is the money? That's the question."

"I'll discuss it with him, but everything really does seem to be in order." Raleigh wasn't all that sure things were in order, but she wasn't willing to admit it to the nosy neighbor.

Hash and Al Vitello returned with the last of the bags and set them on the counter.

"If there wasn't money, why that fancy alarm deal? Piker like George wouldn't do that 'less he had somethin' to protect. Word to the wise," Emmett said as he put a finger to the side of his nose.

"Get your things together, boys, we'd best be going. Everybody over to our house for lunch," Flossie said. "I set the Crock-Pot going after breakfast and the stew should be done. Put the biscuits in the oven and we're set."

The men obeyed Flossie's order and collected their things and gradually made their way out of the house and down the steps. Al Vitello winked at Raleigh as he left the house. Raleigh and Flossie paused in the vestibule.

"Al, you watch Emmett, see he don't fall." Flossie turned to Raleigh and smiled.

"Don't you worry about Dot. She's just fine, got too excited, being out of the house and all. You were very kind to her, Raleigh. I appreciate it."

"Flossie, what she said about George Mobley murdering Buddy. Who's Buddy? Who's Faith?"

"Buddy was her husband. Dot and him had a little girl, Faith. I don't remember what they call it now, but we called it mongoloid back then. When Buddy died . . . ? There's no good way to say this—one day Buddy up and killed himself. Locked himself in the garage and turned on the car. Dot took it real hard, real hard. Changed her. She got it in her head that George killed him, but he didn't. It was suicide plain and simple. She caused all kinds of trouble, couldn't take care of Faith, then someone called the county and Faith was put in an institution."

Flossie shook her head ruefully. "As if that was better than staying in her own house, her own neighborhood, with all of us to take care of her."

"Where is she now?"

"She's in a group home over in Dimondale, that's about ten miles south of here. She seems real happy. I take Dot over to see her every other week. I still think of Faith as that little girl—she's in her thirties now, though. That's where Dot got that outfit she was wearing today. They keep the residents busy there, doing crafts and things. Faith painted those flowers on."

"Poor Mrs. Bean . . . I am so sorry I said anything."

"It was all so long ago. The things Dot gets in her head sometimes . . . even talked about killin' George. Emmett finally got her to leave off that idea. Don't know how, but he did." Flossie's shoulders drooped and Raleigh gave her a quick hug.

"You get on home, Flossie. If I heard right, you have a bunch of hungry men waiting for their lunch."

"You're a good girl, Raleigh. A real good girl."

And with that, Flossie walked across the porch and down the steps. Raleigh stood on the other side of the screen door and watched Flossie walk down the driveway and through the side door of her house. She could hear her ordering the men around the minute she stepped inside.

A car horn honked and Raleigh looked out to the street. Jon opened the door of his PT Cruiser and waved.

"C'mon up! You have to see the house!" She gestured toward the house. If he could pretend to be her friend, she could pretend to believe he was—and keep her eyes open.

Jon parked blocking the driveway and loped up the steps. Today he was wearing a deep blue dress shirt and black dress slacks—and only one earring.

"What's up with the Armani?"

"Armani? In Greenhaven? The best you can get around here is the department store house brand. The key is having a good tailor."

"You have to take a look at the kitchen, for which I am not responsible. And the bathroom, for which I am."

They walked through the living and dining room and into the kitchen, the deteriorated linoleum cracking more under their feet.

"Well, it's an improvement, not."

"I'll want to do a more thorough job in here. The men worked all morning . . . I don't understand why they didn't get more done—even for men. I'd like to put some ant traps in the cupboards, things like that."

"The men?"

"The neighbors. The senior citizens on the block seem to have adopted me. They arrived en masse this morning. The only two women I've met so far escorted me to Kroger and the various aged males set to cleaning the house. That was the idea anyway. All they got to was the kitchen."

They walked into the hall and Jon stopped at the first bedroom door. "What's up with this? Did you lose the keys already?"

Raleigh bent down to look, then checked the door of the spare room. "They told me they wanted to clean in here, but they rushed me out so quickly I didn't think to unlock these."

There were scratch marks on the locks and it looked like someone had shoved a screwdriver into the wood at the edge of one and tried to force it.

"It looks like someone tried to pick the locks. I don't like this one bit." Inadequate *help* was one thing, but breaking and entering was another. Maybe it isn't really B and E if you're already inside, Raleigh thought.

"You'll still need Randy and Naomi, that's obvious."

"I'm not going to leave the neighbors here alone again. Helping is one thing, but trying to pick a lock is another." Now Raleigh was suspicious of Jon and all the neighbors, too.

"Afraid they'll find the buried treasure first?"

"No, but that reminds me. Emmett wants me to grill you about the missing cash. He's the one with the portable oxygen tank."

"The only one I've seen is a scrawny woman who tried to poison me with toxic brownies. I saw her leave them on the porch and scuttle back next door."

"That's Mrs. Bean. She uses saccharine or something. She brought me peanut butter cookies, but Flossie took them away and fed me tomato soup and a grilled Velveeta sandwich."

"Ouch! And that didn't kill you?"

"It actually tasted kind of good, in a salty, greasy, artificial way. It was a Saturday tradition at my house, the only thing my father could cook."

"You probably ate frozen TV dinners, too."

"Yeah, they were a big treat. We'd all sit around our TV, Banquet turkey dinners on those metal trays, and watch *Lawrence Welk* on Saturday night. Or was it Sunday?"

"Sunday. We had the frozen potpies. It's a wonder either one of us survived."

Chapter Twelve

Over a giant veggie burrito no radishes for her and crab cakes with shoestring fries for him, Raleigh told Jon about George Mobley blackmailing a neighbor, not mentioning Flossie and Hash.

"A blackmailer, huh. I wonder what he had on them, or him, or her." Jon didn't seem surprised by her revelation if Raleigh gauged his expression correctly.

"What difference does that make?"

"Oh, just idle curiosity. Did they . . . he give you a hint?"

It didn't sound like idle curiosity to Raleigh and she wasn't going to tell on the Peterses. She dropped that subject abruptly to broach another one.

"Jon, is Mr. Newton absolutely certain that the list of George Mobley's assets is, well, comprehensive?"

Jon bristled at the subtle, once-removed accusation, though Raleigh had tried to keep her tone neutral.

She continued before he could make the expected protest of innocence. "It's the neighbors . . . one of the neighbors . . . he seems so sure."

"I don't know where else to look for assets. I personally checked all the banks, savings and loans, and the credit union. He had listed only the one savings account, but I checked everywhere else anyway. He was pretty doped up at the end, I suppose he might have forgotten something. If he did I haven't found it."

"Let's assume for the moment that he had money, possibly from blackmail." Raleigh knew Flossie and Hash hadn't paid off in cash, but someone else might have. "He wouldn't put it in any of the usual places. I wonder if he would declare it on his taxes . . . probably not. How about his accountant? Can I talk to his accountant?"

"I had our accountant file the final return. Your cousin died before it could be prepared. Don't you have a copy in those files I gave you? You seem to have gone through everything else."

"Probably. I'll look later."

"There are a bunch of old returns in a box in the spare room, but I didn't notice anything out of the ordinary when I skimmed through them. I took them back to the office and ran them through the shredder."

"That's . . . unfortunate. Who was his accountant? There should be copies of his old returns for seven years back."

Jon ignored her question and they ate in silence for a few moments. Raleigh had to wonder if Jon destroyed the returns to eliminate evidence.

"You know, it's funny. All the neighbors coming around today to help you out like that. If they were all such good friends of his, how come they weren't in the will? Makes me wonder, you know?"

Raleigh wondered if Jon was trying to divert her suspicions from him and Andrew Newton. "Me, too. Not about them, but about my cousin. What was your impression of him when you were drawing up the paperwork?"

"That he needed a bath. I was glad I had to see him only twice, once at the house, then once at the hospital when he signed everything. At least he was clean at the hospital. I take that back, I saw him three times. I went to the funeral mass. Newt-face and I were the only ones there."

"Really? None of the neighbors went?"

"We were the only ones there. That's kind of funny, too. Me and Newt-face in a Catholic church, or any church—we're both agnostics."

"He left specific instructions, had already bought the cemetery plot, written the obituary, everything. You'll have to see the monument he bought, it's something else. Maybe that's where all the *alleged* money went."

"Do you have a copy of the obituary? I'd like to see it."

"There should be one in the office files. I'll e-mail it to you when I have time."

Raleigh put down her fork and pushed the plate away resolutely. Half of the massive burrito remained uneaten.

"Want a box for that, hon? Any dessert for either of you?" the waitress asked.

"Sure, I'll take a box. No dessert for me, though, I'm stuffed."

"Nothing more for me, either. We'd better get going if we're going to beat the kids to the house. You can see the bank across the parking lot . . . that's where his savings account was. I changed it to the branch where we have our client trust account."

"That's fine. Let's head back." Raleigh felt like nothing more than a nap, but two energetic teenagers were waiting for her to put them to work.

* * *

"Jon, could you look into something for me? Just to satisfy my curiosity?" Raleigh asked as they pulled out of the parking lot.

"That depends on what it is."

"Find out what you can about Buddy Bean's death. His wife says George murdered him, but Flossie says he committed suicide. Mrs. Bean seems harmless and pathetic to me . . . and somewhat unbalanced, but . . . just in case?"

"Ohhh, a mystery. Can I be Ted Nickerson to your Nancy Drew?"

"Ned. His name was Ned. And I'm sure there isn't any mystery, just a crazy story, but since it involves my cousin I'd like to find out the truth."

"It was Ned in the books and Ted in the movies. Or the other way around. All right, I'll help. Even though you make it sound so boring. Do you know when he died? Or if Buddy was his actual name?"

"Nope, I don't know a thing about him. They had a daughter, that might help. Her name is Faith and she was taken away from Mrs. Bean after her husband died, I'm guessing in the seventies, and put in an institution. She has Down syndrome and Flossie takes Mrs. Bean to see her at some group home in Dimondale."

"Well, I can work backward from there . . . I suppose."

"C'mon, Ned, you can do it. Nancy's counting on you. And if you're real good, you can come over and we'll look for the secret staircase."

"In that house? If there's a secret staircase it doesn't go anywhere. Besides, I already looked."

They pulled up in front of the house where a VW Bug, painted chocolate brown with a white squiggle on the roof, had replaced the Impala in Raleigh's driveway. A teenage boy and girl were sitting on the steps with a golden retriever, a pink print bandana around its neck.

The teenagers got up and Raleigh could see they were both clearly athletic and well able to move boxes and furniture around. They walked down to the car while Raleigh and Jon got out.

"We had to bring Molly, Mom couldn't pick her up from the groomer's on time and they were closing early for Chet's graduation."

"That's okay, Naomi. Raleigh loves dogs. Don't you, Raleigh?"

"I'm more of a cat person, but as long as she's house-broken it's fine. The back yard is fenced if you want to put her out there."

"Randy, take Molly out back and come in through the kitchen." Jon pointed to the rickety gate between the garage and the house.

Raleigh unlocked the door and disarmed the security system and they walked through the house to the kitchen. Molly could be seen through the window as Randy tossed the Frisbee for her one more time, then he joined them.

"I'm glad you could give me a hand clearing things out and cleaning. How long can you stay?" Raleigh asked.

"Mom wants us back by five today, but we can come on the weekend and work longer." Naomi was casting a critical eye over the kitchen. "Someone went over this sink with a lick and a promise." She looked through the cleaning supplies with an approving eye and pulled out a package of rubber gloves.

"Some of the neighbors were helping out this morning and this is a bit cleaner than it was, but . . . I'd like you to start in here."

"And, Randy, I know it's going to be a horrible job, but I'd like you to look through the dumpster, see what's already been thrown away. I'm concerned that the neighbors may have inadvertently pitched something of value."

"Miss Raleigh, you are incorrigible." Jon shook his head.

"No, I'm just checking for letters, clippings, something that might get tucked in a cookbook or something and, yes, money. When Aunt Lily died I threw her accumulation of catalogs in the trash, then noticed there was money between some of the pages. I had to haul everything back out and check each one—found almost seven hundred dollars by the time I was done. And she wasn't even strange. My mother used to do the same thing, figuring on ordering something or other, had set aside the money for it."

"That's treasure hunting as far as I'm concerned. It's the dumpster for me!" Randy charged outside.

"Watch out for broken glass!" Raleigh called after him.

"I'll get started on the cleaning, Miss Killen. Any particular way you want it done?"

"Please call me Raleigh. As long as it's clean when you're through . . . knock yourself out."

Naomi popped open the package of rubber gloves and started running water in the sink. "J. J. said you didn't have anything to eat here, so we brought along some Cokes and snacks. Okay if we use the fridge?"

"Sure, but let me wipe it out first." Raleigh located a container of antibacterial wipes and opened the refrigerator. The "boys" had wiped it out as well as they had done the other cleaning and Raleigh could see some mold and grime in the area underneath the crisper drawer. She set to work really cleaning it.

"Randy!" Naomi had opened the window on the driveway side of the house and was screaming outside. "Bring in the cooler! And you better get Molly some water, there isn't much shade in the back yard!"

"It looks like you'll keep the kids busy for a while. I have to head over to Carlock for my presentation. Same estate planning package as for the seniors, but geared toward college personnel."

"You go on, we'll be fine."

"Good luck with the treasure hunt. And don't forget that I get a cut of whatever you find."

Jon waved and left through the kitchen door.

Randy came back in and thumped the cooler onto the floor and filled a dog dish with water at the sink, then took it outside for Molly. He had obviously already been in the dumpster when his sister called to him. His work boots were covered with baked beans, canned yams, rotten tomatoes, flour and who could tell what else.

"Randy, you are such a pig. Do not come into this house again unless you hose off your boots first," Naomi called through the kitchen screen door.

"Boys," she added under her breath.

"And don't think they get any better when they grow up. If they grow up." Raleigh finished cleaning the refrigerator and Naomi loaded a six-pack of Coke, several sandwiches, a box of granola bars and a carton of milk inside.

"Randy's still a growing boy. It'll be empty by the time we leave and he'll still be hungry. Was J.J. kidding about that? You're treasure hunting?"

"Yes, but he could be wrong. Everyone, not just old people, leaves things in odd places. Me, every time I put something in a safe place I never see it again."

"Why? Was your cousin a spy or secret agent or something?" Naomi had removed the shelves from the pantry and was scrubbing the walls inside.

"You know, you're not too far off. He was kind of a spy, at least he meddled in other people's business. If we look real hard we may be able to show your uncle how clever we are and find something."

"J. J. isn't really our uncle, it's kind of . . . an honorary title. He and Mom were an item back in the old days, but he couldn't decide what he wanted to do with his life. At least that what Mom says. Took off one day without a word. Tried this, tried that, traveled all over the world. Finally wound up back here. He stayed with Mom and Dad for a while, babysat both me and Randy. We never ate so good as when J. J. was in charge of our kitchen. Mom's the best, but her idea of cooking is frozen meatloaf, canned green beans, white bread and a pie from the grocery store. It was a dark day for our stomachs when he moved out."

"The day I got here he did fix me the best omelet I ever had, but I didn't quite believe the chef thing."

"The omelet with the hash browns inside? Man, I love that. That was one of the brunch specialties when he had the restaurant out in California. That and his eggs Benedict—grilled polenta, sauteed spinach and mushrooms, too. That béchamel packs on the pounds, but I work 'em off in soccer practice. I'm on an athletic scholarship over at Carlock."

"What about your brother?"

"Him, too, but he's track."

Randy appeared outside the kitchen door, but didn't come inside. "I haven't found anything yet, just a lot of funky food. Man, it stinks. Even I wouldn't eat it."

"And that's saying something. So, are you finished, brother mine?"

"Nah, I'm just looking for something to sort the recyclables into. No sense in throwing that away. Can I get into the garage, Miss Killen? See if I can find some bushel baskets or crates?"

"Sure, I'll come and take a look, too. If not the garage, maybe we can brave the cellar. And please call me Raleigh."

"Grab me a Coke and a sandwich? I've worked up an appetite already."

Raleigh walked into the dining room and found the house keys next to her tote bag on the table. She stuck her cell phone in her pocket, grabbed the requested Coke and sandwich, and joined Randy in the back yard. Molly had found some shade underneath a hydrangea and was snoring peacefully.

Randy dispatched the sandwich in three bites and chugged the Coke while Raleigh unlocked the garage door.

"You have nice neighbors around here. The skinny lady next door brought over some molasses cookies earlier."

"Gray hair in a bun? You didn't eat them?"

"Yeah, that's her. Great cookies."

"Do you feel okay, Randy?"

"Sure, great. She said she'd make me macaroons on Saturday. Here, I was saving one for later, but you can have it."

Randy pulled a napkin-wrapped cookie from his shirt pocket and handed it to her. Raleigh took a tentative sniff. It smelled good enough, but . . . she broke off a tiny piece and held it in her mouth for a moment. Molasses, sugar, ginger, cinnamon—not a trace of anything unpleasant. Raleigh swallowed and rewrapped the cookie, unwilling to commit herself to eating the whole thing.

There wasn't a light inside the garage, but Randy rummaged gamely through the shelves and trash and unearthed some five-gallon paint buckets underneath a pile of rotting rope and rusting garden tools.

"You want to try and salvage any of this?"

"It can go straight to the dumpster, but set aside any boxes or other containers you find and I'll go through them later."

Randy took the buckets outside and started filling them with the rescued glass containers which he had rinsed off with the garden hose. Flies were swarming around the dumpster and the muck in the driveway.

"When I'm done I'll hose this all out into the street, get it away from the house. There's a cookbook and recipe file over on the gas meter. The rest is just garbage."

Raleigh spotted the cookbook and file and took them into the house to look through later.

* * *

By five o'clock the kitchen was spotless and Raleigh and the kids had decided on a schedule for the upcoming weekend. The dumpster was full and Raleigh put in a call to the number on the lid to request a new one or an emptying. Randy had hauled the useless washer and dryer into the driveway and Raleigh arranged for those to be picked up, too.

Tomorrow she would take a closer look at the living room and dining room furniture and decide what Randy could haul out for immediate disposal. He had convinced her that he and Naomi could pull up the peeling, cracked kitchen linoleum—even a bare subfloor would look better. She and Naomi would vacuum and steam clean the carpet and see what lay underneath the apparent decades of dirt.

Raleigh waved the kids on their way and worked on her next shopping list. She checked the refrigerator and added Coke, bottled water, and she'd see what sort of teenager-friendly snacks the health food store carried and stock up before the weekend.

She set the alarm and locked up the house, then walked wearily down to the car. Luckily she made it without being accosted by any of the well-meaning neighbors, with or without cookies.

Chapter Thirteen

It was drizzling when Raleigh pulled up to the house the next day. The dumpster company had come and gone and the rain had washed the last of the garbage muck away. Even the house smelled a little better inside when she opened the door. In spite of the coolness, and the risk of neighbors dropping in, she decided to leave the front door open to maintain the improving smell.

Jon had e-mailed her the names of three real estate agents, but showing the house would have to wait until it was as presentable as she could make it without investing in actual remodeling. He had also sent George Mobley's obituary, which was short and unenlightening. She had reread the trust and will over breakfast and realized that one of the witnesses was his doctor, Fred Kober, the other she supposed, a nurse at the hospital.

Raleigh had stopped at Kroger on her way to the house and she now loaded the bottled water and pop into the refrigerator. She had also picked up a loaf of bread and one jar each of peanut butter and jelly in case she didn't feel like trying to find someplace for lunch. The kitchen was clean enough to eat in now, though not off the floor, and the dishes and cutlery had been washed more thoroughly and replaced in the clean cupboards by Naomi.

She carried a bottled water back into the living room and decided to start with the rickety end tables. Raleigh spread a yellowed sheet from the hall closet out on the floor and pulled on one of the drawers. It wouldn't budge, warped into place. She tugged and tugged and succeeded only in separating the drawer front from the drawer itself. But she was able to pull out the contents a handful at a time and she set everything on the sheet. Then she got a knife from the kitchen and pried at the rest of the drawer until the bottom came free. She pulled it out one side at a time. Nuts, no money or anything taped to the bottom, back or sides.

The bottom drawer was larger and came free without coming apart and Raleigh repeated the earlier procedure, again without discovering any treasure, then turned her attention to the end table itself. Nothing on the outside except dust and cigarette burns. Nothing on the inside except the supports for the drawer. The bottom was a treasure trove of tiny, dust-covered cobwebs, but little else. She carried the end table out onto the porch with the drawers and tackled the second end table. There was only one drawer on this one, with a stack of magazines in the rack beneath it. Nothing taped underneath the drawer, on the inside, on the bottom. Not even one secret panel. It went out onto the porch with the first and Raleigh started looking through the drawer contents.

A greasy pack of cards, mismatched dice, rusted thumbtacks rolling around loose, AA batteries that were corroded and stuck together, matchbooks from what she supposed were the local bars, a rusted pair of cheap nail scissors, string, assorted keys, a measuring tape that broke off when she tried to extend it—useless junk. Raleigh dumped it into an empty grocery bag. The magazines weren't old enough to be collector's items, if anyone collected outdated electronic magazines, or new enough to want to read. A stray *Newsweek* caught her attention—November 1992. Why would anyone keep this stuff?

Raleigh shook out the magazines in search of cash, stock certificates, or the like, but all that fell out were the blow-ins. She added the magazines to the bag and turned her attention to the TV. She felt underneath it carefully—more cobwebs—then pushed it away from the wall and checked the back. Again, nothing. She didn't have a screwdriver or she would have removed the back and looked inside. She'd look out in the garage for tools when it stopped raining.

She pushed the console back into place and turned one of the dials. The TV started humming. After a moment, a picture began to appear, albeit in black and white. Jon was right, the ancient console model actually worked. So far, this seemed to be the most valuable thing in the house. The door on the right side yielded a box of miscellaneous tubes, which she put back, and the door on the left was a fake one, apparently added for symmetry.

Raleigh was about to start on the bookshelves, which did not hold a single book, when she heard steps on the porch. She had remembered to latch the screen door to at least slow down the neighbors if they decided to descend upon her today.

"Hold on, I'm coming."

"I see you've taken precautions." It was Jon, back in his Nebraska sweatshirt today, but with baggy khaki shorts exposing his pale, knobby legs.

"Yes, it's the only early warning system I have." She opened the door and latched it behind him.

He spotted the TV. "Hey, what's on?"

"No remote. You have to get up and turn the dial yourself."

Jon started cruising slowly through the stations, the dial clicking loudly. He found *Have Gun Will Travel* on the Hallmark Channel and sang a few bars of the theme.

"Why do I have the feeling you know the theme songs for all the old shows?"

"Because I am a Renaissance man, Miss Raleigh. A jack-of-all-trades."

"Peter Pan, if you ask me."

"Be nice. I came over to help you out today since the kids can't come back until Saturday. They said you're going to keep them busy all weekend."

"Most of Saturday, Sunday afternoon. Randy's going to pick up a carpet steamer on Sunday."

"The carpet'll probably dissolve, but it's your funeral—and a messy one, I'm sure." He looked into the bag.

"If this is treasure I'll eat my hat."

"Give me a break, I just got started. If I had a screwdriver, I'd get the back off the TV and check in there, too."

"Don't you dare. You might break something. If you're not going to keep the console I know someone who'd love it in his apartment, hint, hint, hint."

"I am going to check inside the cabinet, then you can have it. I am not moving that monstrosity clear across the country."

Jon went out into the kitchen and returned with a roll of paper towels, furniture polish and glass cleaner. He cleaned the screen first, then rubbed the polish lovingly into the wood.

"It's beauteous, thank you. I knew kissing up to an heiress would pay off eventually."

He grabbed Raleigh and tangoed her back and forth across the living room. At least Raleigh thought it was a tango, being a rhythmically-impaired person she couldn't be sure. Jon stopped in the vestibule and twirled her dramatically.

"Oh, I'm sorry. I didn't mean to interrupt. I'll just leave this." On the other side of the screen door Mrs. Bean blushed and stuck a sheet of yellow copy paper under one corner of the doormat and ran.

"Now there's no hope of convincing them you're not my boyfriend."

"Your what?! Ackkk!"

Jon released Raleigh as if burned. She opened the door and retrieved the sheet of paper.

"Thank you so much for that compliment." Raleigh read the sheet of paper. "There's a block party this weekend. I'm supposed to bring enough chips and dip for twenty."

"Here, let me see." Jon took the invitation from her. "Setup starting at eleven-thirty, party from noon to two. Sounds like fun. You'll get to meet the rest of the neighbors."

"If they're like the ones I've already met I'll pass. I take that back, Flossie and Hash Peters are very nice and quite sane."

"Don't be such a grouch. I'll fix a couple kinds of dip, you buy the chips. Get those baked kind, I like them better. Potato chips or corn chips? Better get both."

"You're inviting yourself? After insulting me?" Raleigh sniffed and went back into the living room. "I don't have time for a party. The kids will be here all day Saturday."

"And they'll need a break for lunch." He consulted the invitation again. "Looks like Mr. Wahl's in charge. I'll tell him you're bringing three extras."

"Three? Why not bring all your relatives and friends?!"

"Nah, I have too many."

Raleigh rolled her eyes dramatically.

"It's a great opportunity, Raleigh. Remember, we're Nancy Drew and Ted Nickerson. We still have the mystery of the hidden doubloons to solve. C'mon, it'll be fun."

"For the last time, it's Ned Nickerson. Oh, all right. But you show up early, bring and set up the chips and dip, clean up afterward and . . . and stay here right now and help me finish the living room."

"You drive a hard bargain, but . . . it's a deal. What do we take apart next?"

"I was about to check the bookshelves when you tangoed me into embarrassment."

"That was the merengue."

"Whatever. Shake out the rest of the magazines and newspapers, see if anything has been tucked inside. Then, Mr. Nickerson, see if there are secret panels in the back of the bookcase."

Jon went back to the kitchen and returned with two packages of rubber gloves and two white fiber dust masks. Properly attired for the job, he and Raleigh started working.

Forty-five minutes later they had located several innocuous, undated newspaper clippings, but nothing else. Raleigh and Jon carried bags of periodicals out onto the porch and turned their attention to the built-in bookshelves themselves. Jon pulled his dust mask onto his forehead.

"I need a break. Is there anything to drink around here?"

"In the fridge. Bring me back a water, please."

Raleigh tapped on the back of the bookshelves, starting from the bottom and working her way up. Jon finally returned, bearing a Coke, a bottled water and two peanut butter and jelly sandwiches.

"What's a hidden compartment supposed to sound like?" Raleigh took her water and one of the sandwiches.

"Different. You know, tap, tap, tap, klunk. Something like that. A hollow sound."

"It all sounded the same to me."

Jon finished his sandwich in four bites and tapped the bookshelves from the top down. "It isn't the same, but the hollow spots are uniform, the spaces between the studs."

"Maybe the furniture?"

"You're going to break that apart, too? What do you expect to use for furniture while you're living here?"

"Oh, I gave up on that. It's better to go back to the hotel at night than to live in this mess. I'll spend the days here, that's enough."

"You've seen the light of reason, unbelievable." Jon actually seemed relieved.

"Let's see if there's anything in the sofa."

They pulled off the cushions and inspected them one at a time and, though none showed signs of being slit open and sewn back shut, Raleigh insisted on cutting them open and checking. One after the other, Jon slit open the cushions and pulled out the stuffing and dumped it onto the sheet. Nothing. Raleigh restuffed the cushions and fastened them shut with some rusty safety pins she found in a kitchen drawer. They stepped back and looked at the lumpy sofa.

"I suppose I should keep it here? There's only the one chair otherwise."

"Aren't we going to rip that apart, too? Have you finally given up on the treasure hunt?"

"You're right, let's take the chair cushions apart, too."

Jon rolled his eyes and sighed loudly, but obediently slit open the cushions and pulled out the stuffing. "I could have told you. There isn't any treasure."

"Are you always so negative?"

"Yes. And I'm done. We finished the living room and I'm free to leave. Unless you think there's something hidden in the legs of the coffee table."

"I hadn't thought of that."

Jon picked up the flimsy coffee table and banged it against the floor. It broke into several pieces.

"This is definitely a disappointment. Maybe there's something."

"No, there isn't anything. And I'm taking this kindling out onto the porch and leaving. And I'm not sure I'm coming back." Jon didn't sound like he was joking.

"You have to, you're bringing the stuff for the party. Remember? If you want the TV."

"Saturday, eleven-thirty."

Jon hauled the remains of the coffee table outside and Raleigh started restuffing the chair cushions, all the time wondering why Jon was lying to her. But about what?

Chapter Fourteen

"It was very nice of you to drop in, Mrs. Bean. But you don't have to bring me baked goods every day."

Raleigh put the dented but clean kettle on the stove and turned on the heat, glad for an excuse to stop working. Mrs. Bean was sitting at the kitchen table, a plate with slices of banana bread in front of her.

"It's no trouble, dear. But I had to use sugar again I'm afraid."

Raleigh got two mugs from the cupboard and set them on the table with the two boxes of herbal tea she had gotten that morning.

"Then those molasses cookies you brought over for Randy had sugar, too? Good. There's nothing wrong with a little sugar now and then."

"I'll have to remind Emmett I don't need the saccharine anymore. Now that George is gone. He was diabetic, George was."

Raleigh wanted to ask Mrs. Bean to explain how she thought her husband was murdered, but didn't want to risk upsetting her. "Does Emmett do your shopping for you? I wouldn't have thought he should be driving."

"Oh, you can't tell Emmett not to do anything. Lord knows, Hash and the rest of the boys have tried. And all he gets me is the saccharine. No one else could ever find it. I had to have it for George, him being diabetic and all." Mrs. Bean smiled.

The kettle whistled and Raleigh poured the boiling water into the mugs and sat while they waited for the tea to steep.

"So you used sugar in the banana bread?" Raleigh wanted to make sure before she tried any.

"Lots of folks don't like the sugar calories, but I always thought that saccharine tasted awful. Diet this, low-calorie that. George couldn't tell the difference, though. Probably ate so quick he couldn't taste it at all." Mrs. Bean smiled to herself.

Raleigh took a sip of her tea and picked up a piece of the banana bread. She sniffed it cautiously first, but it smelled fine. She nibbled on a corner—very good.

"It's just as well. Otherwise I couldn't have poisoned him so easy."

Raleigh inhaled a bite of banana bread and started choking. Mrs. Bean got up and whacked her on the back several times.

Raleigh took too large a drink of her tea and scalded the roof of her mouth, but was able to stop coughing. Mrs. Bean was looking at her curiously.

"Are you all right, dear?"

"Uh . . . yes . . . I'm fine now." Raleigh put the banana bread down and looked askance at Mrs. Bean.

Mrs. Bean resumed her seat at the table, ate some of the banana bread, and sipped her tea daintily.

"Mrs. Bean. Did I hear you correctly? Did you say you poisoned George Mobley?"

"Well, of course, dear. I wouldn't say a thing like that if it wasn't true. I told you he murdered my Buddy. Don't you remember? No one would believe me, though, so I had to kill him. I'm awful surprised it took so long."

"It took a long time to poison him?"

"I couldn't figure out how to do it, not at first. Emmett wouldn't get me a gun . . . he was quite adamant about that. Then George got the sugar diabetes, had to use that saccharine. When they found out it caused brain tumors. Emmett and I put our heads together. He'd been Buddy's best friend, and Emmett said he knew where he could get the saccharine, even though it wasn't legal now. I could make cookies and such for George, use the saccharine, and give him brain cancer."

"So Emmett got you the saccharine?"

"Never thought it'd take . . . more than ten years. Oh well, better late than never." She took another sip of tea.

"Mrs. Bean, I was under the impression George Mobley died of liver cancer."

"Liver cancer, brain cancer, long as he's dead that's all that matters. Here, have another slice of banana bread. You know the secret to good banana bread? Freeze the bananas until they're black, then thaw 'em. They slip right out of the skins like a limp willie."

Chapter Fifteen

The next day Raleigh decided she deserved a vacation from fancifully murderous neighbors and cleaning house and she left a message on Jon's voice mail inviting him out for lunch. He should have received her samples from the contractor by now and she wanted to hear what, if anything, he had learned about Buddy Bean's death.

She slept late, took a longer-than-usual morning walk, ate breakfast in a café she had noticed the previous day, and in general didn't do anything productive—if she didn't count checking her e-mail. Raleigh ambled back to the hotel and placed a call to Pam back in Phoenix.

Luckily, Raleigh caught her friend between classes.

"Pam, it's me. And before you ask, yes, I'm still stranded in Ohio, with a crazier bunch of old coots and biddies than you could ever imagine."

"You've met my parents. Do they come any crazier than that?"

"Well, one confessed to murdering my cousin yesterday."

"I thought he died of liver cancer."

"That's what the death certificate says, but Mrs. Bean says she poisoned him with saccharine. With the aid of the neighbor who lives behind me and got her the banned substance."

"You win. Even my loopy uncle never said he killed anyone."

"Actually, Pam, that's why I'm calling. I know your expertise is in environmental science, but . . . is it possible? Do you suppose eating saccharine for ten years or more could cause cancer?"

"You're right, it's outside my area of professional expertise, but I do know it's been off the market since the sixties. Diabetes runs in the family, knock on wood, but I'm sure saccharine hasn't been available for decades. Even if it could cause cancer, you can't buy it. I can check the FDA and NIH Web sites if that might help, but . . . your confessed murderer may have some dementia issues."

"That's what I'm assuming, some kind of mental instability. Mrs. Bean sure is an odd one, like everyone else I've met in that neighborhood, but she was so matter-of-fact about it. 'Oh, by the way, I killed him and here's how I did it. I'm surprised it took so long,' to paraphrase her."

"Ask her *dealer* about it, see what he says if you're that curious."

"And how do I bring that up? Hi, Emmett, I hear you've been providing Doretha Bean with an illegal carcinogen. How do you feel about being an accessory to murder?"

"Did she say why she allegedly committed this murder?"

"My cousin murdered her husband Buddy."

"Did he?"

"Well, I'm looking into that. Or, Jon Bluff over at the lawyer's office is. Flossie says Buddy committed suicide. *She* seems perfectly sane, so I believe her."

"Since you're apparently playing Perry Mason, the least I can do is be your long distance Paul Drake. I won't have time until tonight, but I'll see what I can find out about saccharine. Check your e-mail over the weekend."

"Thanks. I'm sure it's a waste of time, but . . . from what I understand, George Mobley *was* asking to be murdered."

"Don't be so dramatic. Gotta go or I'll be late for class. 'Bye."

* * *

Just as Raleigh hung up the phone it rang.

"Can I pick the restaurant?" Jon didn't give Raleigh time to say hello.

"Sure. Did my samples get there?"

"They're on my desk as we speak. And I have the dope on Buddy Bean from my cousin over at the police department. I'll bring it along, but it isn't very interesting reading."

"How many cousins do you have?"

"I don't know, twenty, thirty. My relatives are keen on keeping their DNA in the gene pool."

"I guess they are."

"Let's meet at Giancarlo's. It's right around the corner from your hotel and down two blocks. You won't even have to drive. Walk an extra few blocks and work up an appetite. Noon. Ciao."

Jon hung up and Raleigh dumped her tote bag onto the bed and started sorting things into stacks. Several yellowed clippings fell out. Oh yes, the only find from the search of the living room yesterday. She reorganized her tote bag and sat down to read the clippings.

Gus Trout got promoted to supervisor, no date on the clipping. Jake Wahl graduated from college with a degree in engineering. Joe Wahl joined the navy. And a very tiny clipping, a two-line mention . . . Faith Bean had been made a ward of the county.

Raleigh already knew about Faith from Flossie Peters and the other items were just local news about the neighbors, nothing scandalous or suggestive about any of them. She put them into one of the estate folders anyway and turned on the TV.

Speaking of Perry Mason, look what was just starting. Her brain needed a rest and she closed her eyes and listened to the courtroom drama unfold. It was an odd habit, *watching* television with her eyes closed, but by now she had seen all of the episodes numerous times and she could recognize the various character actors by their voices alone.

Chapter Sixteen

The aroma emanating from Giancarlo's promised extraordinary culinary delights. Roasted garlic, basil, fresh-baked bread, the smells lingered in the warm air. Jon was waiting for Raleigh at one of the tables on the outdoor patio, thoughtfully shaded with big, round umbrellas, and he had already ordered eggplant bruschetta.

A Priority Mail box and a manila envelope were on the seat next to him. Jon got to his feet at Raleigh's arrival and held out her chair. There was a pitcher of iced tea on the table and he filled her glass.

"I hadn't walked over this way yet. Smells like you made a good choice."

"Try the bruschetta while you peruse the menu, but leave room for dessert. And there are always the specials."

Raleigh opened the menu and took a bite of the bruschetta as she read. "Ohhh, squash-filled tortelloni topped with a light cream sauce and fried sage leaves. That's for me."

The waiter approached their table and Raleigh and Jon placed their order. She decided to try the salad special, baby spinach, sun-dried tomatoes and grilled eggplant. Jon opted for the halibut in a lemon and white wine sauce.

"This must be my samples." Raleigh reached over and took the box off the chair. Three six-by-eight-inch pieces of Marmoleum slid out. One was green with multicolored flecks, another cream color with earth-tone marbling, the last was dark blue with lighter blue marbling. "I like this one. What do you think?" She held up the green one.

"Marmoleum, very cool. The blue, yuck, too nautical . . . the earthtones are neutral and unobjectionable. The green is very fresh and . . ."

". . . will look good with the yellow walls. That was easy enough."

Raleigh replaced the samples in the box. "You said the police report wasn't helpful?" The waiter delivered her salad and Jon took another bruschetta.

"You can read it for yourself later, but it's really straightforward." Jon handed her a #10 envelope. "Buddy Bean, his given name was actually Buddy, locked himself in the garage, doors and window closed, and taped around all the openings. He got behind the wheel, started up the car and that's it. His wife found him when she came back from somewhere with her daughter."

"How sad. Was there a note?"

"A very terse one. 'George made me do it.'"

"Well, that must be why Mrs. Bean blames him."

"Unless your cousin hypnotized Buddy Bean, I don't see how he could have made him kill himself."

"Have you ever been hypnotized?"

Jon shook his head.

"I was once, to help me get over my fear of flying. It didn't really work. He might have badgered him about something, hounded him somehow?"

"Even if he did that still doesn't make him guilty of murder."

"Mrs. Bean doesn't believe that. She confessed to poisoning him yesterday, remember."

"That sweet old thing? We're talking about the one who bakes everybody cookies, right?"

"That's how she says she did it. Fed him cookies laced with saccharine. Emmett got her the saccharine, though it hasn't been manufactured since the sixties as far as I remember."

"Those brownies were inedible, but she gave Randy some molasses cookies and he didn't get sick. They were fine."

"Flossie just made her throw the saccharine away. George Mobley was the only one who got whatever it really was, because he was diabetic."

"Well, it makes sense in a crazy way."

"I asked a friend of mine to see what she can find out about it. She has access to technical and medical Web sites."

"You're not taking this seriously, are you? Even if the old lady did feed your cousin saccharine? Lots of people ingest artificial sweeteners every day. Like you and your Pepsi."

"The stuff in that is supposed to be safe. And I have only one a day, two at most."

"Yeah, yeah, yeah. Manufacturers never lie."

The waiter cleared her salad plate and the bruschetta and returned with their entrees.

"I declare a moratorium on anything but savoring our food." Jon raised his glass with a flourish.

"Agreed."

They clinked their glasses in a toast and set themselves to the enjoyable task of eating.

* * *

Jon had cannoli for dessert and Raleigh tried the apple polenta tart. Jon might be able to afford all those calories, but Raleigh figured if dessert had fruit in it she wouldn't feel quite as guilty.

"What else do you have on your schedule today, Jon?"

"No, I am not doing any more housecleaning. No way, no how. I have to roast eggplant for the dip I'm making for the party you've blackmailed me into attending tomorrow."

"It isn't blackmail and you invited yourself."

"All right, bribery. And besides, you want me to play detective, too. All right, I'll be Paul Drake. Who am I supposed to pump for information?"

"The role of Paul Drake is already taken. You're Ted or Ned Nickerson, remember? And you're not supposed to pump anyone, just chat with *the boys*. Emmett's the one who's beefing all the time, but the others seem pretty friendly. They used to play poker once a week, maybe still do. I'll introduce you to Bailey and Gus and Al's the greasy little one who thinks he's Casanova."

"This should be a barrel of laughs."

"If you want that console television." Raleigh let Jon think about that.

"I said I'll be there, I'll be there. I'll probably come with the kids, bring Dave's truck and pick up the television before you raise the price." He gave her a meaningful look.

"Fine, take it with you tomorrow. After I get the back off and look inside."

"You're an intransigent woman, Raleigh Killen."

"No, just determined."

Jon paid the check and took his leave somewhat abruptly, but Raleigh remained at the restaurant for a while and read through the sketchy police report on Buddy Bean's death.

And sketchy it was. One page long and with a death certificate. If George Mobley did kill Buddy Bean it was the locked room mystery of all time.

Chapter Seventeen

Saturday dawned sunny and humid and when Raleigh unlocked the house at eight-thirty the thermometer on the front porch was already hovering just above eighty degrees.

A large envelope was stuck between the doors and she took it inside with her.

The house was stifling and she opened all the windows and doors in hope of letting in a breeze. She walked down the hall and unlocked both of the bedrooms and opened the windows in those rooms, too.

Raleigh checked the hall closet and found a cheap box fan and set it in the kitchen doorway, blowing outward to vent some of the stale air. Curious, she opened the envelope and found a black-and-white photograph with a sticky note on the back. *George is third from the left in the back row.*

The photograph appeared to have been taken at a picnic sometime in the late fifties or early sixties judging by the women's clothes and hairstyles. She counted three people from the left and got her first look at George Mobley. He had a disagreeable expression on his face, but she didn't like having her picture taken either, and he was shorter than she expected, probably not more than five-five. One arm was longer than the other, but not by more than two inches. Raleigh didn't know what a blackmailer was supposed to look like, but he looked pretty ordinary to her.

She didn't recognize the two men to his left, but Hash and Flossie were on his right, arms linked together, Flossie's hair dark and lustrous. Next came Bailey Wahl and Gus Trout, laughing into the camera. Mrs. Bean was alone and decades younger, as were the others. She was smiling in the same direction George was scowling. Two boys kneeled on the ground in front of Bailey, probably his sons, but no sign of his wife Lou, the hoochie dancer-cum-felon. A teenage couple was stretched out on the ground and didn't look like anyone she had met, they would be too young to be any of the current neighbors Raleigh guessed. Emmett was standing to one side, tall and cocky, a cigarette in one hand, the pack visibly rolled up in his shirtsleeve—you could tell he was a real hell-raiser. No sign of Al Vitello, so maybe he was taking the picture or maybe it was Buddy Bean behind the camera.

The people in the photograph didn't look like they had a care in the world, except for George Mobley, and he might have been squinting because the sun was in his eyes. There was nothing to show that he was the kind of man who would take advantage of anyone's weaknesses or secrets.

She turned the envelope over and saw that it had been reused and was originally addressed to Bailey Wahl. When she saw him at the block party later she'd have to remember to thank him and see if she could get him to talk about George Mobley.

In the meantime, the dining room awaited. And from the contents, it wouldn't take long to search it. Raleigh checked underneath the table and the seat of the chair, nothing but cobwebs. Inside the built-in china cabinet—no china, no secret compartments that she could find. A few crumbling paper napkins in the one drawer, a card of thumbtacks and a roll of tape, now glued to itself.

She heard doors slam out on the street and walked over to the vestibule. Molly was running around in circles while Naomi teased her with the Frisbee and Randy and Jon dropped the tailgate of the truck in which they had pulled up.

Raleigh walked out onto the porch. "Jon, what's with the truck today?"

"I'm taking that console before you change your mind again, remember? You're not using it to blackmail me into catering another party."

As if some dip and a few chips were such a big deal. Raleigh was sure he would charge it to the estate anyway.

"You just like to complain."

Randy took the Frisbee from Naomi and led Molly into the back yard while Naomi and Jon unloaded a couple of grocery bags from the back of the truck.

"Here, the dip has to stay chilled." Jon shoved two covered dishes into Raleigh's hands and they trooped into the house.

"I didn't expect to see you so early. You don't have to set up for the party until eleven-thirty."

"It was easier to ride with the kids as long as we were moving at least one piece of furniture out of your house."

"All right, all right, take it already."

"Where do you want us to start today, Raleigh?" Jon took the bags into the kitchen while Naomi and Raleigh looked around.

"There's a vacuum cleaner in the hall closet, why don't you get it out and see if it works?"

Raleigh and Jon could hear Naomi struggling to remove the vacuum cleaner from the closet. She returned to the living room with it, an old Electrolux canister model on chrome runners instead of wheels.

"If that runs, it might be worth saving." Jon looked at the Electrolux appraisingly while Naomi went back into the hall and returned with the chrome extension wand and assorted tools.

Randy entered through the kitchen and joined them in the living room. Two screwdrivers were stuck in his back pocket. "You want the back off this?" He nodded toward the console.

"Yes, but be very careful. It still works, believe it or not." Jon and Randy wrestled the console into the center of the room.

"You might as well try it out in the dining room first, Naomi. We'll vacuum up as much dirt as possible and, if the carpet survives, I may send you out to rent one of those steam cleaners."

Naomi dragged the Electrolux into the dining room and plugged it in. "Where's the switch on this thing?"

"Here, the switch is the big chrome button on the end. My mother had one just like it. There's a fabric bag inside instead of those paper ones. You empty it out onto newspaper when the bag gets full and wrap the dirt up."

"If you say so."

Naomi stepped on the button and the vacuum roared to life obligingly. She tested the suction and attached the wand and carpet-cleaning tool. The old Electrolux actually worked and Naomi set to cleaning the carpet.

Raleigh went back into the living room, where Jon and Randy had removed the back of the TV and were looking inside.

"This is so weird. These great big tubes, they're like light bulbs or something. This is way cool, J. J."

Raleigh knelt down and joined them. "Is there anything in there besides the insides?"

"It's a bust, Raleigh. You're going to have to face facts. There isn't any treasure or secret staircase."

"Maybe you're right, Jon, but I still have two rooms and several closets to search."

"There's nothing to find. I don't know why you don't believe me." Jon's tone was undeniably exasperated.

"How about you, Randy? Are you game for pulling up the kitchen linoleum today?" Raleigh hoped Jon's negativity wouldn't rub off on the kids.

"Sure. I brought a scraper in the truck." Randy dashed outside and returned quickly and set to work scraping up the kitchen flooring.

Jon finished securing the back of the console and coiled the cord on top. Then he picked up the box of extra TV tubes and dusted each one off.

"I think the bag must be full already. I'm not getting much suction now." Naomi stepped on the button and the Electrolux stopped.

Raleigh went into the kitchen and got a grocery bag, noticing how easily the linoleum was breaking up under Randy's energetic scraping. She rejoined Naomi and tore the bag open, then showed Naomi how to open the vacuum and empty the bag.

The bag had obviously been used, though just as obviously, not too recently. When Naomi lifted the bag carefully a solid mass of lint and dust was left behind. Raleigh started to wrap up the mass when a thought occurred to her. She spread the bag back out and carefully worked through the cylinder of dirt with her fingers.

"Raleigh, nobody hides anything in a vacuum cleaner bag." Jon stood in the dining room with his hands on his hips.

"Why not?" She continued digging and was rewarded when she felt something solid. "Eureka!"

"I thought it was an Electrolux."

"Scoff you may, but what do you say to this?"

Raleigh opened her hand and revealed a safe-deposit box key. "And you told me you checked at all the banks for anything in my cousin's name."

Jon took the key and turned it over in his palm. "There's nothing on it to say where the box is located . . . if you're right about what it is. I'll check it out and let you know what I find." He dropped the key into his pocket before Raleigh could protest. "I'll go see if they're setting up outside yet."

Jon walked abruptly out of the house, leaving Raleigh and Naomi staring after him.

"He probably feels stupid that he missed finding the key. He's always so thorough."

"Maybe it isn't to a safe-deposit box at all, I was just guessing. He's done nothing but make fun of my treasure hunting." Raleigh didn't want to voice her suspicions of Jon to Naomi.

"Nah, he's a real mystery buff. Randy and I were out here for a whole weekend once the snow was gone, went over the yard with a metal detector. Front and back. It sure wasn't our idea of fun."

"Really? Did you find anything?"

"There was some burned metal out back where someone had an incinerator once, a rusted padlock . . . and an old lawn sprinkler. Can't call any of that treasure."

"It's funny he didn't tell me about that."

"Nothing to tell."

"Did you look through the house, too? Or down in the cellar?"

"We hauled a lot of moldy stuff out of the cellar. If it wasn't moldy it was full of termites—yuck! Took it all to the dump."

"Yuck, indeed."

"J. J. went through the boxes in that spare room, pulled out a bunch of notebooks and papers, took those to the office, I guess. The stuff from the cellar went to the dump that day."

Naomi reinserted the dust bag into the vacuum and went back to work.

Raleigh walked over to the front door and looked out into the street—now blocked off. Jon was helping Mrs. Bean set up a card table. Bailey and Gus were wheeling a barbeque down the sidewalk under Emmett's loud supervision.

Jon turned and looked toward the house. Raleigh stepped back from the screen door and watched him for a moment. *What was in those missing notebooks and papers?*

Chapter Eighteen

When Raleigh walked outside later Naomi was already in place at one of the tables handing out tiny plastic cups of dip and paper bowls for the chips. Randy was supervising Molly playing tug-of-war with two little kids over a chew toy of some kind.

Bailey and Gus were working the barbeque in earnest, assisted by two men about Raleigh's age. Two women were riding herd on children of assorted ages in his yard. A basketball hoop had been set up and some of the older kids were enjoying a rowdy game.

Emmett was sitting in a lawn chair underneath a canvas canopy with Mrs. Bean hovering nearby. People were still arriving on foot and Raleigh spotted Al Vitello dogging a couple of teenage girls. *Eeew*. Flossie and Hash were presiding over the salad table, also under a canopy, and Raleigh walked over and joined them. A woman in her late forties came out of the house with a dish of pickles.

Flossie introduced her to Raleigh as her youngest daughter Jessie. "She's up from Columbus for the weekend with the grandkids."

Flossie bustled around rearranging the dishes while Raleigh and Jessie made small talk about the weather until a minor fight erupted across the street that Jessie had to stop.

"It looks like a good turnout," Raleigh said to Flossie. "Are those Bailey's grandchildren over there?"

"His boys and their wives and kids. They're enough to make a party all by themselves. Gus is kind of an extra grandpop. Don't know why he never married, he was quite a looker in his day."

"I know. Bailey left a photograph at my door. I recognized a lot of you. Looked like it was from the late fifties or sixties. George Mobley was in it."

"If we were all in it, musta been one of the company picnics. What'd you think of old George?" Hash looked at her curiously.

"Well . . . he looked kind of ordinary. Grumpy, but ordinary."

"Knowing what you know about George now, you gotta admit he sure wasn't ordinary."

"No, that he wasn't." Raleigh was silent for a moment, looking at Jon as he checked the snack table, then helped an older man tap a keg of beer. "You don't really know about anyone."

"I don't know what you're thinking, but your young man is all right."

"He's not my . . . you and Hash are all right, too, Flossie."

"Here, you must be getting hungry." Flossie filled a plate with a scoop of macaroni salad, another of potato salad, and topped it off with one of the pickles.

"You've never tasted another pickle like that, mark my words. Floss won the blue ribbon for her pickles at the Greenhaven County Fair, last fifteen years." Pride was evident in Hash's voice.

"That's because no one else bothers to enter anymore."

Raleigh walked over to the drink table with her plate and waited her turn and got a Diet Pepsi. Jon was refilling one of the dip bowls and Raleigh walked over to him next.

"Looks like the dip is a big hit. What gourmet treat did you whip up?

"Sour cream and French onion soup mix. I know my audience. I left some roasted eggplant spread in the kitchen for you."

"Thanks, Jon."

Several younger kids ran up to the table and helped themselves. "I told the kids to take a break. They're in the back yard with Molly."

"Why didn't you tell me you went over the property with a metal detector?"

Jon paused a moment. "We didn't find anything. What was to tell? You were having fun being Nancy Drew. I didn't want to spoil it. And you actually found that key."

"You're jealous that I found something and you didn't."

"Look, you were right and I was wrong. And I would have told you about checking the yard if you wanted to start digging it up or something. It wasn't important."

"Well, I'll forgive you. Especially since I found something." Raleigh couldn't resist the dig. "I'll do my part with the chips for a while. You circulate. Information-gather."

Jon rolled his eyes, but walked over to the barbeque and joined the other men.

* * *

The block party was winding down and even the kids were too full of hot dogs to be running around any longer. Raleigh had taken shelter on Bailey's porch with Gus Trout. Al Vitello and a man about Raleigh's age walked onto the porch.

"Raleigh, I thought you'd like to meet Fred. Fred was George's doctor."

The other man extended his hand. "Fred Kober, Miss Killen. I was with your cousin George . . . at the end."

"Dr. Kober, this is fortunate. Do you live in the neighborhood, too?"

"No, I have a condo near the hospital. I usually stop by and check on Mr. Potter every few weeks, though. He's not good about making regular appointments."

"A doctor who makes house calls?"

"Well, Emmett was a friend of my dad's and I keep tabs on him. Try to make him take better care of himself. It falls on deaf ears, unfortunately."

"Never could tell that Emmett anything." Gus shook his head in exasperation.

"Yes, Emmett Potter is his own man. He reminds me a lot of your cousin George, Miss Killen."

"Dr. Kober, could I talk to you privately?" Raleigh got up and Fred Kober followed her down the steps and into the yard.

"What can you tell me about George Mobley? You must have known him as well as anyone."

"Well, I didn't really know him. He showed up in the ER down at the hospital one night, they ran some tests and referred him to me when the results came back. As far as I know he didn't have a regular doctor. The cancer was already so far advanced I could provide only palliative care. He was on a morphine drip for the last two weeks."

"The little I've learned about him is somewhat . . . disturbing. He seems to have been quite an unpleasant man."

"Anyone can seem unpleasant when they're ill, especially terminally ill. I tried to keep him comfortable, called the local hospice for end-of-life counseling, but he threw them out fast enough. He did seem unusually bitter, that's about all I can tell you."

"Did he have many visitors? Do you know of anyone else who might have known him better?"

"I don't recall any visitors while I was there. Mr. Potter and the others here, they knew him best."

"Let me ask you one more question, Dr. Kober. I know this is probably silly, but do you know if it's possible for the liver cancer that killed George Mobley to be caused by saccharine?"

"It isn't a silly question, not at all. We don't know the causes for many types of cancers. If I recall, saccharine was linked to brain tumors in mice some decades ago, but that's been pretty well debunked. Other, more palatable, artificial sweeteners have come along in the interim . . . but no, even if he had eaten it every day of his entire life, it couldn't have caused liver cancer. Particularly the form he developed. Angiosarcoma is related very specifically to workplace exposure to PVC, polyvinyl chloride. It was invented in the 1920s, you know, and was and still is widely-used."

"PVC? Then why don't we all develop cancer? You're talking about stuff like PVC pipe, right?"

"Yes, and it doesn't pose a danger unless you inhale it as a gas, or dust, or somehow ingest it. The danger lies in industrial settings with inadequate ventilation, or lack of respirators, handling it in a liquid form—and for many years. Your cousin didn't suffer, Miss Killen, you can be sure of that."

"Thank you, Dr. Kober, you don't know how relieved I am." Raleigh was relieved that there was absolutely no way Mrs. Bean could have poisoned George Mobley, in spite of what she said. Raleigh and the doctor chatted about the party and the weather for a few moments, then he was on his way.

Flossie and Hash were folding up their table and the extended Wahl family was assembling in two different cars.

Raleigh joined Jon and Emmett sitting on her porch steps. Randy and Naomi had gone back to work and they were ferrying bushel baskets of linoleum scraps to the dumpster.

"Guess what we found, Raleigh?" Jon said.

"The buried treasure?"

Emmett snorted loudly and heaved himself to his feet, nodded to Raleigh and walked over to supervise the Peterses.

"It's better than treasure. Come and see."

Jon led Raleigh into the kitchen where Naomi was sweeping the last of the crumbled flooring into a trash bag.

"Hardwood floors!" Beneath the remaining chunks of adhesive and dirt was a hardwood floor. "I bet it's under the carpet, too."

"I'd better not steam-clean it then. We'll pull up the corners and see if that looks like hardwood, too. But that can wait until another day. I don't know about any of you, but I'm all in."

"The kids can help me with the console and we'll get out of your hair."

"Naomi, would you load two or three of those boxes from the spare room into my car? I'll start looking through them back at the hotel."

Jon and Randy hoisted the console TV and carried it carefully through the front door and settled into the bed of the pickup. Raleigh grabbed some old blankets from the hall closet and they used them to wedge the console in securely.

"I left you a snack in the fridge if you're hungry. Not French onion dip."

Randy retrieved Molly from the back yard and they all piled into the pickup and backed carefully out onto the street.

Raleigh went through the house and closed the windows and locked all the doors. As she walked from the kitchen to the dining room her foot caught in the now-exposed edge of carpet. She flailed her arms and managed not to fall, then checked the carpet. She had jerked several inches free and she peered under it to see if the floor was hardwood. She pulled more of the carpet free, nearly falling on her ass, and found a long envelope covered with grit and yellowed with age.

Raleigh pulled the envelope out and noticed the letter "P" written in one corner. The flap was unsealed and she opened it and spilled the contents onto the floor. Yellowed newspaper clippings. About former residents whose son had become a rabbi in Toledo. Raleigh leafed through the clippings, obviously the ones stolen from Flossie and Hash, and returned them to the envelope.

Out on the street, the barricades had been removed and the neighborhood was quiet. Raleigh was about to go next door and return the clippings to Flossie right then, but their daughter and grandchildren were still there and Raleigh thought it best to wait. Flossie had kept her secret all these years, Raleigh wasn't going to violate it now.

Raleigh put the envelope in her tote and set the alarm and locked the front door. She would see Flossie tomorrow and return the clippings, but she wouldn't mention her discovery to Jon, unwilling to confide in him about anything until she knew what he was keeping from her.

* * *

The cars were gone from the Wahl driveway and Raleigh walked across the street and knocked on the door. Gus answered.

"Miss Killen, how'd you like the party? I hope those vegetarian hot dogs were okay."

"They were fine, Mr. Trout. It was very thoughtful of you to remember. Is Mr. Wahl home?"

"Nope, they took off down to Moose Park, the nursing home. Wanted to visit with the grandpa of one of the wives."

"Oh, I hoped to thank him for the photograph he left at the house. A group shot of a company picnic or something."

"Yeah, he hunted that up last night. Things sure were a lot different then. We all had our health . . . the war was over."

Gus remembered his manners belatedly and invited Raleigh in and ushered her into the living room. Photographs lined the mantel and filled the walls, Bailey's two boys in every stage of their growth, their marriages, their families—three generations of the family displayed with obvious pride.

"Is Bailey's wife in any of these?" Raleigh asked as she looked around, finding a few more group shots of the neighbors, one of seven men clustered around a table, poker chips in the center, cards scattered on the surface.

"Not many, not that she didn't like to have her picture taken. That woman loved being the center of attention." Gus looked around, too, took down one of the framed photographs.

"Here. This would have been right after Joe was born."

A black and white photograph of a woman holding a baby, looking anything but motherly in her tight sweater, short skirt and high heels.

"That Lou. Thought she should be a movie star, did herself up like Betty Grable. Bailey and I knew her from kindergarten. She thought she was Shirley Temple then."

"It's a little surprising he never remarried. It must have been hard to raise two children by himself."

"Lou wasn't meant to be tied down. And I guess Bailey wasn't meant to be married any more than I was. Flossie and Doretha helped with the boys, and the Wests when they lived next door. They're both in a nursing home now. Young couple bought their place, seem like real nice people. You met them at the party."

"The Castillos? Yes, they do seem like good neighbors."

"What ever happened to Lou Wahl?" Raleigh asked as she returned the photograph.

"We never tried to find out. It wouldn't have been anything good, that's for sure. We were all better off without her." Though Gus's words were harsh, his tone was rather sad.

"Do Jake and Joe take after her? In looks, I mean."

Gus shrugged.

"Well, please tell Mr. Wahl how much I appreciate the picture. If I find any in my cousin's things that any of you are in I'll let you know."

"I'll tell him."

Chapter Nineteen

Refreshed by a soak in the tub, Raleigh ordered out for a pizza and opened the smallest of the four boxes Naomi had managed to get into the Honda. It, like the others, had already been slit open, so Raleigh upended it onto the coffee table and started looking through the papers.

Cash register receipts were fastened together with rusted paper clips, the ink faded into invisibility. She pulled a wastebasket over and started throwing things out. Several more packets of receipts were held with crumbled rubber bands, these also now illegible, but a flat paper bag held something that was of interest. The carbons from money orders. Raleigh read through them—the year was 1963—but all were for utility bills, a subscription to *Reader's Digest,* his property taxes (barely two hundred dollars back then), one for an insurance company. Nothing the least bit suspicious or interesting. Raleigh threw those out, too, and kept digging. By the time her pizza arrived she had finished with the first box and the entire contents were in the wastebasket.

As she ate, Raleigh started on another box and halfway down through mundane receipts and more money order carbons she was rewarded with a few magazines from 1952. One didn't have a cover, but was obviously an ancient porno magazine. As she shook it out for anything tucked between the pages, as she had the others, the rusted staples gave way and the pages fluttered to the floor.

Raleigh picked them up, wondering how she could throw them away without embarrassing the maid or herself, when a grainy photograph caught her eye. She took a closer look. It was Lou Wahl, her hair still platinum blonde, but she now was completely naked, striking what she must have thought was a sexy pose. Worse yet, Raleigh recognized the sofa on which she was lolling in feigned passion. It was a lot dirtier now and a lot lumpier, but it was the sofa in George Mobley's living room. Now Raleigh was even more embarrassed and, in spite of being alone in her room, she blushed beet red.

* * *

It took a while, but Raleigh cut all the pages of the porno magazine into tiny pieces and flushed them a few at a time down the toilet. She was more than flustered by the time she was done and couldn't help wondering if Bailey Wahl knew anything about the photograph or the magazine. Flossie had said Lou ran around with George for a while, but had Lou given him permission to put her photograph in the magazine, maybe hoping it would make her a star like Marilyn Monroe?

Or had George done it to spite Lou? Or did Bailey refuse to be blackmailed over the affair and George sent the photograph to the magazine for revenge? Bailey Wahl was an imposing man when he was younger, he might have stood up to whatever threats George Mobley made.

Whatever the reason, the evidence was gone now and Raleigh wasn't going to mention this find to anyone. She was almost afraid to continue her search, but she finished sorting through that box without anything more unpleasant turning up.

Unwilling to tackle another box, Raleigh checked her e-mail and had a brief message from Pam confirming what Dr. Kober had told her earlier. Regardless of the potential as a carcinogen, saccharine had been off the market for decades. Whatever sugar substitute Emmett got for Mrs. Bean, it wasn't saccharine.

Marty had ordered the floor covering for the kitchen and was nearly done installing the new tub in her bathroom. The tile setters would start on Monday and should finish by Wednesday. All good news. Raleigh was anxious to go home all of a sudden, though home was still a work in progress, and she hoped the remodeling would be done early. What . . . ? Dahlia Bible was back and belatedly trying to *supervise* Marty? *What unbelievable nerve!*

Raleigh sent Marty a message assuring him he could dispose of Miss Bible as he saw fit—short of murder, then logged off and looked at the two remaining boxes for a long moment.

Somewhat depressed at what she might find, Raleigh opened another one anyway. Unless she was willing to throw out everything sight unseen, and she wasn't, she had better continue.

This box had receipts from 1974, still legible, but for mundane items like light bulbs, batteries, a magazine. Raleigh stopped to figure out that her cousin would have been in his midfifties then, still working at the factory, though she had yet to locate any pay stubs or tax returns that Jon had missed. Judging by the receipts he kept and his money order carbons, George Mobley hadn't been a big spender. One of the neighbors mentioned a weekly poker game, perhaps he lost a lot of money gambling. Maybe one of *the boys* could tell her more about that.

Raleigh put the papers back in the box, thankful she hadn't found any more dirty pictures. She approached the final box with less trepidation and some relief now that she was almost done, at least for this day.

Something had melted in this box and many of the papers were stuck together permanently. Raleigh looked through it as best she could and pulled a manila envelope on the bottom of the box free. Underneath there was an audiotape enclosed in waxed paper and tied around the middle with string. The waxed paper was stuck to the box, but she was able to untie the string and retrieve the tape. Inside the unlabeled plastic case, the tape seemed unharmed. Raleigh was curious, but didn't have a tape player so she set the tape aside and checked the envelope. There was nothing inside. Relieved, Raleigh shoved all the boxes around the wastebasket and left a note on it for the maid.

She stretched out the kinks, put the Do Not Disturb sign on her door and went to bed, the tape tossed on the coffee table.

Chapter Twenty

Raleigh had forgotten to cancel her wakeup call and was up earlier than she had planned that Sunday. She decided to try brunch at the hotel restaurant, but first took her walk and headed into the historical district instead of circling the downtown area.

The trees arched over the street and sidewalks, providing welcome shade as the sun rose higher in the sky and the humidity climbed. Church bells were chiming nearby and Raleigh soon reached a red brick church that obviously held early morning services. The parking lot was about half full and several elderly people were making their careful way toward the entrance, the men wearing jackets, many of the elderly women wearing hats and gloves. Raleigh's mother used to dress like that for church. She would have disapproved of the ongoing trend toward jeans and T-shirts in church as disrespectful. Raleigh had to concur.

Raleigh reached a corner and realized Andrew Newton's office was on this block. She followed the numbers down the street and paused in front of the Craftsman bungalow. Jon's car was in the driveway, but the newspaper was still on the steps so he probably wasn't up yet. She walked on and circled back to the hotel. The neighborhood was very like a Norman Rockwell painting, she thought, a lot like the block party yesterday, a bit of idealized Americana—with an extortionist and amateur pornographer living at the end of the cul-de-sac.

Raleigh tried to dispel that unpleasant thought and hurried back toward the hotel.

*   *   *

The neighborhood was quiet when Raleigh parked in front of the house. Perhaps people were still in church, or making the weekly trip to the cemetery as her parents had, visiting her grandparents' graves. Maybe she would drive out to St. Stephen's Cemetery later and find her cousin's grave.

For now, she took the Sunday paper from the seat next to her and went into the house. After fixing a cup of tea, Raleigh went out onto the porch and settled into the swing to read the cartoons and the advice columns, her favorite parts of the paper.

Raleigh read the local real estate section with interest, trying to estimate how much the house might be worth. By midweek she should able to get the agents whom Jon recommended to take a look and give her a better idea. She wouldn't let the kids pull up the carpet in case there were more envelopes hidden underneath, so they might finish this afternoon.

A car door slammed and Raleigh looked up. Emmett had parked in front of Mrs. Bean's house and was hobbling around to help her out of the car. Mrs. Bean must have been braver than Raleigh thought, riding in a car with Emmett driving. She waved at them and Mrs. Bean waved back, but Emmett gave Raleigh his usual grimace. Mrs. Bean came over to the steps, her head covered by an ancient little hat with dusty spring flowers decorating one side.

"Raleigh, dear, are you here all alone today?"

"Just for the morning, Mrs. Bean. The kids are coming this afternoon. I'm going to putter around, sort through a few boxes while I'm waiting."

Emmett rolled his oxygen tank down the sidewalk impatiently. "Dot, quit gabbin' and let's go inside. I gotta sit."

"Come over and join us for lunch, dear, please. It's catch as catch can on Sundays, but please come." Mrs. Bean smiled up at Raleigh.

"Oh, thank you, Mrs. Bean, but I had a late breakfast and I'm not really hungry right now."

"She's got better things to do than sit around with us. C'mon, Dot."

"Well, how about coming over for dessert? In about an hour? I baked a pie . . . it's cherry."

Little did Mrs. Bean know it, but she had just said the magic word—*pie*. There was little in this world that Raleigh liked better than pie. Say what you will about chocolate soufflé or lemon cheesecake; homemade fruit pie was the best as far as Raleigh was concerned.

"An hour it is, thank you for the invitation, Mrs. Bean."

With the thought of pie running through her mind, Raleigh went back into the house and got to work. Randy had left the scraper behind and she pried one side of the already-loose dining room carpet up and rolled it roughly as far as the dining room table, which she had forgotten to move out of the way.

She shoved the table into the living room without too much trouble and finished rolling the carpet. No more envelopes, but the floor was hardwood here, too. Raleigh left the rolled carpet blocking the doorway to the living room when she realized she'd have to move all the furniture into the vestibule and hall to go any further.

Randy and Naomi could probably lift the furniture into the dining room, but she'd have to keep them busy elsewhere and pull up the rest of the carpet alone.

Raleigh still had half an hour before pie time, so she unlocked the bedroom door and started to go through the furniture. The dresser was closest and she pulled out all the drawers and laid them on the bed. One held dingy shorts and socks, several wadded handkerchiefs—nothing taped to the bottom or sides. The next contained a few equally dingy T-shirts and a moth-eaten gray cardigan sweater—nothing taped to that drawer either. Threadbare, faded navy blue sweatpants and a cracked leather belt were next.

And finally several pairs of folded jeans that didn't feel clean, stained with grease. Raleigh checked the pockets—lint—and there was nothing concealed on or in either of those drawers.

She went out to the kitchen and got a trash bag and stuffed the clothes inside. These weren't good enough to donate to even the most desperate homeless person or even wash your car with. Raleigh started to replace the empty drawers when the second one wouldn't go all the way in. She jiggled it around and heard something drop inside the dresser. In the bottom drawer was another audiotape, the plastic case cracked. *Okay, I'm going to have to find a tape player somewhere.* She tucked the tape in her pocket and carried the trash bag out into the vestibule, checked her watch and saw that it was time for pie.

Raleigh relocked the bedroom door and made a beeline for Mrs. Bean's house.

* * *

Emmett was sitting on the pink love seat, looking grumpy as usual, when Mrs. Bean ushered Raleigh into the front room. She hustled out to the kitchen to get the pie.

"Good afternoon, Emmett. Thank you for letting me join you for dessert."

"Don't thank me, it's Dot's doin'."

"Do you usually take Sunday dinner with Mrs. Bean?"

"What's that supposed to mean?"

"I wondered if she's repaying your kindness. The shopping you do for her?"

"I don't do her shoppin'. Flossie takes care of that herself," he snorted for emphasis.

Mrs. Bean returned with two slices of pie and napkins and forks. "The tea isn't ready yet, but you two dig right in."

Emmett hadn't waited. He dug right in the minute he had fork in hand.

"Aren't you going to have any pie, Mrs. Bean?"

"I'll have some later. I made a pig of myself over the pot roast. Sunday's the only time I make a roast or fix a chicken. Emmett takes me out to the cemetery, then has dinner with me."

Raleigh took a bite of the pie and was thrilled. The crust was flaky, the filling not too sweet.

"Mrs. Bean, this is delicious. The crust is just like my mother's. And where did you get the cherries?"

"Crust recipe's right off the Crisco can and the cherries were canned up last summer. It's the only way to make a pie."

"Can I have another, Dot?" Emmett's pie was gone and Mrs. Bean went into the kitchen to get another slice.

"Dot's the best pie baker around here. Cherry, apple, peach, nobody can top Dot, not even Flossie Peters. Cripes, I sure hope I get to taste her pumpkin again."

Emmett's tone was undeniably wistful. Raleigh liked pumpkin pie, too, but not as much as Emmett seemed to.

"Won't Mrs. Bean make you pumpkin pie?"

"Can't have pumpkin 'less it's Thanksgiving. T'aint right. Pumpkin for Thanksgiving, mince for Christmas. Boy, it'd sure be nice to have mince pie again, too. Sure hope I make it to Christmas."

At that moment Mrs. Bean returned with a second slice of pie for Emmett and a cup of coffee, a cup of tea for Raleigh.

Raleigh finished her pie and Mrs. Bean offered to wrap up a piece to take with her. Raleigh accepted happily and Mrs. Bean refilled her tea and poured one for herself.

"Sunday's my favorite day of the week. Emmett and I go out and talk to Buddy, then sit and have a nice dinner. I wish *Ed Sullivan* was still on."

"I understand your husband and Emmett were best friends."

"Oh yes, thick as thieves they always were, up to some mischief or other like spiking the eggnog at the Christmas services down at First Baptist. Not a bit of harm in either one of them, though."

Emmett looked decidedly uncomfortable.

Mrs. Bean got to her feet and walked over to a cabinet and took out a photo album. "Here, I'll show you a picture of Buddy."

"Dot, she isn't interested in ancient history."

But Mrs. Bean ignored Emmett and handed the album to Raleigh. The first picture was a black-and-white wedding snapshot, enlarged and a little grainy. The happy couple was standing on the courthouse steps, Buddy in his army uniform, Doretha in a print sundress with a corsage pinned to one shoulder. They both looked so impossibly young and Buddy was quite thin and not much taller than Mrs. Bean.

"Emmett was Buddy's best man." Raleigh wouldn't have recognized the man next to Buddy as Emmett. Emmett was smiling and looked quite sharp in his army uniform.

"My sister Stella stood up for me. Buddy and Emmett were being shipped out the next day."

Emmett got to his feet and took the album away from Raleigh and put it back in the drawer. "Now don't you start, Dot. You'll just get to cryin' again. There's been enough cryin' around here to last a lifetime."

Mrs. Bean sniffled and looked up at Emmett. "That's just what Buddy would say." She wiped her eyes and got up resolutely.

"I'll wrap you up a piece of that pie to take with you, Raleigh. You're bound to be hungry later on, the way I hear you working over there."

Mrs. Bean went into the kitchen and Raleigh got to her feet.

"Emmett, sometimes it's good to cry. It gets things out of your system."

"Not for her. She's cried an ocean since she lost Buddy, then to have Faith taken away from her. At least since George went she's been a little better."

It was now or never. "Emmett, I'm a little curious about something."

"Buddy's gone, leave him be, kiddo."

Raleigh forged ahead. "It isn't that. Well, Mrs. Bean says you've been getting her saccharine for some years. You know she says she poisoned George Mobley with saccharine?"

"You save your curiosity for that skinny lawyer you got. He hand over George's money yet?" Emmett set his jaw defiantly.

"It's just that saccharine was banned back in . . . ," Raleigh stopped short as Mrs. Bean returned with a tin pie plate that contained the remaining half of the pie. "Here, dear. If those kids are coming over later they'll need a snack, too."

Raleigh thanked Mrs. Bean warmly while she walked her to the door. As the door closed Raleigh could hear Emmett inside.

"C'mon, Dot, girl. Let's see to those dishes." His voice was very kind.

* * *

Raleigh was walking up the steps to her house when Bailey came running across the street holding a foil-wrapped package in his hand.

"Hello, Mr. Wahl. I stopped by your place late yesterday, but you had gone out with your family."

"Gus told me. Made a copy of that picture since you didn't know what old George looked like. Oh, here."

He handed her the package. "Had some of those veggie wieners leftover, didn't know anyone else who'd eat 'em."

"Thank you. It was nice of you to think of them in the first place. If you have a minute, Mr. Wahl, I'd like to ask you something about that picture."

He followed her up the steps and waited while she unlocked the door and went inside. Raleigh returned with the photograph.

"I didn't recognize either of these two men on the left. Or the young couple on the grass."

"That's the Hansens on the ground. He died in Korea. She went back somewhere to live with her folks. The other two gents are Chuck and Pete, from the plant. They're long gone now."

"Oh, well, thanks for the explanation. By the way, I couldn't help noticing that George and Mrs. Bean seem to be looking in the same direction, but he's scowling and she's smiling. Do you have any idea what was going on?"

"Faith was probably acting up or she and Buddy would have been in the picture, too. She was a sweet kid, but she did throw a tantrum when she didn't get her way. Wasn't much worse than most kids, though George took a dislike to her soon as he set eyes on her. Thought she should have been a cage or something. That George, he liked to give people grief when they already had more'n they could handle."

"So I understand. He seems to have been quite . . . unpleasant."

Chapter Twenty-One

After Bailey left Raleigh realized she didn't have much time before the kids would arrive. Jon hadn't said anything about joining them today and she hoped he didn't come along, too. She could keep the kids busy, but she didn't want Jon following her around and seeing whatever she might find.

Luck was with her and when the kids got there they were in the Bug and hadn't brought either Molly or Jon. She first had them move the dining room table and chair back into the dining room and free up the vestibule, then she set Naomi to mopping and drying the kitchen floor. Randy was exiled to the garage to try and create some kind of order from the chaos and throw out anything that was no longer usable.

As Raleigh sat gingerly on the edge of the dusty bed and looked through the first nightstand she could hear the clank and crash of metal and wood hitting the dumpster. The one nightstand drawer didn't hold much, an ancient package of condoms, a cheap crossword puzzle book, a throwaway lighter, one stray, tattered cigarette and a couple of rubber bands that crumbled into fragments. The other nightstand held a paperback book with a lurid cover, a shoestring, a pack of Chiclets (stuck together), another lighter and a suction cup with a jack at the end of the attached wire.

Naomi stepped into the open doorway and saw the jack. "Oh J. J. was looking for that."

"He was? What is it?" Raleigh looked at the suction cup curiously.

"It's one of those things you stick to a telephone to record your conversation. There was a tape recorder by the living room phone, and he thought there might be one of those, too. Don't know why, but you can see he was right."

"I didn't see a tape recorder anywhere."

"He probably took it back to the office with the other boxes of stuff. Want me to give it to him?"

"Thanks, I'll take care of it."

Naomi had been looking for something to finish drying the floor and the two women rummaged through the hall closet and pulled out the worst of the towels and sheets for her to use.

Raleigh sat back on the bed when Naomi resumed work on the floor. She put the jack in her pocket. Jon had appropriated the tape recorder and perhaps other things. That would explain why the house was so bare. But would he steal from the estate right in front of witnesses? Even if they were honorary relatives? It didn't make sense. Raleigh decided to see if she could get a cheap tape player on the way back to the hotel. She wanted to listen to the two tapes she had already found anyway. Maybe George Mobley left an audio treasure map.

Naomi finished with the floor and Raleigh had her clean the two nightstands. The dresser was beyond salvaging with most of the veneer peeling off and Naomi hauled that through the house and out to the porch. Raleigh could hear the two kids breaking it up in the driveway and wondered what she could keep them busy with next.

Before she tackled the closet, Raleigh went into the kitchen and started to heat the hot dogs Bailey had given her. At the first smell of food, Randy was in the doorway.

"I thought I smelled something. Is there enough for me, too?"

"Randy! That is so rude! Wait until you're invited."

"There are four here and you and Naomi are welcome to help yourselves. Mrs. Bean sent over a cherry pie, or half a cherry pie. It's in the fridge."

Raleigh fixed her lunch and the kids devoured the excess hot dogs and pie, with Randy licking the pie plate clean. Luckily, he hadn't finished the garage and Raleigh sent Naomi out to work with him. She didn't think they were spying on her, but they'd surely tell Jon what, if anything, she found in the house. It was better to let them work out the day as planned and do the rest of the cleaning and searching unobserved.

Raleigh went back to the bedroom and opened the closet door. There was the one wooden rod and a shelf with a couple hatboxes. She took out the clothes and laid them on the bed and checked all the pockets, then put them into a trash bag. Everything was so dirty and greasy, armholes rotting in some shirts, Raleigh wished she had put on rubber gloves first. The rusted hangers went in with the last of the clothes and Raleigh dropped the trash bag in the hall. She pulled the hat boxes off the shelf and opened them to find—hats. Vintage hats in good condition, but only hats.

"Raleigh, we're done with the garage. What's next?" Randy thundered down the hall and looked into the bedroom. He spotted the hats.

"Way cool. Where did those come from?" Randy wiped his hands on his jeans and carefully took a fedora from one of the boxes. He put it on his head at a jaunty angle. "Do I look like Humphrey Bogart?"

"You look like Hubert Humphrey," offered Naomi.

"Who?"

"Never mind."

"The one you have is a fedora and I think this one is a homburg." Raleigh took a hat from the other box. "This is Bogart in *Sabrina*."

"Even better. These are so phat. What are you going to do with them, Raleigh?"

"Give them to you, apparently."

Randy repacked his new acquisitions carefully, there were two hats to each box, and took them out to the car so he wouldn't forget them. Raleigh and Naomi agreed that males of any age were too weird to be understood.

With that, Raleigh sent off Randy and Naomi with her thanks and a promise to call them as soon as she needed more heavy lifting. Both were eager to continue with the treasure hunt, but Raleigh was determined to follow through on her own. The fewer people who knew George Mobley's secrets, the better.

* * *

Raleigh settled herself into the Honda and pulled away from the curb. She suddenly smacked herself none too gently in the forehead. One answer was right in front of her. The tape player in the dash! She rooted through her tote and came up with the tape she had found stuck in the dresser. She popped it into the player and listened as she drove back toward the hotel.

"February 2, 1967. 6:15 p.m." George's voice, Raleigh supposed. Thin, high-pitched.

"Hello . . ." Raleigh had no idea whose voice this was.

"I'm still waiting, Trout. You know I'm not a patient man."

"It's not up to me, George, you know that. We all have to agree before someone joins. Bailey and Hash are with me, but . . ." Gus Trout wasn't begging, yet.

"You know what's gonna happen if I don't get in. There's gonna be a mighty interesting article in the paper about you and Wahl . . . mighty interesting."

"The others have to agree, too. Al thinks we have enough with the six of us. Buddy'll go along with what Emmett says, but Emmett's dead set against having you in."

"I already persuaded Emmett to change his mind. Now you'll have to let me in."

"Emmett said it's okay? I don't believe you."

"Ask him yourself. Bet he won't tell you why he changed his mind, though. I want that invitation formal-like before the next game, you hear?"

There was a long pause in the tape.

"Next Monday, George. Next Monday."

"Just you see that you and Wahl lose twenty-five each or you know what will happen. Hate to see something like that in the paper for everyone to read."

"You win, George, you win."

"I always do."

Raleigh could hear the click of a receiver and the tape ran for a moment longer, George Mobley chuckling with apparent glee. The tape hit a blank spot.

"February 8, 1967. 5:45 p.m."

"Hello . . ."

"Al, old buddy, old pal."

"Hi, George. What can I do you for?" Al's voice sounded worried.

". . . like to know I've been looking over . . . down at St. Stephen's . . ."

The tape stopped abruptly and the player whirred. Raleigh tried to eject the tape, but it was jammed. She pulled the car over and tried again. The cassette came free, but the tape was twisted and knotted beyond salvation.

Well, she thought to herself, I didn't really want to hear the rest anyway. One by one, George Mobley had discovered his neighbors' and coworkers' secrets—and used them to his advantage. Whatever form the payoffs took, it was over now. Or was it?

What had Jon taken from the house in boxes? Was it financial records as he claimed, or did he plan to take over where George Mobley left off? Raleigh had accepted Jon Bluff at face value and had warmed to him immediately. Well, almost immediately, but she didn't really know anything about him, or Andrew Newton, Esq. for that matter. Maybe they were in it together, fleecing senior citizens one way or another.

As Raleigh wound the ruined tape around the cassette and dropped it into her tote she realized she had stopped down the street from the lawyer's office. Perhaps a surprise visit from her was in order. Catch Jon unaware for a change. She locked the car and walked down the sidewalk. Jon's car wasn't in the driveway, but maybe it was in a garage around back.

Raleigh rang the bell and waited. She could hear someone moving around inside and, after a moment, a tall woman in her early forties came to the door.

"You must be Raleigh Killen. I would have recognized you anywhere from J. J.'s description." The woman held out her hand. "I'm Addie. C'mon in."

Addie was tall and solidly built, her graying hair curly and cut short. A few crinkles formed at the corners of her hazel eyes as she looked Raleigh up and down.

"J. J.'s not here right now, but . . ." A timer went off in the kitchen and Addie hustled after it. Raleigh followed her and waited while Addie took a round loaf of bread from the oven. "He should be back in an hour at most."

"I just stopped by to drop this off." Raleigh took the phone jack from her pocket and put it on the table. "Naomi told me he had taken the tape recorder from the house, but hadn't found this."

Addie picked up the phone jack and walked back through the dining room and into the reception area, where she dropped it on the desk. "I'll let him know."

Raleigh would have liked to look through the office herself, but didn't have any plausible excuse for staying any longer. She took her leave of Addie and walked back to her car wondering who the younger woman was. Another relative in Jon's vast family tree or a girlfriend?

Chapter Twenty-Two

Back at the hotel, Raleigh pulled out all the correspondence and estate documents, finally locating a note from Andrew Newton that included his cell phone number. She picked up the phone and was ready to call him, but had no idea what she would say. She had no proof that Jon was doing anything unethical and, if he was, Andrew Newton might be in on it, too. Raleigh dialed room service instead of the lawyer and ordered dinner, disgusted with herself that she couldn't figure out what to do.

She threw the ruined cassette tape in the trash and located the one she had found the previous night. Housekeeping might be able to locate a tape player for her, but—what was the point? She knew what George Mobley had been, listening to the painful details wouldn't change anything now. Raleigh had always been a naturally curious person, but in this case she felt her cousin's victims deserved to keep their secrets. She pulled the tape from the cassette and wadded it up as thoroughly as she could, then cut through it with her nail scissors before throwing it in the trash, too.

Raleigh realized right then that she'd have to get into the Jon's office—and his apartment—and see if there were any more tapes or other kinds of blackmail evidence. However, breaking and entering were beyond her area of expertise, much like car repair. Who could she get to help her? She would have to do the searching herself; she couldn't trust anyone else to do that. But the locks, and there must be a security system to disable.

It was at that point that Raleigh picked up the phone book and started looking for private detectives. Divorce, security services, employee screening . . . industrial espionage. Industrial espionage? In Greenhaven, Ohio? The idea boggled Raleigh's mind, but they could surely pick locks, that's really all she needed if there wasn't an alarm system. She left the phone book open and would call one or more of them first thing in the morning. The illegality of the idea didn't bother her one bit, she realized with surprise.

While she waited for room service, Raleigh looked through a box she had brought from the house and lugged to her room. The year was 1977 and, though receipts were legible, nothing was of interest in the first batch she checked. More money order carbons . . . why didn't that man have a checking account? Obviously because he didn't want anyone to know how much money he had, Raleigh told herself. Which made her think of Jon again. He must not have found any money, or as much as he thought there should be, otherwise why hang around her and the house? He'd already searched the house thoroughly and taken everything of real or potential value. But he had missed the two tapes she found and he might have missed something else.

She'd better find a locksmith and change the locks at the house tomorrow. And figure out how to change the alarm code, too. No one was going to have access to that house except her.

She continued with the contents of the box, shaking out magazines, reading newspaper clippings and checking more money order carbons. Unless George Mobley was a gambler or gave a lot of money to charity, which Raleigh didn't believe for a minute, he hadn't been spending as much as he was taking in. Emmett Potter was right after all. There had to be money hidden somewhere and if it was in that house Raleigh was going to find it. She had no idea what she'd do with it, but she would find it or tear the place down trying.

Chapter Twenty-Three

Monday dawned hot and humid, but Raleigh wouldn't be deterred from any of her several missions. She located a locksmith who could change the locks that morning and she had an appointment with a real live gumshoe to discuss her idea for B and E. They agreed to meet at the Mexican restaurant for lunch, which would give Raleigh time to also stop at the bank branch where George Mobley supposedly had the savings account Jon closed.

While the locksmith was busy Raleigh called the number on the alarm keypad and they talked her through changing the code and password. She also gave them her cell phone number and instructions to call her in the event someone, someone being Jon, tried to get in while she wasn't there.

The locksmith left and Raleigh was about to get to work rolling up more of the carpet when the doorbell rang. In spite of the heat Raleigh had closed and locked the front door, leaving only the front window open, the box fan stirring up the dust. Apprehensive that it might be Jon, whom she did not relish confronting at the moment, or ever, she was relieved to see Flossie and Hash on the porch.

Raleigh invited them in, locking the door behind them. They noticed, but didn't say anything about her precaution.

"I'm so glad you came over. I might have forgotten this otherwise." Raleigh found the envelope in her tote and handed it to Flossie.

"We were busy with the grandkids yesterday and church and you had your helpers here . . . ," Flossie stopped short as she opened the envelope and recognized the clippings.

"What is it, Floss?" Hash took a look over her shoulder, then looked at Raleigh. "Where'd you find 'em? I looked all over the place when I was here with the boys . . . ," now Hash stopped short and blushed.

"It's all right, Hash. I realized later that you and the others must have spent more time looking for . . . whatever . . . than cleaning. The envelope was under the carpet in the dining room."

"I don't know what to say, Raleigh. This is such a weight off my mind." Flossie sniffled and pulled a handkerchief from the pocket of her apron.

"What with the alarm system we couldn't get in to look before, even after old George was in the hospital. Then when he died your fella was in and out . . . took a lot of stuff with him. We didn't know if there was anything here at all."

"So no one else has contacted you? Wanting to take up where George left off?"

"No, and no one can, not as long as we have this back." Hash gestured with the envelope.

"How about any of the others? Has anyone contacted them?"

"The others? What makes you think there are any others?" Flossie's expression was very guilty and she twisted her handkerchief nervously into a knot.

Raleigh thought for a moment, then decided she could trust the Peters. "I found some other . . . things. We both know you weren't his only victims."

Hash Peters looked every bit as ashamed as his wife.

"Well, all right, if you must know. We were each looking for something when the girls got you out of the house that day. Danged if we didn't come up empty. 'Course we couldn't get into the two bedrooms, none of us knew how to pick a lock." Hash seemed quite disgusted with himself.

"It was devious and I'm sorry for that, Raleigh." Flossie sniffled again.

"I was going to destroy the clippings, but then I thought you might want to do that yourself."

"Hash, how about we barbeque ourselves some pork chops tonight?"

"That's a fine idea, Floss. A fine idea."

"You'll join us, Raleigh. It'll be kind of a celebration. I'll make you another grilled cheese."

Raleigh accepted the invitation and declined their offer of assistance in rolling up the carpet. Though she trusted Flossie and Hash, she didn't want even them seeing what, if anything else, she found. Raleigh relocked the door and started cutting through the carpet with a sharp knife she had gotten at the hardware store that morning. She would have the kids back on the weekend, if they could come, and have them haul the carpet to the dump if the trash company wouldn't take it.

The air got even dustier as Raleigh loosened the short edge of the carpet and started to roll it up. She belatedly remembered the dust masks and ran into the kitchen to get one. Something moved in the back yard. She stopped to take a look. It was Emmett, ducking through the fence and back into his yard, not that he could move quickly with his cane and the oxygen tank. He'd never make it as a secret agent. She watched him replace two loose boards in the fence so that it looked whole again.

Emmett was spying on her. Or looking for whatever George Mobley used to blackmail him. Raleigh made sure the kitchen and side doors were locked and went back into the living room with her dust mask.

Half an hour later Raleigh had succeeded in rolling up the living room carpet and revealing another old, dirty envelope. She shoved the furniture back into place and went into the kitchen and got a Diet Pepsi.

Raleigh washed her hands and face and sat down at the table and opened the envelope, which bore a return address for the

County Mental Institution. Her heart fell as she read the letter inside. The depths to which George Mobley sank were simply unbelievable.

He was responsible for Mrs. Bean's daughter being institutionalized, having lodged numerous complaints by phone and letter to the county about her destructive, violent behavior. Raleigh didn't have a lot of knowledge about people with Down syndrome, but she didn't recall that they were violent. Flossie Peters hadn't given the least hint that Faith Bean was anything but a loving little girl, regardless of her chronological age. If she and the other neighbors had been willing to help raise her she couldn't have been much of a problem.

Whatever his warped reasoning, old George had deliberately broken Mrs. Bean's heart and consigned an innocent child to life in an institution. If he had still been alive, Raleigh would have been tempted to throttle him right then and there.

Raleigh sighed sadly, but was thankful she had found the record and could destroy it. Knowing what George had done wouldn't help Mrs. Bean or her daughter now. Though if Mrs. Bean did know George was responsible for her daughter being taken away it would give her even more motive for wanting to kill him.

Perhaps George did kill Buddy Bean by tormenting him over some . . . past sin until he committed suicide.

Raleigh shook herself out of that morbid thought and stuffed the letter in the bottom of her tote and looked around the house. She had the bedroom carpet to pull up, and the carpet in the spare room, but it was still full of boxes and would have to wait. When she got back from lunch she would check the mattress and box spring for a hiding place, then put the furniture on one side of the room and deal with the carpet.

She checked her watch and saw that she just had time to change her clothes and get to the Mexican restaurant to meet her own personal Hercule Poirot and see if she could persuade him to break into Andrew Newton's office.

* * *

Arnie Szkolnik didn't look much like a detective to Raleigh, being somewhat on the short side, thinning reddish hair and the annoying tendency to whistle off-key while he thought. But it had been, all in all, amazingly easy to convince him to break into the legal office and Jon's apartment.

Raleigh regretted that her well-rehearsed rationale for the break-in was unnecessary. It had been quite a convoluted story on which she had worked since the previous night. All she really needed to persuade the detective was money.

For a mere one hundred dollars an hour he would put the premises under surveillance, then get her inside and open any locked doors or filing cabinets for her. She agreed to his insistence that she not remove anything, but she could photocopy whatever papers she found that were of interest.

Raleigh had a secret plan that involved stopping at the hardware store and purchasing a magnet, with which she could destroy any tape recordings she found. Arnie didn't need to know about that, she'd just have to be subtle in the execution. She remembered it worked for Perry Mason once. Though she couldn't conceal it in a pack of cigarettes like he did since she didn't smoke.

She gave Arnie her cell phone number and he was going to stake out the office and tap the phone to monitor Jon's schedule. As soon as the office would be empty for a while they would meet in the alley behind a nearby liquor store and walk from there.

Satisfied that her plan was in motion, Raleigh said good-bye to Arnie and walked across the parking lot to the branch bank.

A helpful bank representative pulled up George Mobley's information on the computer, once Raleigh had produced identification and the trust agreement and will.

"Yes, your cousin did have a savings account here. It looks like he closed it out . . . hmmm, two weeks before he died. The balance was $21,003.78. We transferred it to Ohio Western, to an account in the name of the trust."

"Two weeks before he died? He was in the hospital then. Are you sure it was him? Maybe it was a tall, skinny guy in his midforties, someone representing his lawyer."

Raleigh waited while the bank representative went into the back to retrieve the original signature card. She returned quickly with a file folder.

"Everything is in order here. He signed in person, Janine was the teller who processed the transfer."

"Could I talk to her? See if she remembers George Mobley?"

"Sure. She's over on window three, but it's about time for her break. Why don't you take a seat in the lobby and I'll get her."

Janine walked over to Raleigh carrying the file folder and introduced herself. Though it had been months ago, the teller remembered George Mobley vividly. He had been swearing and barking orders and wore an overcoat on top of pajamas. A plastic ID band had been visible on his left wrist. He closed the account and transferred the balance to a different bank, then he and his lawyer went over to the safe deposit box desk.

"His lawyer was with him? He had a safe-deposit box?"

"Well, I think he was his lawyer. He had on a suit, carried a briefcase, tall, skinny guy with glasses. You'll have to check on the safe-deposit box with Chuck, he might be able to tell you more."

Stunned, Raleigh walked over to Chuck and introduced herself and produced her identification and legal papers yet again. Chuck also remembered George Mobley and his lawyer.

"The lawyer went outside and came back with a banker's box. Your cousin was making rather rude remarks about one of the tellers as I recall. They went into one of the privacy booths together, emptied the box, returned the keys and left. No, that's not right. They were short one key. We issue two keys to each box holder."

He pulled the original paperwork from a file and showed it to her.

"You should have heard Mr. Mobley squawk when I told him there would be a fifty-dollar charge for the missing key. His lawyer wrote us a check and hustled him out."

A business card fell from the folder and onto the floor. Raleigh picked it up. Jon Bluff.

Chapter Twenty-Four

When Raleigh returned to the house she was too distracted to go back inside. She had missed her morning walk in order to meet the locksmith so, in spite of the increased heat and humidity, she set off down the street and tried to calm her thoughts.

If the safe-deposit box had been full of money then it was gone for good and there wasn't anything Raleigh could do about it now. Her suspicions weren't enough with which to approach the police—unless she could turn up some kind of proof when she searched his office. She was sure Jon wasn't stupid enough to leave a banker's box stuffed with cash and covered with George Mobley's fingerprints sitting around, but then again, he wasn't expecting her to break in.

And if the box they took from the bank wasn't full of money—what had it contained?

Raleigh was giving herself a headache and she was sweating uncomfortably when she paused in the shade of a tree, then realized she had stopped in front of Emmett's house.

* * *

"Well, come in if you're comin' in, kiddo. No sense in coolin' the whole neighborhood." With that cordial greeting Emmett ushered Raleigh into the front room.

The air conditioning was on high and the sudden change in temperature made Raleigh sneeze several times.

"Set yourself down."

Raleigh took a seat on the sofa and looked around. Emmett hobbled from the room and returned with a box of tissues, to which Raleigh helped herself.

"Allergies . . . sorry."

"Whataya want, kiddo? I got things to do. A house don't clean itself."

Raleigh offered to give him a hand, reciprocating his help around her house, and they went into the kitchen. Mason jars were soaking in the sink and Raleigh started washing them. Emmett dropped into one of the kitchen chairs.

"Do you can, too? Like Mrs. Bean?"

"Yeah, my apple butter took first prize last year at the fair." Emmett's tone was sarcastic.

Raleigh scrubbed hard at one jar, trying to remove a crusted white powder. "I'm pretty sure this isn't apple butter. My mother's was brown from all the cinnamon."

"Canning jars are good for keeping all kinds of stuff. Use 'em down in my workshop."

Raleigh got the rest of the jars clean and dried them. "Where do they go?"

"Don't bother. I'll get 'em down to the basement later."

"It's no bother." Raleigh gathered the jars in her arms and spotted the door which led to the basement. She flipped the light switch with her elbow and started down the stairs.

"Don't you mess around down there! Leave 'em on the floor and get right back up!" Emmett's voice sounded a little panicked instead of his usually bossy tone.

Raleigh reached the bottom of the stairs, ducked underneath some piping that had been suspended from the rafters and looked around. There was a wooden workbench with pegboard above it, every tool in its place, jars of nails and screws labeled clearly on the adjoining shelves. A band saw stood on the floor and a smaller, metal workbench held a belt sander, vise, and power tools she didn't recognize. Though tidy, nothing had been used for some time, judging by the amount of dust that covered everything. There was quite a bit of white dust on and surrounding the belt sander and Raleigh saw space on the shelves on the right side for the jars.

"What're you doin' down there?! I said get back up here!"

Raleigh heard him struggle to his feet and roll the oxygen tank across the floor. His shadow fell down the stairs as he stood in the basement doorway.

"I'm coming, Emmett. I had to find a place to put the jars."

As she walked back to the stairs she banged her head on the lengths of pipe, thankful that it was plastic instead of metal. Emmett backed into the kitchen and out of Raleigh's way as she reached the top of the stairs. She flipped off the basement light and closed the door, noticing Emmett's sudden pallor with alarm.

Raleigh pulled a kitchen chair over to him and he sat down wordlessly. She filled a glass with water and tried to hand it to him, but he pushed it away.

"Stop fussin', kiddo. You're as bad as Dot." Emmett was gasping for breath in spite of the oxygen tank, and his lips were taking on a bluish tinge.

"I'm calling 9-1-1, Emmett. Right now."

Raleigh grabbed the kitchen phone and did just that. Emmett didn't have the strength to protest; he sagged more heavily into the chair and dropped his cane.

Thankfully the 9-1-1 operator was able to trace the call, since Raleigh didn't know Emmett's address, and she was assured that help was on the way. Raleigh located the phone book and called Dr. Kober's office and left a message, then called Flossie and Hash since she didn't know what else to do.

Emmett's color was a bit better by the time Raleigh got off the phone and Flossie and Hash were at the front door even before the paramedics. Flossie held Emmett's hand and stroked his forehead while they waited.

"What happened, Raleigh?"

"I don't know. I came up from the basement and he was all pale, then he couldn't talk."

"Tell your woman to stop fussin', Hash."

"She's her own woman, you oughta know that by now, Emmett." Hash picked up Emmett's cane and pressed it into his free hand, giving him a reassuring, gentle pat on his shoulder.

"I'll outlive you all . . ."

"Out of pure cussedness, I have no doubt."

They could hear a siren scream up the street and Hash went to the front door and let the EMTs in and directed them to the kitchen. In no time flat, Emmett was on a gurney, an oxygen mask over his face and in the ambulance with Flossie alongside.

"I'd better get back to the house, find the health care thing Emmett signed . . . just in case." Hash sighed as he and Raleigh walked down to his car. He offered Raleigh a ride back to the adjoining block and she accepted it.

"Hash . . . Emmett got really upset when I went down into the basement. I mean, really upset. Do you have any idea why?"

"Can't imagine. He has quite a workshop down there, but it's nothing that special. Don't know how he still manages the steps. Figured he'd probably kill himself falling down them some day if his heart or lungs didn't give out first."

Hash pulled into his driveway and they both got out of the car.

"Raleigh, would you go tell Doretha about Emmett? It'll take me a few minutes to find his paperwork—she can ride over to the hospital with me then."

Raleigh nodded and walked over to Mrs. Bean's house and broke the news to her as gently as possible that Emmett had been taken to the hospital. Mrs. Bean darted back into the house and got her purse, then trotted over to the Impala and got in. Raleigh realized no one had thought to lock up Emmett's house. It was too hot to walk back, so she got into the Honda and drove around the block.

Raleigh walked through Emmett's front door and went into the kitchen to look for his keys. She always dropped her keys and pocket change on the counter nearest the door when she came home, but she didn't see his keys anywhere in the kitchen. Maybe he always came in through the front door. She went back to the entry and looked, checked a drawer that yielded winter gloves, then walked into the front room. No keys in plain sight, so she looked in the top desk drawers. Nothing there, either.

Raleigh was about to try Emmett's bedroom when she stopped and looked at some faded photographs on the coffee table. There was a color shot of Emmett and Buddy flanking a young girl who could only be Faith Bean. Clearly affected by Down syndrome, she was wearing a frilly pink dress and smiling happily at her father. Faith appeared to be about ten. Raleigh replaced the photograph and located Emmett's bedroom at the back of the house.

Bingo! His keys were on the dresser with his wallet.

"Hey, pretty lady."

Raleigh stifled a scream and turned around. Al Vitello was slouching in the doorway.

"Mr. Vitello, you nearly scared me half to death."

"Whatcha doin' in Emmett's bedroom?" Al Vitello wiggled his eyebrows suggestively.

"Looking for his keys. So I can lock up."

"Sure, sure. I can be discreet. Didn't think old Emmett had it in him."

Raleigh edged by the harmless, but annoying little man and walked back to the front door.

"Emmett had some kind of attack and he's in the hospital. Flossie went with him, but Hash and I forgot to lock up the house in all the excitement."

"Really? Poor old Emmett. He really wanted to make it to Thanksgiving . . ." Al's leer dissolved.

"And he may still. I have to lock up now."

Al Vitello, looking rather downcast, left without further remarks and Raleigh locked the front door after them.

Chapter Twenty-Five

Later in the afternoon while she worked at her cousin's house Raleigh realized she should have talked to Al Vitello about her cousin, but she hadn't had the energy at the time. She felt as though she had been the cause of Emmett's attack—she assumed it was a heart attack—and possibly his death. All she had done was go down into the basement with those jars. Why had that upset him? There wasn't anything suspicious down there that she had seen—not that she had really looked around.

Raleigh found another tape cassette tucked under a corner of the hall rug, but dropped it in her tote without looking closely at it. She'd destroy it when she got back to the hotel. The hall rug was rolled and ready for disposal with the dining room and living room carpet and Raleigh had given up the heavy work and dragged several of the boxes from the spare room out onto the porch, now an oasis of shade in midafternoon.

She wanted to watch for Flossie and Hash to return and give them Emmett's keys, so the porch seemed like the best place to wait and it was far less dusty than inside the house. Raleigh had set a leaking sprinkler running in the front yard and changed the position every time she finished a box. Since learning about the safe-deposit box, Raleigh wasn't surprised that she hadn't found much of interest in the house, but she was determined to look just in case Jon missed something. After all, she had found three tapes, Flossie's clippings, another envelope and the safe-deposit box key.

Suddenly Raleigh hit the jackpot. Old photographs and letters, some with "Pa" written on the back. Raleigh looked at them carefully and could see a resemblance between the pictures of her cousin and this man. He must be Richard Mobley, her aunt's erstwhile husband. She handled thee pictures gingerly, some were in dreadful condition, and stacked them in a shoebox which she had already emptied of money order carbons. Raleigh added the letters and postcards, checking the postmarks—1920s and 30s, but didn't try to read them now. The paper was dry and brittle and her hands were none too clean at the moment. Here was a photograph of Richard Mobley holding his son at three or four. The difference in George's arms was already apparent.

Though there was no sign of Aunt Sue in any of the photographs Raleigh hoped there was a mention of her in the letters or postcards. A clue that would tell her what had happened so long ago. Raleigh finished with the box and dropped it over the porch railing and into the trash, then saw how full the dumpster was and called the trash company and arranged for it to be emptied by the end of the day. She paused and sat on the steps for a moment. Down the block several kids were playing in a plastic pool with a sodden mutt and she felt like joining them. When she was little and the weather got this hot her mother and father would let her run around the yard in her underwear and hose her off. If she tried that today she'd get arrested or, with her short hair and less-than-ample bosoms, perhaps no one would even notice.

Raleigh contented herself with moving the sprinkler and letting it get her bare feet wet in the process. She squished her toes in the mud for a moment, then heard a car coming up the street. It was Jon's PT Cruiser. If there was anyone Raleigh didn't want to see it was him. But she waited while he parked and got out of the car.

"Making mud pies?"

"No, just watering the yard."

"Find any more treasure?"

"Some photographs and letters from when Richard Mobley could have been married to my aunt. That's treasure to me."

"Are you okay? You look kind of funny."

Raleigh wanted to tell him she knew he was a thief and a liar, but she stifled that urge. "Emmett had a heart attack. I'm waiting for Flossie and Hash to get back, see if he made it."

"Oh . . . sorry. He was the blowhard, right?"

"Is. Don't talk like he's dead already."

"Sorry. Well, can I help you with anything here? More treasure hunting?"

"I have a feeling the treasure is long gone," she said meaningfully.

"Yeah, he probably spent everything. Gambling or something."

"Or something. Look, it's been an upsetting day and I'm not in the mood for company." A car could be heard coming up the street. "And the Peterses are back. I have to go now."

"Sure, okay. Give me a call if you need anything. Sorry about the old geezer."

"Yeah, me too."

Flossie and Hash got out of their car as Jon roared away.

"Raleigh, honey, I'm glad you're still here. Emmett's going to be just fine. Well, as fine as Emmett can be these days. Dr. Kober's keeping him overnight just in case, gave him blood thinners or something. He thinks it was a little clot, not a heart attack."

"I am so relieved. I really feel responsible for what happened. He got so upset with me, over nothing. It would have been so awful . . ." Raleigh remembered the keys in her pocket and she handed them to Hash.

"We forgot to lock up his house. I went back over after you left with Mrs. Bean. Where is Mrs. Bean?"

"She wanted to stay with Emmett a while longer. Al showed up and he's going to bring her back when visiting hours are over. They're going to join us for supper. You can still come, can't you?"

"If you're making grilled cheese."

They went home and Raleigh loaded several of the smaller boxes from the spare room into the Honda and went back to the hotel for a shower and change of clothes. She had already disposed of nine boxes today and figured she would have the room emptied by the coming weekend. While she was in her hotel room she checked her e-mail. There was one from Pam with an attachment labeled "liver cancer," but she didn't have time to read it right now. The contractor informed her that the wallpaper in her bedroom had been attached with something like Crazy Glue and they would have to replaster. Since they were two days ahead of schedule the work should still be done on time—thank goodness. The sooner Raleigh got out of Ohio, the better.

* * *

"When can we pick him up?" Raleigh heard Hash ask as she walked around to the back of their house.

Hash was lighting a small charcoal grill and Al Vitello and Mrs. Bean were sitting in two lawn chairs.

"The doc decided that while he has Emmett in his clutches he's going to make him have a couple of tests he's been ducking." Al Vitello put down his Budweiser and jumped to his tiny feet at Raleigh's arrival and offered her his chair. "Ah, the heroine is here!"

"Hello, Mr. Vitello," Raleigh said, ignoring both the proffered chair and his calling her a heroine. "Mrs. Bean, how are you today?"

"Fine, dear, fine. Emmett was barking at all the nurses when I left, so I know he'll be coming home soon."

"They'll probably throw him out tonight if he doesn't shut up." Flossie walked into the yard with a plate of pork chops, which she gave to Hash.

"Here, Flossie. I didn't know what else to bring." Raleigh handed Flossie a grocery bag that contained two six-packs of assorted beers and one bag each of organic, unsalted, baked corn chips and potato chips.

"I'm not much of a beer maven, so I got one of every kind they had."

"Let's see." Hash flipped the chops onto the grill and he and Al Vitello checked out the beer. Raleigh had apparently chosen brands they had never tried, especially the Japanese and Mexican varieties. They popped the tops and swapped the bottles back and forth.

Flossie went back into the house to get bowls for the chips and Raleigh followed her. Flossie handed her the griddle, spatula and a plate with an as-yet-ungrilled Velveeta sandwich on it.

"Do you suppose Emmett would mind if I stopped in and saw him tomorrow?"

"He'll gripe and moan, but if you can put up with him . . . he'll like it."

"His bark is worse than his bite. I've seen how nice he is to Mrs. Bean . . ."

"Don't sell him short, girl. Emmett was a hell-raiser in his day and I wouldn't want him for an enemy even now."

They walked back out into the yard with Flossie carrying the bowls of chips and a plate of sliced tomatoes. A card table had been set up with macaroni salad, cutlery and old Melmac plates. Mrs. Bean was sucking on a Dos Equus.

"Raleigh, just put the griddle on the grill and let it heat up then I'll start your sandwich."

"I'll watch it, Flossie. You relax."

"Buddy would have liked this. We mostly had Pabst because of the plant being here, but he would have liked this." Mrs. Bean took another long swig.

"Don't you be getting tipsy, Doretha Bean. We don't want you embarrassing the young lady here." Flossie smiled as she scolded Mrs. Bean.

Raleigh got herself a Rolling Rock and kept an eye on the griddle. It was probably hot enough so she flipped the sandwich on it and tried to stay out of Hash's way as he shifted the pork chops around.

Flossie checked on the pork chops, annoying Hash with her fussing.

Hash switched on a propane-powered contraption at the back of the yard, explaining that it attracted and killed any mosquitoes within a quarter mile. Raleigh was glad when the pork chops were done, afraid that the oldsters were consuming far too much beer on empty stomachs.

She flipped her sandwich back onto the plate and took a seat on the glider, then moved quickly to a lawn chair when Al Vitello tried to sit beside her. She savored her grilled cheese, surprised to realize how much she had looked forward to it, then worked on a scoop of Flossie's macaroni salad.

Flossie took a lawn chair next to Raleigh and they compared the various advantages and disadvantages of nonstick cookware, agreeing that there was nothing like an old aluminum griddle for making grilled cheese sandwiches or pancakes. Mrs. Bean provided a blueberry pie made from one of the last batches of fruit she had frozen the previous summer.

The boys had agreed to skip the poker game until Emmett could join them again, so Bailey and Gus had gone on down to the Elks Hall for the mah-jongg tournament. The early evening passed pleasantly, but as the sun was starting to set Raleigh said her good-byes. Al Vitello wanted to see her home, but Hash rescued her by insisting that he needed Al's help with the grill. Flossie walked her down the driveway.

"I don't know if you noticed, Raleigh, but Hash used some real old newspaper to get the charcoal started tonight."

Chapter Twenty-Six

While Raleigh waited for her room service breakfast she called the hospital and checked the visiting hours, and that Emmett was still allowed visitors. Then she opened one of the boxes she had carried up the previous night and went through it. This one held quite a few magazines from the fifties, which she riffled through, but they were mainly electronics journals and a few about deer hunting. If Raleigh hadn't hoped to find more family photographs or letters she would have been very tempted to give up right then and there.

She worked her way through the rest of the boxes, all dating from the fifties, without finding anything of interest. She switched on *Leave It to Beaver* and checked her e-mail, noticing the message from Pam again. She opened the attachment and skimmed the first paragraph of a very technical analysis of the causes of angiosarcoma. Oh dear. Footnotes and statistical analyses. Her brain wasn't ready for that this early.

Raleigh's breakfast arrived just as *Mister Ed* was starting and she switched off her laptop and concentrated on the horse's quest to overcome his agoraphobia.

* * *

The hospital was within walking distance and Raleigh started out from the hotel, hoping to arrive there just as visiting hours started. She stopped at a florist on the way and bought a potted cactus instead of cut flowers. She preferred to buy something living, arrangements withered so quickly that Raleigh found them rather depressing. For anyone else she would have purchased an azalea, or even an African violet, but Emmett reminded her more of a cactus than anything. She hoped he wouldn't throw it at her.

Raleigh reached the hospital and stepped through the doors and into the usual smell of antiseptic and sickness. Visiting hours had started fifteen minutes ago and one of his allotted two visitors was already upstairs. The Ladies Auxiliary volunteer clipped a plastic tag to Raleigh's shirt and gave her directions. As soon as the elevator doors opened on the third floor Raleigh could hear Emmett complaining.

She walked quietly down the hall and looked into the semi-private room where Emmett occupied the bed nearest the window. Mrs. Bean was straightening the sheets and it was at her whom Emmett was yelling. The noise didn't seem to faze Mrs. Bean—she kept straightening and fluffing until she was satisfied.

"You can't be comfortable in a messy bed, Emmett. There, that's better."

"Better than what, woman? The Spanish Inquisition?"

Raleigh knocked on the doorframe and entered.

"What is it now? More needles? Oh, it's you, kiddo. What're you doin' here?"

Emmett looked even older lying in the hospital bed, faded gown, paper robe hanging on a hook. He had oxygen tubes taped under his nose, and an IV in one arm, but his eyes were alert and, judging by the volume of his voice, he was feeling much better.

"I came to see you, Emmett. I thought this might cheer you up." Raleigh brought the cactus from behind her back with a flourish and set it on the bedside table.

Emmett broke into a cackle upon seeing the spined succulent. "Now I can give them nurses some of their own back. They'll be sorry they stuck me."

"I didn't intend for it to be used as a weapon."

Mrs. Bean busied herself rearranging the things on the bedside table. "It's very nice, dear. And so like Emmett. The doctor says he can come home tomorrow afternoon, once he's had his angiogram."

"Don't talk about me like I'm not here, Dot. That blasted Fred Kober thinks I got nothing better to do than hang around this hospital. Why I have a mind to . . ."

"You have a mind to do just what Dr. Kober ordered, Mr. Potter." A formidable nurse entered the room pushing a wheelchair. "It's time for your X-rays now."

"I'll be going then, Emmett. Good luck with the tests."

"Luck schmuck!"

"Mrs. Bean, I saw a cafeteria downstairs. Why don't I wait down there with you? Unless you're ready to leave, too. I can take you back home."

"I'm here for the day, dear. Emmett needs my support. But I wouldn't mind a cup of tea while he's having his X-rays done."

"Get on outta here, both of you. I'm not gettin' outta this bed and showin' you my backside. Unless you want to see it." Emmett leered at the two women.

"That's definitely our cue, Mrs. Bean."

* * *

Raleigh and Mrs. Bean were settled into one of the cafeteria booths, each with tea bags—plain Tetley—pots of hot water and a chocolate croissant and cheese Danish respectively. The pastry looked a lot more promising than the tea.

"When I was down in Emmett's basement I noticed he had a lot of woodworking equipment. Does he like to build things?"

"Not anymore, it's too hard on him, going up and down those stairs. But when he was younger . . . he made all of the furniture in his house himself—just the wood furniture, not the davenport and the like. He made Faith the sweetest dollhouse . . . I kept it for her while she was in . . . that place. Once she moved to the group home Flossie and I took it over to her."

"It didn't look like it had been used in quite a while. My father liked to build things, but he wasn't very good at it. Whatever he made was always crooked."

"That's his laboratory down there, too. That's where he fixed up my saccharine."

Raleigh didn't want to listen to yet another fanciful account of how Mrs. Bean had killed George Mobley. "Dr. Kober seems very nice. Does Emmett like him?"

"Dr. Kober still takes Medicare. Some of the new ones don't—say the government doesn't pay enough to break even. Most of us see him, even if we don't have cancer. He's a fine boy, just like his pa."

"Couldn't get up to see Emmett, they told me he had two visitors already." Bailey Wahl stood next to their booth.

"He's having his X-rays right now, but I'm going back up and wait for him. Thank you for the tea, Raleigh."

Raleigh took off her visitor badge and handed it to Bailey as he slid into the booth in Mrs. Bean's place. "Here, you can have mine. I saw Mr. Potter earlier."

"How's old Emmett doing?"

"Well enough to go home tomorrow, I'm told." Raleigh added the last of the hot water to her cup. "He and Mrs. Bean seem very fond of each other. It's a wonder they've never married."

Bailey snorted, though not unkindly. "Doretha Bean would try the patience of Job. I think that bun of hers is screwed down too tight, the ideas she gets some times. She's best taken in small doses and preferably with a piece of her homemade pie."

"I've had her cherry and blueberry pie and they were both terrific."

"How you doing over to George's place? Getting ready to move in soon?"

"Getting ready to sell it soon. I should clear out the last of the trash by the end of the week, finish cleaning, then I can get back to Washington." The fatigue Raleigh felt was evident in her voice.

"Find George's hidden treasure yet?"

"The only treasure I've found is some old photographs and letters that I hope will mention my aunt. Some of the pictures are of George as a boy with, I presume, his father."

"That's too bad, all that work you've been doing over there."

"No gold bars or bags of jewels, unfortunately. Just a lot of old receipts and money order carbons . . . he must not have had a checking account."

"Old George was a cash kind of fella, that's for sure."

"Well, I'd better be getting over to the house, get back to shoveling it out."

"I'll see how Emmett's doing. If he's barking about something he'll be okay."

They left the cafeteria and walked out into the lobby. Raleigh headed for the door, then turned back to wave good-bye to Bailey. She saw Gus Trout get up from one of the benches and speak to Bailey, then the two men put their arms around each other.

Oh. Oh . . . maybe that was it.

Bailey's wife didn't have anything to do with the blackmail—it was Bailey and Gus all along.

Raleigh walked quickly out of the hospital and into the parking lot, hoping the two men hadn't seen her, and located the Honda. Her cell phone started to ring and she tried to find it in her tote. It had fallen to the bottom and she finally dumped everything on the passenger seat in order to locate it. Too late, the caller had hung up.

She began replacing her things, leaving the cell phone out, and came across the last tape she had found at the house. Raleigh glanced at the label, "12/02 B." This tape was obviously very recent and the initial could stand for Buddy, Bailey, or Bean, she supposed. Not willing to risk playing the tape in the car tape player, she stuck it in her pocket and drove away.

* * *

A short time later Raleigh was the proud owner of a Walkman knock-off from the local drug store. Leaving the knock-off behind, she parked in front of the house, checked the dumpster—empty, and let herself into the house. It was hot and stuffy inside and she quickly opened several windows, but closed and locked the front door again. She carried the box fan into the bedroom, then dragged the nightstands and dresser into the hall. She stripped the bed of the dusty and obviously dirty sheets, stuffed them into a trash bag and checked the mattress, then the box spring for signs of being slit open and resewn. Nothing. She hauled the bed into the hall and checked out the flimsy bed frame. Nothing. That came apart easily and joined the rest of the furniture in the hall, then she went to work on the carpet.

The carpet came up fairly quickly and Raleigh managed to roll it up and drag that out of the room, too. No more tapes, no envelopes, no nothing. Raleigh was disappointed, but pleased with herself for accomplishing so much before noon. The closet—was there carpet in there, too? She checked and got to work on the scrap of carpet that had been amateurishly tacked in place. The work may have been unprofessional, but whoever fastened it down had used an excess of tacks and Raleigh had trouble getting an edge started. She finally tucked herself inside the cramped space and pulled with all her weight.

And crashed through the closet wall! Through the cheap paneling that concealed an opening about three feet high and as wide as the closet itself.

Raleigh picked herself up, swearing mightily, and checked for broken bones. She had scratches on her arms from the broken paneling and would undoubtedly have some colorful bruises tomorrow, but none of the damage appeared to need medical attention. She turned back to the closet and pulled the cord of the single light bulb suspended from the ceiling.

There was a void in the back of the closet about a foot deep and as Raleigh pulled out the broken paneling she could see there was a row of shoe boxes on the floor inside. *Those must be some valuable shoes.* Once she cleared the debris Raleigh pulled the shoe boxes out into the bedroom. All were tied several times in both directions with string and labeled on the end and top. "Wahl and Trout," "Bean," "Greaseball," that must be Al Vitello, "Peters" and "Potter."

Raleigh left the shoe boxes on the floor and walked into the kitchen, realizing she was about to hyperventilate. She slowed her breathing, got a bottled water from the fridge, then washed her hands. She rinsed her face and walked back into the bedroom.

The doorbell rang.

Raleigh took a deep breath and opened the door. A stranger was standing there, a youngish man in a navy blue suit, crisp white shirt and tie, in spite of the heat.

"Hi, Miss Killen?"

Raleigh nodded, but didn't open the screen door.

"I'm Carl Willerton." He seemed to think she should know him. "The real estate agent? My cousin Jon told me to come take a look at the house?"

The name did ring a bell now and Raleigh should have guessed the real estate agents Jon recommended were probably more of his seemingly endless supply of cousins.

"Mr. Willerton, the house isn't ready to be seen yet. Maybe by next week."

"It doesn't matter if it isn't perfect, I can see past that."

"Perfect doesn't enter into it, Mr. Willerton. I have your name and number from Jon and I'll call you, possibly by this weekend." And she shut the door.

*   *   *

Raleigh stood in the bedroom and looked at the five shoe boxes for a while, then went into the spare room and got two of the boxes of receipts and dumped their contents on the floor. She set the shoe boxes inside and placed some of the receipts on top, stalling, though she didn't know why. Raleigh finally got her things together, locked both the bedroom and the spare room and carried the two larger boxes out to the Honda.

Hash was working in his yard and he walked over to chat, but Raleigh said she wasn't feeling well because of the heat and had to go back to the hotel. She declined his offer of lemonade and drove away.

Raleigh couldn't explain it, but she wanted to get those boxes out of the house without anyone knowing she found them. They seemed far more sinister than the clippings and tapes, being so well-concealed behind the false back of the closet. Jon obviously hadn't found everything for which he had been looking.

In spite of the excited panic Raleigh was feeling, or because of it, she started to get very hungry. It was just past eleven-thirty and Raleigh detoured into the parking lot of a pizza restaurant. She placed her order at the counter and was able to locate a table from which she could keep an eye on the car. As she sipped her Diet Coke she decided the safest thing to do was return to the hotel and open the shoe boxes. If they contained anything of value, and her intuition said they did, she should be able to leave it in the hotel safe. She could always get a safe-deposit box if necessary, she supposed. Raleigh started to relax a bit and when her salad and pizza slice arrived she was able to sit back and enjoy her impromptu meal.

Chapter Twenty-Seven

Raleigh had just lugged the two boxes through the door when the room phone rang. She dropped the boxes, flipped the lock on the door and answered the phone.

"Yes . . ."

"Good afternoon, Raleigh Killen." It was Jon. "I stopped by the house and Mr. Peters told me you weren't feeling well."

"I'm fine . . . the heat got to me, that's all." Raleigh held her breath, wondering if he'd tried to let himself into the house.

"Well, I wanted to let you know you'll be on your own until Thursday. I have to take Newt-face some papers that I'm loath to consign to Federal Express, regardless of their reputation."

"Oh that's all right." The relief she felt was probably evident in her voice. "I don't really need any help right now anyway. I'm nearly done in fact."

"Did you hit the jackpot yet?"

Raleigh looked somewhat guiltily at the two boxes.

"No, no more family things. When the kids shovel the last of it into the dumpster I'll be heading back to Washington. My contractor's ahead of schedule." No matter the actual condition of her house in Pine Grove, Raleigh was going back as soon as she hired a realtor.

"Good, you can get out of Greenhaven early . . . you'll miss the real heat wave we always have at the end of the month."

"Lucky me." Raleigh realized belatedly how lucky she was. Jon would be gone for a whole day at least. If she didn't hear from Arnie, and soon, she'd call him and they'd schedule their breaking and entering for Wednesday.

"I'll stop by the house when I get back. Remember, it's my job to take care of things for you."

"Wait until Saturday, I'll be nearly done by then."

"Whatever you say, Raleigh. À bientôt."

As soon as Raleigh hung up, the phone rang again. Arnie, her paid partner in crime. He knew about Jon's coming trip and he and Raleigh arranged to meet in the liquor store parking lot the next day at nine. She thought they ought to go in under cover of darkness, but Arnie pointed out it would be easier to see in the daytime and, dressed in a business-like manner, they wouldn't draw any untoward attention even if they were observed.

Raleigh hung up and eyed the phone for a moment, but it didn't ring again and she turned her attention to the boxes. She pulled out the receipts that had concealed the shoe boxes and lined the boxes up on the coffee table, then hesitated. She was excited and scared and the pizza slice she had for lunch was churning around inside her stomach.

Pull yourself together, she scolded herself, and open one. She decided to start with the box labeled "Peters" since it was the least likely to hold a surprise. The clippings had already been returned and destroyed, so Raleigh expected to find tapes perhaps, or . . .

She clipped the string securing the lid and opened the box.

. . . money.

Lots of money.

Lots of money banded around with strips of paper into neat stacks of tens, twenties and fifties. She sat back on her heels for a moment, then released the breath she was holding. Raleigh finally took the money out and laid it on the table, pulled off the paper and started to count. An hour later she had counted twice to be sure, then a third time because the totals didn't match (math was never her strong suit)—$13,125.

She sat back and took a long drink of water, staring all the while at the cash. "Holy s'mores . . ."

"Housekeeping!" There was a knock and someone tried the door. Raleigh had hooked the chain and they couldn't get in. She went to the door and saw a maid standing in the hall with a cleaning cart.

"I'm sorry, I'm not feeling well. I forgot to put the sign on the knob." Raleigh slipped the "Do Not Disturb" sign through the opening and onto the doorknob. "Don't bother with my room today." She closed the door and watched through the peephole as the maid went across the hall to another room.

Raleigh restacked the money in the shoe box and looked at the other boxes in more than a little dismay. She salvaged enough of the original string to tie the first box closed again and she set it to one side.

The next box belonged to Gus and Bailey if the label was accurate. Raleigh cut the string and lifted off the lid. More packets of money. And an envelope. Raleigh opened the envelope and pulled out old newspaper clippings. Neither Gus nor Bailey were subjects of the articles, but all the clippings pertained to the erroneous belief that homosexual men are child molesters. One mentioned the arrest of a high school football coach who had been fired when the school board found out he was gay. The threat of exposure must have been why the two men had paid George Mobley to keep quiet. Poor Lou Wahl and her more-than-checkered past didn't have anything to do with the blackmail. When Raleigh pulled out the stacks she found there were some hundred-dollar bills and, at the bottom, an audiotape. Raleigh located the magnet she had purchased and ran it all over the cassette. She'd try to play it later and see if Perry Mason was right and you could erase a tape with a magnet.

Raleigh set to counting the money, only twice this time, and had a total of $23,545. She felt sick inside as she restacked the cash in the box. She tore the clippings to shreds and flushed them down the toilet, then unwrapped her tape player and batteries and tried to play the tape. Noise, nothing but noise. She skipped ahead, then reversed it for good measure. It worked, the tape was erased. Take that, George Mobley! She replaced the tape in the shoe box and tied it shut and set it aside with the first one.

Raleigh opened the "Bean" shoe box next. There was far less money in this one, but Buddy had been dead for some years and Raleigh had no indication that Doretha Bean had been blackmailed. Mrs. Bean had been more than forthcoming about her timed-release murder of George Mobley, Raleigh couldn't imagine she wouldn't have spilled the beans, as it were, about being blackmailed, too. Raleigh took out the money and found some folded sheets of paper in the bottom. They were carbon copies of complaint letters to the county about Faith Bean, nothing different from what Raleigh had already seen. How anyone could pick on poor Mrs. Bean and her daughter like that was beyond Raleigh's understanding.

The money totaled $4,010. Raleigh replaced it in the shoe box and tore up the carbon copies and mixed the scraps in with the other trash.

It was late in the day and Raleigh was tired from her frantic work that morning, aching from the fall in the closet and she was hatching a killer of a headache. She put the completed shoe boxes into one of the bigger boxes and left the other two on the coffee table while she ran a bath and had a long soak.

* * *

Feeling somewhat better, Raleigh called room service and cajoled them into fixing her breakfast instead of ordering off the dinner menu. Until her order arrived, she concealed the last two shoeboxes in her closet and set the larger boxes next to the wastebasket. Everything looked much as it had for the last two days and when Raleigh finished she realized she was being paranoid.

She checked the hotel services guide and confirmed that they did have a safe, then changed her mind about leaving the shoeboxes there. If Jon had even one cousin on the staff he would probably hear about her stash and it would somehow disappear. Raleigh would take the boxes back to the house tomorrow and leave them in the spare room with the other boxes where they wouldn't be conspicuous. With the changed locks and alarm that only she controlled it was probably as safe a place as any until she figured out what to do with the money.

Her dinner arrived and she tipped handsomely, in gratitude for having poached eggs and hash browns instead of the lasagna again. She watched the local news, then changed channels and caught an episode of *SpongeBob SquarePants*.

In spite of being out of sight, the remaining shoe boxes were not out of mind and after she set the room service tray in the hall Raleigh retrieved the boxes from the closet. For some reason she couldn't figure out, Raleigh left Emmett's box for last.

Al Vitello's box contained packets of bills like the others and she started counting. She didn't bother to double-check her figures and she came up with a total of $20,005. No envelopes, clippings or letters, just two audiotapes to which she gave the magnet treatment and replaced in the shoe box.

Raleigh held Emmett's box for a long time and finally put it back in the closet unopened and set it next to the box of old photographs and letters. She really, really did not want to find out what George Mobley had on Emmett Potter—at least, not yet. While she was at the closet she pulled out the only business-like outfit she brought with her, black knit pants and a cobalt blue silk blouse. If Arnie was wearing a suit they would pass muster as a couple of clients or lawyer-type colleagues.

Somewhat depressed, Raleigh went to bed early.

Chapter Twenty-Eight

After a restless night, Raleigh dressed in her casual clothes and took a walk through downtown Greenhaven. She stopped at a bakery and bought a couple of crullers and went back to the hotel. She made a breakfast of the crullers and a Diet Pepsi and then got ready for the daylight break-in she was about to commit with Arnie Willerton. In case they got arrested she wanted to look good for her mug shot, so she took the time to apply mascara, her oil-absorbing powder and lipstick. Make a good-looking felon, she always said.

Raleigh carried the box containing the shoeboxes downstairs and put it in the Honda, hoping it didn't look as valuable as it was. She couldn't leave it in her hotel room and she didn't have time to drive over to the house and leave it there. If anyone had noticed her driving back and forth there was nothing unusual about a grubby cardboard box in the back of the Honda.

She reached the liquor store twenty minutes early and went inside and bought a newspaper and another Diet Pepsi. Raleigh knew more caffeine wasn't a good idea, she was already jumpy, but she got it anyway and sat in the car waiting for Arnie to arrive.

Her Sherlock Holmes for hire was on time and they locked their respective cars and walked down the street, Raleigh obviously nervous.

"I monitored the office and the apartment all night; it's empty. We'll be in and out with no one being the wiser." Arnie sounded matter-of-fact.

"There's a girlfriend, I think . . . you're sure she's not there either?"

"She went to Dallas, too. We can spend the whole day there if necessary."

Arnie was perfectly calm as they made their way toward the office. He hadn't worn a suit, but the dress slacks, linen blazer and briefcase fit right in with their disguise. Raleigh's backpack was a bit off-key, but she hadn't dared leave that in the car.

They reached the office and walked up the steps and onto the front porch. Where Arnie took a key from his pocket and unlocked the door.

"A key?! You have a key?!"

"They keep a spare under a pot of geraniums on the back steps. People never learn."

Arnie opened the door and Raleigh stepped inside listening for the screech of an alarm.

"I rewired it outside. As far as the alarm company is concerned the place is still locked up. I'll fix it when we leave."

Raleigh walked into Jon's area and looked around, wondering where to start.

"Remember, you can't take anything with you. If you want to copy something, that's okay, but I'm not abetting a burglary."

"I promise, Arnie. I won't take anything, I just want to look."

Arnie took a seat in an armchair and removed a hand-held video game from his briefcase. Raleigh pulled a pair of rubber gloves from her tote and started her search by switching on the computer. While she waited for it to boot up she checked the desk drawers, then the unlocked cabinets, which held office supplies and, at the back of one, a tape recorder. Since she had never seen George Mobley's tape recorder she couldn't know if this was his, but it looked rather low-tech to her and out of character for Jon. She pushed the eject button and found that it was empty.

The computer was ready and Raleigh started checking the various folders and file names. She found one for the Mobley Estate and she opened it. A scanned copy of the signed and notarized trust and will were in one file. Another held the genealogical information that led from George Mobley to her. Copies of her e-mail correspondence with Andrew Newton were in another file. It all seemed very straightforward and aboveboard. Frustrated, she switched the computer off and checked the file cabinets. All were locked.

"Arnie, can you open these?"

He got up without taking his eyes off his game and walked over to the file cabinet. "Keep it going for me." He handed her the game and took a lock pick from his pocket.

Raleigh had no idea what the game was about, but she pushed buttons quickly and randomly and hoped for the best. Arnie made quick work of the locks, popping them one after the other, then took back his game and resumed his seat.

Raleigh checked the file drawers until she found a folder for Killen and one for Mobley. Both folders contained hard copies of the computer information, though there was a household inventory in the Mobley file that she hadn't seen. She scanned the list and found the tape recorder entered with the notation, "at office." This was really embarrassing. Jon hadn't stolen the tape recorder after all. The trust checkbook was also there with several bank statements. There was a deposit slip for twenty dollars with the notation "tape recorder." And he had even paid for it—she figuratively smacked herself in the forehead.

With an eye out for audiotapes, Raleigh felt underneath the furniture, looked behind it, went back and checked the undersides of all the drawers. Nothing. Finished with this room, Raleigh punched the file cabinet locks down and went into the dining room. There were rows of law books on the shelves, china in one hutch, silverware in the hutch drawer, table linens in another. She checked beneath the table and chairs, but found nothing.

Arnie was still playing his game and Raleigh went into the kitchen. The cupboards held a fantastic array of professional cooking equipment and utensils and the pantry was as well stocked as she expected. She was starting to get hungry and looked for something to eat that wouldn't be missed. The cookie jar. Even Jon wouldn't miss a cookie or two. She reached in and pulled out two cookies, oatmeal with dates and orange zest, and got herself a glass of water. Raleigh sat at the table for a moment, trying to deduce what Jon would consider a good hiding place for audiotapes. They were there somewhere, she was sure.

Raleigh checked the toaster, the appliance garage, the big stockpot, the freezer and the refrigerator. She even checked the cookie jar and took another cookie while she was about it. She looked in and behind the washer and dryer in the adjacent laundry room, finding nothing except a partial load of dirty clothes.

She went down into the basement where she found shelves of banker's boxes labeled and covered with dust. She scanned the names for Mobley or Killen, but these files looked to be ten years old and older if the hand-lettered dates were accurate. That left the upstairs storage to which Jon had referred and—his apartment.

"Arnie, can you let me into the upstairs?"

Arnie managed to negotiate the stairs while still playing his game, which he again surrendered temporarily to Raleigh while he picked the locks on the three upstairs doors. He retrieved his game and sat on the steps and continued to play.

One room was a powder room. No place to hide anything there, but Raleigh checked inside the toilet tank and behind it just to be sure. The storeroom was row after row of shelves filled with more banker's boxes, more current files than those in the basement. Nothing for Mobley or Killen, though.

Raleigh hesitated for a moment before going into Jon's apartment, but there might be evidence in there and she was going to look, squeamish or not. A parlor, bedroom and quite a luxurious bathroom. The furniture was very fifties modern/Danish and the console TV fit in perfectly with the other blond wood. It wasn't to her taste, but it was quite streamlined and unfussy with few places to conceal things.

In the bedroom, she didn't think Arnie would help her slit open the mattress, so she made do with feeling around between the mattress and springs. The dresser was painfully neat, socks and underwear folded uniformly and arranged by color. She looked carefully through the drawers and replaced everything as precisely as she could. Nothing in the pockets of the clothes that hung in the closet, no hidden panel in the back that she could tell. The shelves held out-of-season woolens in opaque plastic storage bags.

The only place left to search was the bathroom. Fluffy towels concealed nothing in their folds, extra toiletries and toilet paper were in the vanity. Tissues were in the vanity drawers with a blow-dryer, Q-tips and other personal care paraphernalia. There were two heads for the Sonicare and a lipstick and two types of deodorant in the medicine cabinet. His girlfriend obviously lived elsewhere. Raleigh's stomach growled again and she decided she had done as much as she could. She wondered briefly if she had been wrong about Jon. Perhaps if Emmett hadn't planted the seed of doubt—and if she had asked Jon point-blank about the tape recorder—she wouldn't have wasted the morning.

"All set?" Arnie asked as Raleigh walked back to the top of the stairs.

"I guess so. I couldn't find anything."

Arnie pocketed his game and locked the three doors, then they walked downstairs.

"If I'm not being too nosy, what is it you're looking for?"

Raleigh debated for a moment before answering. "Tape recordings. Audiocassettes."

"Like that?" Arnie pointed to a banker's box stuck behind a huge ficus in the vestibule. The word 'tapes' was printed in black marker on one end.

Oh no, it can't be that easy. Or can it? Arnie pulled the box from behind the plant and Raleigh looked inside. The box was full of tape cassettes. Raleigh started pulling them out, checking the handwriting—it was George Mobley's. Tapes with dates and times, the names or initials of the neighbors and others. But what could she do with Arnie breathing over her shoulder?

"It's going to take a while to look through these . . . ," she hinted.

"Take your time, we have all day." Arnie went back to the office chair he had occupied earlier and continued playing his game.

Raleigh spread out the cassettes and passed the magnet slowly back and forth over them, then returned them to the box, leaving the magnet in the middle. Arnie's game was beeping in the other room and Raleigh felt quite proud of herself for pulling this off right under his nose. She replaced the box where Arnie found it and joined him.

"I've seen all I needed to see." Raleigh stuffed the rubber gloves into her tote.

Arnie replaced his game in his briefcase. "I hope you won't be insulted, Miss Killen, but I'll have to pat you down before we leave. Just to make sure something didn't make it into a pocket by accident."

Glad that she had thought to stash the magnet in the box, Raleigh held her arms away from her sides and stood still while Arnie frisked her. "Do you want to check my bag, too?"

"No, it's been in my sight the whole time. But thank you for cooperating."

Arnie ushered Raleigh through the vestibule and out the front door, which he locked behind them. She followed him down the driveway to the back porch and waited while he replaced the key under a pot on the steps, then tinkered with the wiring in the alarm system box. The garage! They hadn't looked in the garage!

"Arnie." Raleigh nodded her head toward the old, one-car garage.

Arnie picked that lock easily and they stepped inside. It was immaculate and filled only with gardening tools and cans of paint. While Arnie relocked the garage door Raleigh looked inside a wheeled recycling can. It was full of shredded paper in grocery bags.

"If you're going to pick through the trash we'd better get out of sight."

Raleigh dropped the lid. "No, that's okay."

They walked silently down the driveway and onto the street, heading back toward the liquor store.

"Well, if you need me for anything else, you have my number. I'll e-mail you the bill, okay?"

"Sure, that's fine."

Raleigh was relieved to see the Honda was still there with the box intact in the back seat. Arnie waved her on her way and Raleigh drove off.

* * *

Raleigh stopped for lunch at a nearby diner that offered both Gardenburgers and a black bean patty. She ordered the black bean patty with avocado and took a seat in one of the turquoise-upholstered booths and thought over what she had learned from her daylight felony.

One, Jon hadn't stolen the tape recorder. He could have told her he bought it from the estate, but that issue was fairly trivial.

Two, he had lied by not telling her about the safe-deposit box and emptying it out with George Mobley before he died. Raleigh assumed that the box Arnie found at the office contained tapes from that self-same safe-deposit box. Why hadn't Jon turned them over to her? Well, if he planned to take up where George left off and blackmail the neighbors he wouldn't be able to now. She could take some satisfaction in that.

Three, he must have known there was money hidden somewhere in the house or he wouldn't have gone through every single box in the place and, according to Naomi, searched even the yard. It also explained why he had been so helpful, hiring Naomi and Randy to work for her and spy for him at the same time. Well, he wasn't going to get that money now. And the kids wouldn't have any information to share with him. After this weekend she would be done with the house and Greenhaven, Ohio.

Four, she needed to hire an agent and get the house listed, but not anyone Jon recommended.

And finally, she had to figure out what to do with the money. Raleigh wouldn't keep it, that was out of the question, but how could she best give it back to everyone? Or should she give it to charity or something?

Raleigh set her many questions aside and dug into her black bean burger and fries, which were the best she had ever had.

Chapter Twenty-Nine

Raleigh was carrying the box up the steps to the house when Mrs. Bean called to her from next door.

"Raleigh! Raleigh! Have you heard the news?!"

Fearing Emmett had taken a turn for the worse, Raleigh walked over to Mrs. Bean's with the box still in her arms.

"I must not have heard, Mrs. Bean. What is it?"

"Emmett's coming home any minute! Bailey and Gus went to pick him up from the hospital. We're going to have a little party over at Emmett's as soon as they get back. Will you come, too? Flossie and Hash are fixing things up for him and I'll be going over as soon as my pie's done."

"That's wonderful, Mrs. Bean. I'm so glad he's coming home." Raleigh had been expecting the worst when Mrs. Bean called to her and was delighted that the news was good.

"It's apple pie, Raleigh. He asked me to make pumpkin, but I told him he'd have to wait until Thanksgiving."

"Why not make him one now?"

"So he'll have something to hang on for . . . just a little longer." Mrs. Bean started to sniffle, but pulled herself together quickly. "Emmett's been taking care of me since Buddy . . . passed. Pays the bills, has one of the boys come over when I need something fixed, takes me down to visit Faith if Flossie can't go. Don't know what I'd do . . ." Mrs. Bean gave another loud sniff, then blew her nose.

"If there's anything that would make me want to live it would be your pie, Mrs. Bean. And I'll be happy to join you and the others as soon as I take care of a few things at the house."

Mrs. Bean nodded and went back into her house. Raleigh shifted the box and cut across the grass and went inside.

Raleigh locked the door behind her and carried the box into the spare room. She set it in the closet and closed the door, then carried several more boxes out to her car. In case she was being watched she wanted to continue with what had become her normal routine. Back in the house, she sorted through two boxes, spreading things out on the floor, but didn't find any more blackmail material. She dumped the boxes and their contents into the dumpster and paused when she heard her name being called. She looked into the back yard and saw Hash peeking over the fence.

"Raleigh, Emmett's back. Dot's saving you a piece of pie."

"I'll be right there, Hash."

She washed up, checked the bedroom, now containing only the rickety bed frame, mattress and springs. She would have to drag them into the hall later and keep the door locked so the kids wouldn't notice the mess in the closet. Her back groaned in protest at that idea. She locked up the bedroom and spare room and went out the kitchen door.

Raleigh checked the fence and found the spot where Emmett had shifted some loose boards and come into her yard before. The boards were still loose and she was able to get through the opening and onto Emmett's property. She walked over to the kitchen door and knocked. Gus let her in.

"I took a shortcut," she explained at his surprised look.

"Everyone's in the front room. I was getting the napkins." Gus led the way to the front room, a pack of paper napkins in his hand.

"Well, look who snuck in the back way. You practicin' to be a cat burglar, kiddo?"

Raleigh started guiltily, remembering the morning's sort of felony, or maybe it was a misdemeanor. "Uh, no. Too lazy to walk around the block."

She took a seat in one of the kitchen chairs that had been brought in, next to Bailey. Emmett was stretched out on the sofa obviously feeling well enough to enjoy all the attention he was getting. His oxygen canister was on the floor next to him, but his color was good and from the way he was digging into Mrs. Bean's apple pie his appetite hadn't diminished.

Flossie and Mrs. Bean were serving the pie, coffee and tea while Gus handed out paper napkins. Raleigh was pleased to see the cactus she had given Emmett was in the center of the coffee table.

The welcome home party went on pleasantly, but it was soon evident that Emmett was getting tired and Bailey and Gus took their leave first. Flossie was cleaning things up in the kitchen and Hash convinced Mrs. Bean to let him drive her home. She had spent most of her time at the hospital and was obviously exhausted. Raleigh picked up the last cup and saucer and took them in to Flossie.

"What can I do to help, Flossie?"

Flossie lowered her voice so Emmett wouldn't overhear. "Keep an eye on Emmett if you would. He's awful wore out."

Raleigh nodded and went back into the front room and moved the furniture back into place, surreptitiously watching Emmett. His eyes were closed, but he was breathing regularly, so she tried not to worry. She was about to take the last chair back to the kitchen.

"Don't go, kiddo. Have a sit and tell me what you've been up to. 'Sides buying a cactus for an old coot."

"Not much really. I'm still going through old boxes full of receipts. It's all useless—straight to the dumpster it goes."

"Receipts, huh."

"And money order carbons. Some of them dating back fifty years. It's kind of crazy when you think about it."

"Well, old George was kind of crazy. Nothing interestin' in any of those boxes?"

"Oh yes, I did find something interesting. Photographs and letters back from the twenties. George Mobley as a little boy with, I think, his father. I hope there'll be some mention of my aunt Sue in the letters. I haven't had time to read them yet, though."

"Yessiree, that's mighty interestin', kiddo."

"I'm almost done with it. I'll probably be leaving next week, go back to Washington, get moved into my house."

"You don't say? Next week already? Well, I know how you feel, kiddo. We all like being home."

"Emmett, I'd like to ask you something." Raleigh paused, not sure how to proceed. "You've no reason to satisfy my curiosity, but . . . what did you give to Mrs. Bean? The saccharine? What was that really?"

Emmett gave a little chuckle and actually smiled. "Well, kiddo, Dot was right crazy after Buddy died, then having Faith taken away—it was too much for her. All she talked about was killin' George and I was afraid she'd go and do it. Buy a gun or somethin', shoot him. Then where would she be? So I got me this idea. Let her think she was killin' him . . . keep her from really doin' it. He'd got the sugar diabetes, that saccharine thing came out in the news—I told her she could give him cancer and no one would be any the wiser."

"I have to admit, that is an ingenious plan. Especially if it kept her from really killing him."

"You can't imagine, kiddo. First Buddy, then Faith." Emmett shook his head ruefully. "It was all too much for her. Dot's kinda, I don't know, kinda fragile."

Raleigh thought that Mrs. Bean being willing to commit murder put the lie to her fragility.

"You were Buddy Bean's best friend, Emmett. Do you know why he committed suicide?"

At that question Emmett bristled and his expression was stony.

"That's something that's between me and Buddy. It's nobody else's business. I will tell you this. Dot was right about it all being

George's fault. He drove poor Buddy to it, then sat there in his house while that car was runnin' in the garage right next door. He heard it all right, he told me so later, George did. He coulda called for help, stopped the whole thing, but he didn't. If I hadn't been down to Columbus that day."

Flossie came into the front room, wiping her hands on a towel. "Kitchen's all redd-up, Emmett. You set there for a while?"

"Don't fuss, woman. I'm fine. Get on outta here, both of you. Let a man get some rest." Emmett closed his eyes and Flossie and Raleigh tiptoed to the front door and out.

The two women walked down the street.

"The visiting nurse will be by later to get him set in bed and Al's bringing him supper. Al's gonna sleep on the davenport tonight."

"Will he be homebound from now on?"

"The doc wants to keep an eye on him for a few days, make sure the new pills are working right. Emmett being Emmett, he'll likely be driving around by tomorrow. Lord help us all."

They turned the corner and started up Spruce Circle.

"I'll be leaving soon, probably next week, Flossie."

"So soon? You just got here, girl."

"By this weekend all the trash will be out of the house and I can list it with a realtor. I don't have to be here for the sale, we can FedEx or e-mail the paperwork back and forth."

"I reckon you're anxious to be getting back home, now that I think of it. Get yourself settled in there."

"Yes, I am. I'm glad I got to meet you all, you've been very kind to me, but the more I've found out about George Mobley the more I want to get away from his, oh I don't know, bad karma."

"Kind of like fire blight, George was. Until *it's* dead it tries to kill everything else."

"Interesting analogy, Flossie Peters. You're quite poetic."

"Go on with you, Raleigh."

They reached the end of the cul-de-sac and paused.

"I'll be right sorry when you leave, that I will." Flossie patted Raleigh on the shoulder and went home.

As Raleigh unlocked the front door and disarmed the security system she realized Emmett had never answered her question. What had he given Mrs. Bean instead of saccharine?

Chapter Thirty

Raleigh spent the balance of the afternoon removing the paneling that remained over the hiding place in the bedroom closet. Underneath the debris she found another tape, which she tucked into a pocket. There were a few nail holes in the plaster, but with the broken paneling gone the closet looked fairly ordinary, if unfinished. She managed to wrestle the rest of the bedroom furniture into the hall and locked the door.

She quickly sorted through several more boxes in the spare room and dumped the contents over the paneling pieces she had earlier thrown in the dumpster. While Raleigh took a break and had a bottled water she called Naomi and Randy and left a message about the coming weekend. If they could spend most of Saturday at the house Raleigh would, indeed, have no more work for them. Before long Randy returned her call and they decided to start at eight and the kids would stay until the job was done.

Raleigh finally decided to call it a day and she loaded one more box into the Honda to take back to the hotel. After she locked up the house she stopped at the hardware store again and bought another magnet since the first one was tucked safely into the box of tapes in Jon's vestibule.

* * *

Back at the hotel Raleigh pulled out the phone book and made appointments with three agents to look at the house on Monday.

None of them were Jon's recommendations, who were most likely more of his seemingly infinite supply of cousins. Based on Raleigh's unfortunate experience in Pine Grove, she had called what appeared to be the three largest agencies in Greenhaven and would confirm the company she chose would have backup staff in case her listing agent decided to abandon her in mid sale. No more mom and pop, or mom and daughter, agencies for her.

Raleigh checked her e-mail and informed the contractor that she would be returning early, but would book a hotel room and not expect to move into the house immediately. She didn't want Marty to rush and perhaps do a less-than-satisfactory job. Then she noticed the attachment that Pam had sent earlier and settled down to read it, if she could understand the technical jargon. From what Raleigh could tell as she read, it was a report on the causes of angiosarcoma. She skipped through the rather weighty article, looked at the highlights, and came to the gist of the whole thing. Angiosarcoma, wherever it appeared in an individual, had only one cause—workplace exposure to plastic. Just as Dr. Kober had explained.

Raleigh called Pam to thank her and let her know about her early return to Washington.

"What? You can't take the heat or the humidity?"

"Well, no, not at the same time. But what I really want is to get as far away from George Mobley as possible. He's like when you get a whiff of mildew—even after you get rid of the stuff, the smell sticks in your nose for days."

"Your cousin may be pretty moldy by now, though with embalming, he should look as good as he ever did."

"Which wasn't very good, judging by the photographs I've seen."

They chatted for a while and Raleigh almost told her friend about the shoeboxes of money. But she decided it was her problem and she'd have to figure it out by herself. Pam wished her luck selling George's house and told her to make sure the guest room in Pine

Grove was ready. Pam had a conference coming up in Seattle and she had already scheduled a few extra days off work to come visit Raleigh afterward.

Raleigh was at loose ends after talking to Pam and she finally decided to take a walk through the downtown. It was going on five o'clock and maybe the air wouldn't be quite so hot and humid. Raleigh was wrong in that hope and she returned quickly to the air-conditioned haven of her hotel room after only one lap around the block. The message light on the phone was blinking and Raleigh found that Jon called while she was out. He didn't leave a call-back number in Texas, but he told her he would drop by the house tomorrow morning and give her a hand if she needed his help.

While Raleigh didn't feel quite as distrustful of Jon now, he still had the box of tapes to explain. And since she had broken into his office, she couldn't ask him straight out about them as she would have preferred. Of course, if the bank clerk was correct, George Mobley and Jon had removed the tapes together. Since her cousin was obviously alive at the time, it was arguable that the tapes didn't belong to the estate at all. Old George could have given them to Jon—and Jon might not know what was on them. Maybe if she mentioned the tapes she had found at the house he would tell her about the boxful at the office. In any event, it seemed that she would see him tomorrow. Maybe if she figured out what Mister Ed would do in a similar situation . . . or June Cleaver when she knows Beaver is hiding something from her. Yes, June Cleaver was a better model than Mister Ed in this case.

Chapter Thirty-One

Thursday dawned hotter and sunnier than the previous day and Raleigh donned a sleeveless shirt, arm flab be damned, and shorts. To hell with the cellulite, too.

Raleigh arrived at the house before eight, hoping she could finish and leave before the heat inside became unbearable. She started the sprinkler going in the front yard and shuddered to think what the water bill would be, but as seedy as the house looked inside it would look even worse in an island of dead grass.

The house was stifling, but Raleigh opened the windows, positioned the fan to blow out of the spare room window, and got back to work on the boxes. She had to clear it out and pull up the carpet before the kids came Saturday morning. Since this room and the bedroom both had double deadbolts on the doors she still expected to find more of value, be it blackmail material or additional cash.

As the morning wore on Raleigh sorted through the contents of one box after the other as quickly as possible, carting them outside and dropping them into the dumpster. A few more photographs had turned up and Raleigh slipped them into an old envelope to take with her. A postcard here and there she would read later and several tiny, rectangular boxes that held folded rolls of negatives. She dropped these into her tote with the other things to examine later. She suddenly noticed there were two tapes inside her tote that she had forgotten about, including the one she had found in the closet cubbyhole.

Raleigh took a break about ten and got a Diet Pepsi from the kitchen. She remembered the sprinkler and ran outside to move it, pausing for a moment to let the cold water splash her dusty legs and bare feet. Mrs. Bean, wearing a sweat suit and looking cool and unruffled, walked over to the house bearing a plate of chocolate chip cookies.

"Good morning, Mrs. Bean." Raleigh waved as the older woman approached, her hair tight in the habitual bun.

"You look like my Faith, Raleigh. She always liked to splash outside in the sprinkler when it got hot like this. Sometimes Buddy would join her and they'd both come back in all soaking wet."

"I have to admit the cold water feels really good right now."

"Oh, here, I almost forgot why I came over. I couldn't remember if I made you chocolate chip yet. I put in black walnuts, too."

"This is very kind of you, Mrs. Bean, but how can you bear to have the oven on in this heat?"

"I've never been one to get hot, unless I was sick. Always been skinny and cold. Winters are mighty hard on me, but summer is another story."

"The house is stifling, but would you like to come up and sit on the porch for a while? I'd love an excuse to take a break."

"Thank you, dear, I was hoping you'd ask."

Mrs. Bean made herself comfortable on the porch swing and Raleigh went inside to retrieve her Diet Pepsi and bring one for Mrs. Bean. Raleigh took the chair and they shared the cookies between them.

"What's this? You didn't invite me to the party!" Jon walked up the sidewalk and onto the porch.

"We're taking a break. Have a cookie?" Raleigh offered the plate and Jon took a seat on the steps. Where was his car, Raleigh wondered. "Where's your car?"

"At the shop. Something was wrong with the battery or the starter . . . I don't know. Brad dropped me off at the corner. I thought you might take me back to the office later."

"Sure. I'm about ready to leave anyway."

"Oh dear, I left the last sheet of cookies in the oven!" Mrs. Bean jumped to her feet and hustled down the sidewalk.

"Baking in this heat?"

"That's what I said. You're looking mighty sharp today, Jon."

And he was. Crisp navy slacks and white shirt, tan linen blazer slung over one arm. "I had to drop some things off at the courthouse for Newt-face on my way to the airport, had to look good for the judge."

Jon got up from the steps and sat on the swing. "How's it going inside? Find any hidden treasure yet?"

"A few more photographs and postcards, that's about it." Very casually, she added, "Oh, and a couple of tapes, audiotapes."

"Oh really? Country or Tommy Dorsey?" Jon was also acting casual.

"They're blank—except for the dates someone wrote on the labels. One is from the sixties, I think. Too bad I don't have a tape player."

"Oh, so you haven't listened to them yet? I have a tape player back at the office, how about I check them out? Maybe they contain clues to the hidden treasure."

"In that case I'll listen to them myself. There's a cassette player in the car—why didn't I think of that before? We can both listen to them while I drive you back to the office."

Raleigh got up and went into the house, Jon right behind. She grabbed her tote with the tapes and locked up the spare room. "Would you close the windows, please?" Jon obliged and shut and locked the windows while Raleigh locked the back door and walked through to the vestibule. She set the alarm and locked the front door behind them.

They walked down to the Honda, where Raleigh unlocked the passenger door and the trunk. While Jon got in she found the older of the two tapes in her tote, locked the bag in the trunk and got behind the wheel. The magnet was in a paper bag on the floor and Raleigh grabbed it while Jon tried to adjust the seat. She managed to pass the cassette over the magnet twice and hoped it was enough to erase it, then dropped the bag in the back seat.

"Here's the tape. Let's see what's on it." Raleigh handed the cassette to Jon as she started the engine and pulled away.

Jon paused, then popped the cassette into the player. Distorted and filled with static, the tape was unintelligible. Jon looked visibly relieved, Raleigh noted as she snuck a peek at his face.

"The tape must be deteriorated. I'd better take it out before it ruins your cassette player." Jon popped out the cassette and dropped it in the pocket of his jacket.

"Were there more?" Jon asked warily.

"There's another one back at the hotel, but I'll just throw it away. With a tape that old trying to reuse it would be a waste of time."

They rode silently for a few moments.

"How was Texas?"

"Hot, no humidity. Newt-face should be back next week."

"I hope he gets back before I leave. That'll be sometime next week, too."

"Oh, already?" Jon didn't sound disappointed as the neighbors had; he sounded relieved.

"I have three agents coming in at the beginning of the week. I'll sign with one of them and handle the paperwork through the mail."

"It's probably for the best. What can I do to help get you on your way?"

"Nothing, I have it all organized. But thank you for the offer. The kids will haul out the last of the trash, mop the floors—and I'm gone."

"Good, good. You can shake the dust of Ohio from your feet and never look back."

"I wish it was that easy, Jon. I wish it was that easy."

That was her last word as Raleigh pulled the Honda up to the curb in front of the office and Jon got out. She waved and drove away.

As Raleigh headed back to the house, she had lied to Jon about being done for the day, she detoured into the parking lot of the Mexican restaurant to get some lunch. She was retrieving her tote from the trunk when she heard her name being called.

"Miss Killen! Raleigh! Over here!" Bailey Wahl and Gus Trout were standing next to a van and waving.

"Bailey, Gus, what's all the excitement?"

"We were just going to have lunch." Gus nodded his head toward the Mexican restaurant.

"Will you join us?" Bailey added.

"Sure, that's where I was heading myself."

They settled into a booth and Bailey ordered a pitcher of sangria for the three of them. They all ordered their food and dug into the chips and salsa and complained about the weather for a while. Raleigh told them she would be leaving soon and they seemed disappointed that she hadn't decided to stay in Greenhaven. They insisted the house wouldn't take much fixing and they both offered their handyman services, but Raleigh reminded them about the house that was waiting for her in Pine Grove. And how miserable she found the weather in Ohio.

"So you worked at the plant with my cousin?" Raleigh looked at Bailey.

"After the war. Not in the same department. He was floor manager in electrical, I was a lathe operator. The other end of the plant in the machine shop."

Raleigh had asked the question just to make conversation, but then something occurred to her. "Did they use plastic there? Make anything out of plastic, you know?"

"Not in the machine shop, but there was an extruding department, they worked with plastic there."

"The electrical department, did they use plastic?"

"Sure, in the harnesses. Electrical harnesses, for cars, trucks, anything that has a motor."

"Have many other workers from the plant gotten sick? Cancer, like my cousin?"

"Hard to say. Not everyone's still around from the old days. Machinists mostly lose fingers or hands . . . the guys who worked with insulation, they all have lung problems. Like Emmett, emphysema, some lung cancer. There's a class action suit going on that some of the guys from extruding joined; they'll be dead before it's settled, if it ever is. Yeah, the guys in extruding got hit the worst with that angio thing."

"You live long enough, you're gonna die, that's what I always say. If it isn't cancer, it's a heart attack, stroke . . . or you get hit by a bus." Gus was apparently feeling the effects of the sangria and Raleigh realized she had a slight buzz on, too.

In fact, they had already drunk the whole pitcher. Gus ordered another and Raleigh ate more chips and prayed the food would arrive soon.

"You taught at the high school, Gus?"

"Gym, football coach, basketball coach . . . always loved working with kids. Went to college on the GI Bill, taught at Greenhaven High for more'n thirty years."

"And you never had any of your own?"

"Never was the sort to get married. It was a big disappointment to the folks. They counted on grandkids, but that wasn't in the cards."

"I should never have married Lou, it was a disaster for both of us." Oh, dear. Bailey was tipsy, too. "Except for the boys, they're my pride and joy. And they're as much yours as mine, Gus. They've always thought of you as a second father."

"Always liked kids. After I retired from the school I became a Boy Scout leader. Campouts, wilderness skills, all those things a boy needs to know."

"Girls need to know those things, too. I was thirty-two before I learned how to use a miter box. Nearly cut my finger off. Here, you can still see the scar." Raleigh held out her left index finger for them to see.

The two men looked at her in surprise. Raleigh realized *she* was close to being drunk—for the first time in a decade, she thought. Maybe she should take a nap in the car before she tried to drive anywhere. Luckily, the food arrived and Raleigh ordered a Diet Pepsi to replace the sangria. She also rummaged through her tote and found her aspirin and took two in expectation of the headache she was going to have.

Bailey and Trout exchanged looks and set the pitcher of sangria out of Raleigh's reach, then dug into their food. The three ate silently for a few moments.

"Have you known Al Vitello all your lives, too?" Raleigh realized she didn't know much about him. The vague hint of thievery in the scrap of recorded telephone conversation with George Mobley and that he was Catholic was the extent of her knowledge.

"Well, I knew him from the plant. He was in electrical, under George. They were thick as thieves for a while there and George converted to Catholic, not that he was ever anything religious from what I could tell. Things weren't so friendly after that, but Al's sister died about then and there were lots of bills the insurance wouldn't cover. Insurance companies—phooey!'"

"He was part of the regular poker game? Al, you two, Buddy Bean, Emmett . . . and George?"

Gus snorted rudely. "George wasn't a regular, not at first. He had a way of . . . irritating folks and no one wanted him around."

"But you let him in."

"Yeah, well, old George had a way of pushing until you saw things like he wanted. What he did to poor Lou . . . drove her out of town with the shame of it all." Bailey shook his head, but didn't elaborate.

Raleigh wondered if Bailey knew about the pictures of his wife in that porno magazine.

Gus patted his friend on the shoulder. "You couldn't have done anything about it, you know that. She wouldn't have settled down with anyone."

"I know, but without George Mobley around she might not have gone the way she did. It was a damn shame takin' the boys to the jail to see her every Sunday. A damn shame."

"Lou spent some time in the local pokey. Took off for California as soon as she was released. Still thought she could be a movie star," Gus explained to Raleigh.

"Do you know what happed to her?"

"Said good-bye to her down at the bus station, never heard from her again. Never even called to talk to the boys, nothing. The way she lived I suppose she's been gone a long time now."

"That damn George tried to blackmail Bailey. Said he'd show some pictures he took of Lou all around town if he wasn't paid off."

"Did you pay him off?"

"I punched him right in his damn nose. Knocked him flat on his ass. He didn't mess with me for a long time after that." Bailey took another swig of sangria.

If Raleigh could read between the lines, Bailey was saying that George did "mess" with him later on.

"Then he started complaining about the boys, said they were hooligans, lies like that. So I punched him in the nose that time and he left Bailey alone." Gus waved his gnarled fists for emphasis.

"George got his own back, though. Took him a long time, but he got his own—got into the poker game after all."

"I heard that he was a good gambler, won every week. Is that true?"

"As long as we lost to him he was happy. And we all made sure we lost. Got rid of him quicker that way. Old George was kind of like toenail fungus."

"You're right, Gus. That's George all over, toenail fungus. You can keep it at bay with Vicks VapoRub or you can up and cut off your toe. We just kept him at bay. No offense, Raleigh."

"None taken, Bailey, none taken." Raleigh ordered another Diet Pepsi, not that more caffeine would be very good for her burgeoning headache, but she wanted an excuse to stay at the restaurant a little while longer and sober up.

The two men finished eating and said their good-byes and insisted on picking up the check, but Raleigh nursed her pop until she felt like she could walk without listing to one side. By the time she splashed cold water on her face in the ladies room the unremitting pain was pounding behind her eyes and she drove carefully back to the hotel.

Raleigh left the boxes in the car and managed to get herself to her room without incident. Grateful that it had been cleaned already, she closed the drapes and gingerly lowered herself onto the bed with a wet face cloth on her forehead. The message light was blinking on the phone, but she ignored it and thought to cover the phone with one of the pillows.

* * *

When Raleigh woke it was almost dinnertime, but she wasn't ready to think about food yet. She did open the drapes and drink a whole bottle of water and take two more aspirin. Her tote was a complete jumble inside and she dumped the contents onto the coffee table and started to straighten it out. Without thinking, she tucked the large envelope that had been living in her bag for a few days now into one of the estate folders and set it aside. She tossed out the various receipts she had collected, saved the credit card slips, checked the cash in her wallet and brushed out the variety of cookie crumbs.

Cookies. She'd have to remember to get a treat for Mrs. Bean and return her plate. Maybe some muffins from the Starbucks nearby.

Some of her things had fallen onto the floor and she scooped them back onto the table. The tape cassette, a really current one. What had she done with the tape player? Raleigh couldn't find it in the room, so she hustled down to the parking lot and checked in the car. There, under the seat. She also grabbed a couple of the boxes and carried them back to her room. When she walked back in she noticed the pillow covering the phone, took it off, and saw the message light blinking.

It was Jon, inviting her over for dinner that night. Raleigh felt too guilty to accept his hospitality.

"Hi, Jon. It's Raleigh Killen."

"Dinner's in half an hour. You'd better hurry or the soufflé will be flat."

"I can't come, but thanks for the invitation."

"A date with one of the septuagenarians?"

"No, I'm still hung-over from lunch. Gus ordered two pitchers of sangria and my head still feels squishy."

"An assignation in the middle of the day, naughty, naughty."

"Bailey was there, too. We just happened to run into each other at that Mexican place."

"A threesome in the middle of the day, better and better."

"Oh, knock it off. You're worse than Al Vitello." Then Raleigh remembered she couldn't trust Jon and cut off the conversation somewhat abruptly and hung up.

Raleigh ordered out for Chinese again and put the batteries in the Walkman and inserted the tape. It started playing in the middle of a conversation.

"Do it the way I told you!" George Mobley's voice, very angry, but weak.

"Mr. Mobley, this is most . . . unusual. I wish you would consider that . . ." It was Jon Bluff. That's what the *B* on the label stood for.

"I want it the way I want it and that's final! You're my lawyer and you gotta do it like I say!"

"Yes, Mr. Mobley, but this will hurt . . ."

"What do I care who it hurts? I'll show 'em. I'll show 'em all. George Mobley's gonna have the last laugh."

Jon sighed on the other end of the line. "All right, Mr. Mobley, I'll draw everything up just the way you want it."

"You be damn sure you do! If it ain't right I'll get somebody else! You're gettin' everthin' to do what I want, see that you do it!"

"I'll have the papers ready for your signature tomorrow, Mr. Mobley. I'll bring everything over to your house."

"Goin' into the hospital tomorrow, bring it over there. And see that it's right . . . or else."

Raleigh had no idea what "or else" could be, unless her cousin somehow managed to blackmail Jon, too. And what did "you're gettin' everthin'" mean? Jon wasn't the trustee and the heir, she was. How could he get everything? Or anything? There wasn't anything else on the tape, but if George Mobley was hospitalized the following day—this was the last tape he made. She flipped the tape over and checked the other side, but it was blank.

Raleigh ejected the tape and put it in the shoebox that held the family photographs. On the bottom, in case anyone removed the lid and didn't look further. She picked up Emmett's shoebox and carried it over to the coffee table, but didn't open it. Instead, she sorted through the two boxes she'd brought from the house, hitting a minor mother lode of letters from the twenties and thirties, fourteen of them in all. One of the boxes was from 1995 and held a money order carbon to St. Stephen's with the notation, *plot 455*. She had forgotten about the cemetery.

Raleigh's Chinese food arrived and she had a couple of the egg rolls and half her vegetarian lo mein, then stashed the leftovers in the minifridge. It was going on seven, but would be light for at least another hour—she'd go over to the cemetery right now.

Chapter Thirty-Two

The desk clerk gave Raleigh very clear directions and she found St. Stephen's without difficulty. It had once been located at the edge of town, she imagined, but houses had been built around it and the cemetery seemed more like a park.

Luckily, there was a map at the entrance that showed the various plot numbers and, though it was quite a hike, Raleigh made her way toward George Mobley's grave. There were several cars in the parking lot and Raleigh noticed people replacing dead flowers with fresh ones, carefully scraping the moss off an old headstone, two people making rubbings of epitaphs.

Though still humid, it wasn't too hot and Raleigh rather enjoyed reading the inscriptions on the headstones as she walked. Many were merely names and dates, others quite poetic, some newer ones with permanent photographs of the departed. Raleigh was a firm believer in cremation, even if there had been much of anyone to mourn her eventual passing. Scatter her ashes to the four winds and join the universe.

As Raleigh approached the plot she couldn't help noticing an oversized pink obelisk ahead of her and think how tasteless it was. The monument dwarfed the surrounding headstones and was polished pink marble with carved angels jutting from the sides and Jesus on the cross at the apex. Very tasteless. *Oh no. It can't be.* But it was. George Mobley. Ye gods and little fishes, as Raleigh's mother would have said.

What had George Mobley been thinking? Raleigh bent down and read the inscription on the base of the pink monstrosity.

> *"Beloved by All*
> *Cherished in Life*
> *Mourned in Death*
> *George Durbin Mobley"*

Ye gods and little fishes, indeed. He must have been completely crazy. Besides vicious, cruel, controlling and an all-around bastard—he must have been utterly crazy.

"Hey, pretty lady. You come to visit Al?"

Raleigh spun around in surprise. Just what she needed, Al Vitello.

"Hello, Mr. Vitello. I wanted to . . . pay my respects."

"What a headstone, huh?"

"Yeah, it's something all right. Well, I'll be going now."

"I hear you're leaving us soon."

"Yes, I have to get back home. Good-bye, Mr. Vitello." Raleigh walked away rather quickly in case he wanted to follow her, but she didn't hear any footsteps on the path besides hers. As she reached a tree, she paused and snuck a furtive look back. Al Vitello was on one knee in front of the grave. He crossed himself and stood, then spit on the marker and walked away.

Chapter Thirty-Three

Raleigh didn't sleep well that night and, as a result, was up earlier than usual. In fact, even after her walk and breakfast she arrived at the house just before eight. She pulled the boxes she had sorted last night from the Honda and threw them into the dumpster, then jammed the rest of the boxes from the spare room into the car and locked it.

It was too early to drop in on Mrs. Bean, but Raleigh washed the plate and arranged three scones she bought at Starbucks on it and covered them with a napkin.

Since it was so early the house hadn't heated up yet and Raleigh unlocked the bedroom door and set to work mopping the floor with oil soap and drying it off with old towels from the hall closet. The hardwood must have been covered with the carpet shortly after it was installed as it was in good shape once she removed the dirt and grit that had sifted down onto it over the years. If the kids had enough time tomorrow she would have them wash the windows, which were streaked with grime on the outside, a haze of smoke on the inside. She washed the bedroom window inside, wiped down the closet shelf and called it good, or good enough. She relocked the door and hauled the now-ruined towels out to the dumpster. The trash company was coming to empty it in the afternoon so there would plenty of room for the rolls of carpet, padding and furniture once the kids broke it up.

Spurred on by her desire to get out of this house and Greenhaven as soon as possible, Raleigh started washing the rest of the windows. Though still filthy on the outside, they already looked better, now clean on the inside. She went out onto the porch to wash the living room window, when she saw Emmett's car pull up in front of Mrs. Bean's house. Good grief, he was driving again. Mrs. Bean got out of the front seat and Emmett pulled away.

"Mrs. Bean! Wait! I have something for you!"

Raleigh waved and ran inside and got the scones and carried them over to Mrs. Bean.

"Oh, Raleigh, what's this you've brought me?"

"Scones, three different kinds. From the Starbucks downtown. The lemon poppy seed is especially good."

"Thank you, dear. You're so kind to me."

"No kinder than you've been to me. I can't even pretend these are homemade."

"It's the thought, dear. It's the thought."

They chatted a moment longer, Emmett had just taken Mrs. Bean to the bank, then they parted and Raleigh went back to the house. She set to work on the window and was soon joined by Flossie.

"Don't be wasting those paper towels, Raleigh. Newspaper is what you want. Doesn't leave streaks."

"So I've heard, but I don't have any. Paper towels will have to do."

"Hash!" Flossie leaned over the porch and yelled across the driveway. He stuck his head out the side door, cup of coffee in hand.

"Bring over some old newspapers! We're washing windows today. And the stepladder!"

"Windows? What for?"

"Because they're dirty! Get a move on!"

"Can I finish my coffee?"

"If you have to." Flossie walked back over to Raleigh. "Men. Sometimes . . ."

"I agree, but I wouldn't be trading in Hash if I were you. You'll never find another one like him."

"I know, just don't tell him."

Pretty soon Hash was on the stepladder outside washing windows, Flossie and Raleigh touching up the panes on the inside. Flossie checked from time to time to see if Hash was leaving any streaks on the outside and soon the old house started to really sparkle. By the time they finished Flossie had convinced Raleigh to take down the yellowed old roller shades and throw them away. Hash took the measurements of the windows and they all headed down to the hardware store in the Impala where Raleigh purchased new shades that simply by virtue of being new would be a big improvement.

Flossie and Hash let Raleigh take them to lunch at a nearby pizza restaurant that also offered spaghetti and ravioli. They placed their order and chose a table.

"I went out to St. Stephen's yesterday to see if I could find George's grave. The marker is quite . . . something."

"Something isn't the word for it, from what Al tells me. Floss and I don't have any interest in seeing it ourselves."

"Well, it certainly looks expensive."

"I can't imagine who George was trying to impress, buying a plot over with all the doctors and such. He bragged on it like . . . What would you say, Hash?"

"Like it made him somebody, somebody important. Guess he thought he'd get the last laugh on us."

"We decided not to waste money on a plot, a marker, a casket—good Lord, do you know how much all of that costs?" She sniffed with indignation.

"We'd rather spend some of it while we're alive, leave what we can to the girls and the grandkids."

"I have to agree with you both. What happens when you're alive is much more important than how you look dead."

"Wonder what old George looked like. Maybe he had the undertaker cut into that short arm and make them both look the same."

"Oh, Hash, stop it. Don't talk like that when we're about to eat."

"All right, Floss. Simmer down."

Hash turned his attention to Raleigh. "You said Al was out there? Was he . . . paying his respects?"

"Um, I suppose you could call it that."

"Wasn't there some funny business at the church, around when Al's sister died? Flossie?"

"That was so long ago . . . nothing comes to mind. Poor Rita got meningitis, went into a coma . . . died three years later, I think. Al took real good care of her, saw that she had the best doctors, but . . ."

"Let's talk about more cheerful things, gals. Raleigh, tell us about your place in Washington."

Their food was served and Raleigh told them about the remodeling that didn't initially happen, now was happening with her long-distance supervision, and was almost finished. The kitchen was decorated like the fifties, her orange boomerang-pattern Formica-topped table was in storage and she still had to find someone to recover the chairs, but it would be cheerful and sunny with the yellow, even if the weather wouldn't cooperate with sunshine all that often.

Pam warned her it would like a cheese sandwich with mustard, but Raleigh didn't budge from her color combination. She had plans for the yard and would now be starting school in the winter since she'd missed the registration deadline for the fall term, but she still had to time move into the house and add some of the finishing touches.

* * *

When the Impala pulled back into the driveway Bailey and Gus walked over from across the street, toolbox in Bailey's hand.

"Saw you all over here this morning. Thought you might need some handyman help."

"Are you saying I'm not handy, Gus?" Hash bristled slightly.

"I didn't mean anything of the kind. Just thought you might be able to use some *extra* help."

Hash opened the trunk to reveal the bundle of shades.

"Then lend a hand, you won't get anything done gabbing out here." Flossie followed Raleigh up the steps and after she unlocked the house helped her open the windows and set up the fan.

The men set to work figuring out which shade went where and Hash brought in the stepladder. In no time at all the shades were up and, though the clean white accentuated the cheap paneling and decrepit wallpaper, the place did look better.

Gus joined Raleigh in the kitchen to help get cold drinks for everyone.

"How's your head?"

"It was questionable for a while, but I'm fine now."

They carried the pop and bottled water into the living room just as Bailey finished with the last shade.

"There, all set."

"Bailey here's been telling us he and Gus got you drunk yesterday." There was a twinkle in Flossie's eye.

"I wasn't drunk. I was . . . rather tipsy, I admit that. But *they're* the ones who ordered two pitchers of sangria."

Chapter Thirty-Four

After everyone left Raleigh pulled out her cell phone and checked her messages. Dinah Hottel, one of the real estate agents, had called to confirm their appointment for Monday—that was a point in her favor already. Jon wanted to take her to lunch—too late. Marty told her to check her e-mail, he sent her pictures of the nearly finished house and wanted some last minute input from her on the chair rail placement in the dining room.

She called the contractor back at once and they went over his questions, even though she hadn't yet seen the pictures. She promised to e-mail him with her decisions tonight and thanked him for sticking to the schedule. So optimistic was she that she called the moving company and alerted them that they could take her things out of storage within the next two weeks.

There wasn't much else for her to do, so she pulled the last boxes onto the front porch and started to go through them. Same old, same old. Receipts, money order carbons, old magazines. Raleigh was relieved rather than disappointed. She already knew more about George Mobley *and* all the neighbors than she ever wanted to know.

A car pulled up front. It was Jon. He waved and walked up onto the porch.

"Still at it I see. I didn't hear back from you about lunch so I came over to make sure everything was all right."

"Flossie, Hash, and I were out buying new window shades." She gestured toward the bay window where the white of the shades sparkled through the clean glass.

"We stopped for lunch by the hardware store."

"Washing windows, too? You've been a very busy lady, Raleigh."

"Flossie and Hash helped me out. I wasn't doing it right apparently. Bailey and Gus came over later and put up the shades."

"At least from the outside it looks good."

"The inside isn't all that bad, in spite of the wallpaper."

Jon took a step toward the door.

"Don't go in yet, I'm not done cleaning. You can see it . . . Monday, when the real estate people come by."

Jon crouched down over the boxes she had already sorted through. "Find any more treasure?"

"Not a single family picture or letter. Absolutely nothing."

"Well, I suppose if there was anything really interesting I would have found it already myself."

"Yes, you've had plenty of time to go through everything. You've found whatever there was to find." Only she knew her remark was untrue.

"Are you okay, Raleigh?"

"Me? I'm fine. Looking forward to getting back to Pine Grove."

"I'll be on my way soon, too."

"Oh, taking a vacation?"

"No, moving up to Canada. Going to forestry school."

Raleigh was dumbfounded and couldn't tell if Jon was joking.

"What about your law career?"

"I don't like it anymore. I need to get away from . . . death. At least for a while."

"People die in Canada, too."

"But I won't be responsible for settling *their* estates."

"Forestry school. Well, why not?"

Jon fidgeted with one of the boxes as Raleigh looked at him.

"You're done with these?" He gestured at the boxes she had set aside.

"You can drop them into the dumpster. I'm through with them."

Jon dropped the boxes over the porch railing into the dumpster.

"What time on Monday?"

"The realtors are coming between eight and eleven. In there somewhere."

"Okay. Call me if you need anything in the meantime." Jon walked down the steps and got into his car, seeming quite subdued.

Raleigh wondered if she would ever figure out just what he really took from George Mobley, or why. She wiped her grimy hands on her shorts and went back into the house. She closed and locked the windows, made a mental list of cleaning supplies she needed to replace and left.

Chapter Thirty-Five

The next day Raleigh half-expected Jon to show up with the kids anyway and was relieved when the chocolate VW arrived with only Naomi and Randy inside.

The kids started work by hauling the rolls of carpet outside and Randy had raucous fun destroying the furniture and throwing it in the dumpster.

Raleigh had stocked the refrigerator with pop and snacks and it wasn't long before both the kids were looking for something to eat. They descended like two locusts and luckily Mrs. Bean arrived with a whole pan of homemade brownies for them. While the kids were taking a break Raleigh and Mrs. Bean went out onto the porch with glasses of iced tea Raleigh had brewed in a saucepan.

"How's Emmett doing, Mrs. Bean?"

"Fit as a fiddle, thank the Lord."

"I'm glad to hear that. Do you suppose he would be well enough to attend a little gathering before I leave Greenhaven? This coming Friday? I thought I'd have a lunch catered here at the house."

"A party? Catered? With fancy food and everything?"

"With fancy food and everything. I thought I'd drop off the invitations at everyone's houses on Tuesday."

"That sounds lovely, dear. I know Emmett wouldn't miss it for the world."

"Good. It's settled."

Naomi came out onto the porch. "Raleigh, I'm out of that oil soap for the floors."

"There's a grocery bag in my car. I'll go get it."

Mrs. Bean took her leave—Randy returned the already-empty brownie pan—and Raleigh went inside to supervise the cleaning.

"It looks a lot better with the windows clean and the new shades."

"Thanks, Randy. The neighbors helped me accomplish both."

"We stopped by to pick up J. J. on our way, but he said you didn't need him, just us." Naomi brought a bucket of water and a mop into the hall and started cleaning the floor. Randy was on his hands and knees scrubbing the woodwork.

"He's done too much already. And, besides, he told me once he doesn't clean."

"Aw, he'd pitch in for you. You've been his pet project for so long now."

"Pet project? How so, Naomi?"

"Oh, I don't know. He likes things to go right. I guess he feels kind of responsible for you, getting the estate settled."

"He told me yesterday that he's leaving town—the country. I couldn't tell if he was joking."

Randy looked up. "It's no joke. Major bummer for my stomach."

"Honestly, Randy. Do you ever think about anything but food?"

"The hammer throw." And he went back to scrubbing.

"That's his weakest event," Naomi explained for Raleigh's benefit. "We all thought J. J. was settled for good this time, but . . ."

"He probably got sick of all the old coots and biddies he had to deal with. Or the heirs, fighting over who gets the cast-iron frying pan. You couldn't pay me enough to be a lawyer. Me, I'm into marine biology."

Raleigh was just a little amused at that. "Naomi, how can you study marine biology in Ohio?"

"Eventually I'll transfer to UMass. Junior year is when I start getting hands-on experience."

"She'll be getting hands-on experience barfing over the side."

Naomi threw one of the soggy sponges at Randy.

"She gets seasick in a canoe."

Naomi took a step toward Randy with the dripping mop.

"You take that back Randall Maynard Dupree."

"All right, all right, sis. You never got seasick in a canoe."

Naomi went back to work and headed into the vestibule.

"It was a kayak."

Randy ran out the back door to escape his sister's wrath. Raleigh heard screaming and looked out into the back yard. Naomi was chasing Randy around the yard with the hose.

Raleigh replaced the abandoned mop in the bucket and unlocked the spare room. She had forgotten to move the shoe boxes into the bedroom. She could hear the kids laughing and yelling outside and checked her watch.

"Is anyone ready for lunch?!" Raleigh yelled out the kitchen door.

The kids thundered to the back door and shook themselves somewhat dry before they came in.

"I ordered pizza and Chinese since I didn't know which you'd prefer, but you'll have to go pick it up."

Raleigh gave Naomi some money and sent the damp kids on their way to pick up the fast food. As soon as they left she transferred the shoe boxes to the bedroom closet and locked the door. She'd take them back to the hotel tonight rather than have them sitting around while the real estate people trooped through on Monday. And with Jon or his spies around . . . it would be best to have them out of sight. She had finally decided how to dispose of them, but couldn't complete her plan until Tuesday.

When the kids got back and finished lunch she'd have them wash the painted walls, take the sofa out to the dumpster and she would be nearly through with the house.

The VW roared up to the curb and the kids piled out bearing take-out containers and two pizza boxes. Raleigh heard them and walked out to the porch.

"It's a good thing Randy was driving or one of the pizzas would be gone already."

"Let's eat out here, at least we have something to sit on."

Raleigh went back in and returned with a six-pack of Coke for the kids and a Diet Pepsi for her. They remembered to get plastic cutlery and plenty of napkins so they wouldn't have to do dishes later.

"Heard all the commotion, kiddo, thought I better see what you crazy people were up to over here."

Emmett walked out of the house and onto the porch.

"Come through the back way," he said by way of explaining his unorthodox arrival.

Raleigh didn't appreciate having him walk right into her house, but it was probably better that he hadn't driven over.

Naomi nudged Randy and they got off the porch swing so Emmett could sit down. They settled onto the steps and continued eating.

"Thank you kindly, folks."

"Would you like to have some lunch, Emmett? It's only pizza and . . ." Raleigh could see that the egg rolls, moo shu, lo mein and fried rice were already gone. ". . . pizza."

"Dr. Fred would have conniptions. No salt, no fat, no damn fun."

"Raleigh, we'll finish up inside. Okay?"

"Sure, Naomi. I unlocked the spare room so you can mop in there now. And when you're done with the woodwork, Randy, see if you can scrape the last of whatever that gunk is off the back porch."

The kids picked up the wrappings and boxes and pitched it all into the dumpster.

"Seem like good kids."

"They've been very helpful."

"Hear you're throwin' a party."

"It's the least I can do to thank all of you for your kindness."

"Did you find what you were lookin' for?"

Raleigh started guiltily, thinking about the money inside the house—and Emmett's as yet unopened box in her hotel room.

"Yes, Emmett, I did. I can't say I like it very much, though."

"That's the way it is sometimes, kiddo. You don't want to know a lot of the things you do know, if you get my drift."

"Emmett . . . the other day. You never answered my question." She hesitated for a moment. "What did you give Mrs. Bean to use instead of saccharine?"

"Kiddo, when you came here you were expectin' to find what was left of old George's life. You did. It wasn't pretty. Let it be."

Raleigh had a pretty good idea of what Emmett had done, she started to put it together when her hangover subsided the other day. Even if Emmett admitted to her that he had poisoned George Mobley with polyvinyl chloride over the course of years, what was she going to do about it? She didn't have any evidence, that was long gone. She had destroyed proof of the motive herself, all she had was a theory—and several shoeboxes full of money.

Though Raleigh had a strong sense of justice and felt that the truth was paramount, she could see nothing to be gained by acting on her suspicions. George Mobley was dead and very unlamented. Exposing Emmett and Mrs. Bean, who had been more right about her role in old George's death than anyone but Emmett knew, served no purpose. The thought of her in jail was unsupportable. And Emmett might not make it to Thanksgiving, let alone Christmas.

"You're very wise, Emmett. And quite the *boomer*, quoting the Beatles."

"Quoting what?"

"*Let It Be*. It's the classic song by the Beatles."

"That rock and roll group?"

Raleigh didn't want to explain how the Beatles were the seminal musical artists for her generation—and she wished she had a pitcher of sangria handy.

* * *

It was with some sadness later that Raleigh waved the kids on their way. They had been helpful and so willing to tackle anything she put in their way. Raleigh locked up the house and walked down to the Honda. The box from the closet was in the back seat, Randy had carried it down for her as they left. She told him it contained the family pictures and correspondence she had found.

Raleigh hopped into the car and drove back toward the hotel. She had formulated a plan to return the money, now all she had to do was have the invitations to her going-away party copied in the hotel business center. She soon pulled into the hotel parking lot and carried the box up to her room.

She called down to room service and cajoled them into fixing her breakfast for dinner again. Apparently her previous generous tips had been sufficient motivation and it didn't take much persuading on her part for them to agree to fixing poached eggs, toast and hash browns. While she waited, Raleigh stashed the box in her closet and again pulled out Emmett's shoebox, the string still undisturbed. She would wait until she had eaten, she decided, and she set it under the coffee table.

Raleigh checked her messages and e-mail, nothing important except more photographs from Marty of the house. It looked really good as she enlarged each one and panned around the rooms. The walls had been primed, though not all had been painted as yet. The kitchen was blindingly bright yellow and cheerful and Raleigh could hardly wait to unpack her things and arrange them in the cupboards. The shelves looked ample enough for even her enormous cookbook collection and she looked forward to getting everything out of storage and settling in. She sent the contractor back a quick response, thanking him profusely for how good the place looked.

* * *

After Raleigh finished eating and placed the room service tray out in the hall she resolutely untied the string on Emmett's shoebox and opened it. Hmmm, several sheets of yellow legal paper folded to fit the box. Raleigh took them out, but didn't immediately unfold them. She was stopped short by the bundles of bills underneath. These were thousand-dollar bills. She had never seen a bill that large and she pulled one from its bundle and turned it over in her hands. Were these even legal anymore? And how many were there?

Raleigh was shaking almost uncontrollably as she counted the cash, all thousand-dollar bills! When she was done, the total was $218,000. What could Emmett have done to warrant this sort of blackmail, kill someone? Duh, she said to herself, he did kill someone—George Mobley. Raleigh replaced the money in the shoebox, still shaking, and sat back.

The papers. Where were they? Momentarily frantic, Raleigh found them on the floor under the coffee table. She sat back again and unfolded them. It was a handwritten agreement of some kind. She looked at the last page. Emmett's signature—and George Mobley's. Then she went back to the beginning, which bore a date some months after Buddy Bean's death, if she remembered correctly.

"I, Emmett Potter, agree to pay to George Durbin Mobley the sum of one thousand dollars a month starting now and for as long as I live.

In exchange George agrees to stop harassing, threatening or making life miserable for Doretha Bean and Faith Bean in any way."

Hmmm, this must have been after Faith had been sent to the institution. If it had been before, why would Emmett continue paying off her cousin? She resumed reading.

"George also agrees to demand no more than twenty-five dollars a week from anyone else he's blackmailing.

George will also be accepted into the Monday night poker game."

So it looked as though Emmett didn't have a secret after all. He paid George to leave Mrs. Bean and her daughter alone, and to minimize the extortion of his friends. Twelve thousand a year, tax free, what a bonanza back then and what a supplement to his Social Security after George retired. Now Raleigh knew how he paid for that monument.

How could Emmett afford to pay so much, year after year, especially after *he* retired himself? She'd likely never know the answer to that.

Raleigh retied the shoebox with the string, hid it in the closet, and went to bed.

Chapter Thirty-Six

Raleigh tossed and turned all night, unable to sleep. She finally gave up, took a bath and got ready for her day. She didn't have much to do, just print out and copy the invitation she had drafted on her computer. She decided to take an extra long walk in spite of being so tired and she actually felt a little better by the time she returned to the hotel. She changed clothes and had breakfast in the restaurant, then packed all the shoeboxes into one old carton, stowed it in her trunk and went in search of a copy place since the hotel copier was down.

She found one next to a bookstore and made five copies on neon yellow paper, then went into the bookstore and was happy to see the latest Janet Evanovich was out in paperback. She snapped it up and also found the current Simon and Schuster crossword puzzle book. Raleigh made her purchases and went back out to the car, then made the rounds of Greenhaven and stuck her invitations in the neighbors' various mailboxes. She made her stops with the motor running and avoided actually seeing any of the seniors.

Map on the seat beside her, Raleigh drove out of town. She was looking for Duck Lake, a picnic spot Flossie had mentioned. She found it with only one wrong turn and managed to find a place some distance away from the splashing, screaming children and their parents. She opened her mystery, found her yellow highlighter and started to read. She probably wouldn't find many typos or incorrectly used words in a Janet Evanovich book, she seldom did. Other writers and editors, if some books were even edited these days, apparently relied solely on a spell-check program of some kind that couldn't tell the difference between *picaresque* and *picturesque*. She and her former book circle friends each used a different color highlighter to point out errors and oftentimes a particularly illiterate volume would be so multicolored it became difficult to read.

She passed a pleasant couple of hours in the shade of a tree, but it was becoming even more raucous as grills were fired up and kids were starting to throw footballs and Frisbees around. Raleigh gathered her things and walked back to the parking lot.

* * *

Raleigh drove back to the hotel and carried the box and several flattened grocery store bags up to her room. She wrapped each shoebox in paper from the grocery bags, taping Emmett and the Bean's box together. Mrs. Bean's box should go to Emmett Potter since he took care of her finances. She wrote the addresses on the top and called a bonded messenger service to pick the boxes up and deliver them that day.

* * *

An hour later the phone rang. She didn't answer it. Twenty minutes later another call, then another. She didn't answer it either time. Two hours later, the last call went unanswered, too.

A *Have Gun Will Travel* marathon was playing on the television. Raleigh was stretched out on the bed, earplugs in, sound asleep, her crossword puzzle book in her lap.

Chapter Thirty-Seven

Raleigh parked at the bottom of Spruce Circle and waited until she saw the agent who was her first appointment of the day pull up the street and park in front of the house. She hoped that with a stranger present the neighbors wouldn't approach her. She quickly followed the agent to the house and parked in the driveway.

* * *

Raleigh dashed from the house on the heels of the final of the three agents she had interviewed, dove into the car and pulled away quickly. As she and the agent parted on the steps Raleigh spotted the curtains move over at Mrs. Bean's house, Bailey and Gus were sitting on their porch, and she had heard Flossie and Hash's side door open. But she made her escape and headed toward an Indian restaurant on the other side of town.

* * *

Once seated in a booth, her order for *palak paneer* taken and her basket of naan delivered, Raleigh turned her attention to the proposals from the real estate agents. She had already rejected the man who thought he'd endear himself to her by telling a sexist joke, but the other two, Dinah Hottel and Phoebe Martin, had both been prompt for their appointments and thorough in their marketing proposals. Neither seemed to feel there would be a problem selling the house in spite of the amount of work necessary to update it. Raleigh worked her way through the naan and both proposals when she was stricken by a new thought that made her set aside all the paperwork.

Could she make it work? She would still need an agent, but—why not? It certainly made more sense than selling the house. She flipped a coin, pulled out her cell phone and called Dinah Hottel.

Raleigh's entrée arrived with another basket of the wonderful naan, to heck with carbs, and she quickly outlined her plan to the agent over the phone. It was a bit unusual, Dinah said, but certainly possible. Dinah made several suggestions, with which Raleigh agreed, and they set a time to meet the following day.

Real estate business completed, and with a smile on her face that had nothing to do with her savory entrée, Raleigh started to eat.

"He'll roll over in his grave," she thought to herself. And she took another piece of the naan.

* * *

Raleigh drove back to the hotel and started her preliminary packing. Dinah called at the arranged time to confirm she had been able to get the meeting tomorrow organized and they could sign the preliminary paperwork then. Everything else would follow by Federal Express and escrow should be closed by the end of the week. Raleigh thanked her and proceeded to ignore the ringing phone for the rest of the day.

Late in the afternoon Raleigh drove out into the country with a lunch she picked up at the local deli and found a place to park and watch the sunset. She was quite satisfied with the way everything turned out.

You've done what you can to make things right.

Raleigh wished she'd been able to confront Jon and resolve things—find out what he really knew. But she never had been good at confronting people, look how those antediluvian victims of her cousin's blackmail had pushed her around. Even Mrs. Bean could coerce her into doing who knows what, if the coercion involved homemade pie. Raleigh drew the line at store-bought, but homemade was a different story.

As for Jon? Well, she had long ago learned the hard way that closure isn't all it's cracked up to be. Being comfortable with ambiguity wasn't always easy, but she was starting to get the hang of it. Old George's ill-gotten gains had been returned, the issue of the house would be settled tomorrow and she could go home.

Raleigh did hope her neighbors in Washington would be as nice as Flossie and Hash Peters, not as odd as Mrs. Bean, half as helpful as Gus and Bailey, but not at all like Al Vitello. She supposed he must have his good points, though she never saw them. Emmett . . . In a funny way, she was going to miss him most of all.

Chapter Thirty-Eight

Raleigh waited in the mall parking lot the next morning for Dinah Hottel. The real estate agent pulled in next to Raleigh's car and got out with another woman.

"Ms. Killen, you can't imagine how surprised and grateful we are." The other woman grabbed Raleigh's hand and pumped it vigorously.

"Raleigh, this is Maxine Looman." Dinah made the brief introduction and spread documents onto the trunk of her car.

Maxine thanked Raleigh effusively again, then they chatted about the upcoming party. In fact, the party would start in two hours—without Raleigh.

"What?" Maxine was stunned at Raleigh's absence. "You're not going to be there?"

"No, it's best this way. I can't explain why, but it's best that you and Dinah take care of everything from here on."

Dinah paused in her preparations. "She's serious, Max. This is the way she wants it done and I assured her we'd cooperate."

"Well, of course. It's just that, won't the neighbors . . . ?"

"That's exactly why my taxi will be here in twenty minutes. And I'll be on my way back to Pine Grove by the time you make the announcement to the neighbors."

Maxine looked more than a bit concerned.

"Don't worry, they're great people and they'll love helping you out. Believe me, they will be very happy about this whether I'm there or not."

"Here," Dinah handed them each a pen. "You can start signing."

Raleigh and Maxine did as Dinah directed and signed numerous pages of the documents. Dinah ducked back into the car and returned with a notary book and stamp. Two pages were notarized and Diane recollated everything and handed both Raleigh and Maxine a folder. "Your copies, ladies."

Raleigh took the key ring from her pocket and turned over the keys to George Mobley's car along with the title.

"Ms. Killen, if you knew how grateful we all are." Maxine started in again.

"Please, stop. It's the least I could do—for everyone involved."

A taxi pulled in at the far end of the lot and Raleigh waved the driver over. She unloaded her bags from the Honda, gave the inside of the car a quick look to make sure she hadn't forgotten anything and shook hands with Dinah and Maxine. "It's all yours now."

And with that Raleigh got into the taxi and left, Dinah and Maxine waving after her.

Chapter Thirty-Nine

Raleigh relaxed into the back seat as the taxi headed for the airport. Much to her chagrin, she couldn't help wishing it was a limousine instead. She hadn't used the limo service since her driver had been an acquaintance or relative of Jon. Oh well, she still had the chartered plane for the flight back. The trip had already been paid for by the estate and she hadn't been able to talk the charter service into canceling the flight and refunding the money. So she intended to enjoy every luxurious moment of the flight to her new home and gorge herself on pop and cheese puffs and potato chips.

She wasn't interested in the passing scenery as the taxi drove through town and out into the countryside. She was interested in forgetting about her wretched relative and the misery he caused so many people. At least she had managed to close that chapter for all of them. In a way she hoped they would find appropriate.

The taxi pulled onto the road for the airport and Raleigh gave the driver directions to the private hangars. The plane was waiting and the pilot and the copilot hustled to unload her luggage and stow it in the plane. Raleigh held onto her backpack and paid off the taxi driver, then climbed the stairs into the plane and settled down.

The copilot put on his headset and started talking with the tower as he flipped switches and checked various readouts. Raleigh could see the computer display map with their route, a star indicating their location in Greenhaven, and Pine Grove on the other side of the country.

While the pilot went back outside Raleigh closed her eyes and started her preflight meditation. She could feel the plane jostle slightly and she opened her eyes, expecting to see the pilot.

"Thought you could run out on me, Miss Raleigh?"

"Jon?! What are you doing here?!"

Jon's lanky form was bent over as he tried to avoid hitting his head on the ceiling of the cabin.

"We have some unfinished business."

Jon settled into the seat across from Raleigh and handed her something flat that was wrapped in a brown paper grocery bag.

"That was quite a stunt you pulled with the house."

Raleigh checked her watch. "But the party hasn't started yet. How do you . . . ? Don't tell me, another cousin."

"I do pro bono work for Maxine."

"And what do you mean *stunt*? It was my house to do with as I pleased."

"Well . . . actually."

"Jon, stop playing games. Why are you here?"

Jon suddenly looked very uncomfortable. "Hey, open your present." He stalled for time. "It's from Mrs. Peters."

"No. Tell me what's going on. Right now." She set the package on the floor.

"It's good what you did with the house and the car. It's going to make a lot of people very happy."

Raleigh remained silent and simply looked at Jon.

"Actually, since the neighbors don't know about the day care center yet I have to wonder why they all seemed so happy and so anxious to find you."

"My plane leaves in ten minutes, Jon. I've made everything as right as I could and now I'm going home."

The pilot stepped into the plane and spoke with the copilot for a moment, then looked back at Raleigh.

"Are we all ready?"

"I am. Please remove your cousin from the plane so we can take off."

The pilot looked nonplussed for a moment, then turned his attention to Jon. "I thought you were coming with us."

"It's okay, Will." Jon got up and ducked through the hatch and went down the steps.

The pilot followed him out and Raleigh could feel the baggage compartment being opened and closed. The pilot returned and gave Raleigh a quizzical look. He stepped back and handed her a large manila envelope with her name on it and Andrew Newton's return address in the corner.

The copilot pulled up the steps, closed the door and both he and the pilot took their seats.

Raleigh craned her neck and looked outside the plane. Jon was standing on the tarmac, a YSL duffel and backpack at his feet. He saw her and waved. She didn't wave back.

* * *

After the plane stopped climbing and leveled off Raleigh removed her headphones and unbuckled her seatbelt. As she rose to get a snack from the pantry she tripped over the package she had left on the floor and nearly fell. Regaining her footing, she picked up the package and put it on the seat opposite her, then got a Diet Pepsi and small bag of honey-roasted peanuts from the cupboards.

Raleigh buckled herself back in and retrieved the package. She opened the taped-over top and looked inside. Mrs. Peters' griddle and well-worn spatula. There was a note.

> *"I didn't know if the Velveeta would keep going up in a plane, but I'm sure you can get it in Washington, too. Use the griddle in good health. Love, Flossie and Hash."*

Raleigh was sure Velveeta would keep through a nuclear war, but she was nonetheless touched at this kindness. And she would use reduced-fat Muenster instead of Velveeta in her grilled cheese sandwiches.

The manila envelope was still unopened and Raleigh decided procrastination was called for. She drank her Diet Pepsi and nibbled on the peanuts for a while, then started on a bag of cheese puffs for good measure.

Raleigh's curiosity finally got the better of her and she opened the envelope. Inside were a letter and a blue-backed sheaf of papers like George Mobley's will. She read the letter first.

> *"Dear Raleigh,*
>
> *I'm not good at facing the music, but I couldn't let you leave without knowing the truth. Part of it you guessed. I had already used the Perry Mason trick on the tapes, though, and they were thoroughly degaussed before you left the magnet in the box. Arnie thought it was a pretty neat trick. I didn't destroy the tapes immediately because it took quite some time to listen to them all, not that I wanted to, but I felt obligated to your cousin. A penance for betraying a client.*
>
> *As you will see when you read the enclosed will (it's the real one) . . ."*

"The real one?" Raleigh looked at the papers. They looked like a copy of the will and trust documents she already had.

> *". . . he wanted me to do something that I couldn't do. Though his wishes were despicable, they were perfectly legal and I should have carried them out as instructed. I couldn't and I knew I wouldn't the whole time I was drawing up the will for him. If I refused he might have*

> *found someone else to do his dirty work, so I lied to him every step of the way."*

Raleigh took another look at the will, then actually read it. She flipped one page, then another, then another.

What?! George Mobley had really left his entire estate to Jon, not to her?!

She read further. And in exchange Jon had agreed to write a book detailing all the supposed sins of George's neighbors.

> *"I didn't bind the pages of the will until after your cousin signed them. Yes, he really was your cousin. It was simple to substitute the new pages naming any unknown relative as his heir. I didn't know it would be you at that point, but I needed to buy time. George told me about the money, not where it was though, and I wanted to find it and give it back—and any evidence he had on his victims. I never did find the money. Since neither of us found it; it probably didn't exist."*

Raleigh sat back and wondered if Jon really would have given the money back had he found it first.

> *"I'm sorry, Raleigh. It was a choice between lying to a crazy old man or ruining the lives of innocent people. I made the best decision I could. At least, that's what I tell myself.*
>
> *I hope you're happy in your new home. I'm going to commune with the Canadian wilderness until I can put this all behind me. Please forgive me for lying to you.*
> *Your friend, Jon."*

Raleigh slowly replaced the papers in the envelope and stuck it in her backpack.

Epilogue

Raleigh woke from her rum-and-Diet Pepsi-induced nap and realized the plane had landed. She unbuckled her seat belt and got her backpack from the seat across the aisle, then tucked the griddle under her arm.

The pilot and copilot lowered the steps and started unloading her things.

Raleigh stepped down onto the tarmac and spotted a taxi waiting nearby. She was about to wave the driver over to the plane when a man came running toward her.

Marty Hammer? Her contractor? What was Marty doing here? As the man got closer she noticed that he was incredibly dirty, even for a contractor, and that he was out of breath.

"Ms. Killen! Ms. Killen! Wait!"

Raleigh waited for Marty to stop gasping and noticed that he reeked of smoke. "You didn't have to meet me, Marty. I already called for a taxi."

"No, no!" He was interrupted by a fit of coughing that bent him over. "It's gone! Your house! Burned to the ground!"